PRAISE FOR BETHANY BLAKE'S
PREVIOUS MYSTERIES

Bethany Blake is the author of:

The Lucky Paws Petsitting Mysteries

Death by Chocolate Lab

Dial Meow for Murder

Paw Prints & Predicaments

A Midwinter's Tail

Something Borrowed, Something Mewed

The Owl & Crescent Mysteries

A Brushstroke with Death

A Brushstroke With Death

Bethany Blake

k

KENSINGTON BOOKS
KENSINGTON PUBLISHING CORP.

www.kensingtonbooks.com

KENSINGTON BOOKS are published by

Kensington Publishing Corp.
119 West 40th Street
New York, NY 10018

Copyright © 2019 by Beth Kaszuba

All Kensington titles, imprints, and distributed lines are available at special quantity discounts for bulk purchases for sales promotion, premiums, fund-raising, and educational or institutional use.

Special book excerpts or customized printings can also be created to fit specific needs. For details, write or phone the office of the Kensington Sales Manager: Kensington Publishing Corp., 119 West 40th Street, New York, NY 10018. Attn. Sales Department. Phone: 1-800-221-2647.

Kensington and the K logo Reg. U.S. Pat. & TM Off.

First Kensington Books Mass Market Paperback Printing: November 2019
ISBN-13: 978-1-4967-2453-3
ISBN-10: 1-4967-2453-4

ISBN-13: 978-1-4967-2001-6 (ebook)
ISBN-10: 1-4967-2001-6 (ebook)

10 9 8 7 6 5 4 3 2

Printed in the United States of America

To my bewitching daughters,
Paige, Julia, and Hope

Chapter 1

"Oh, goodness!" my friend Astrid Applebee cried, chasing her floppy straw hat down the stepping-stone path that led from my cottage to my studio, the Owl & Crescent Art Barn. The batlike wings of Astrid's unusual poncho flapped as she scooped up the hat, jamming it onto her head and flattening her unruly, dark brown curls. Turning back to me and the third member of our small sorority, Pepper Armbruster, Astrid frowned. "Time to batten down the hatches!"

"It's definitely going to be a wild night," I agreed, hurrying after her and daring a wary peek at the darkening sky. Then I looked down at the path again, being careful not to trip, because I was carrying a basket that held freshly cut flowers, a ceramic rabbit, a flowerpot—and three sharp old garden tools, all props I'd use to create a still-life scene that guests to my upcoming wine-and-painting social could re-create in oils.

Joining Astrid at the studio door, I fumbled with the knob, while the wind, which was rising ahead of a storm, jangled the chimes that hung in my apple trees and rattled the shutters on my cottage. The rooster weathervane atop the pink wooden playhouse where my rescue pig, Mortimer, lived was spinning in wild circles. Finally managing to open the door, I gestured for Astrid to dash inside. "It feels like a tornado's coming!"

"Oh, there's a tornado headed our way," Pepper noted dryly, strolling right past me, too. She appeared calm, cool, and collected in a pair of white jeans and a sleeveless black top, and the gusts weren't even riffling her perfect, blond bob—probably because she was quietly using her skills as an elemental, a witch tuned in to nature's forces and cycles.

I stepped back, making room for her to pull a red wagon stocked with wine from her family's vineyard, Twin Vines, and food from her inn, the Crooked Chimneys, through the door, which I closed behind us all, shutting out the gale.

"We should all brace for a flesh-and-blood cyclone," Pepper added, dragging the wagon toward a mustard-yellow, antique dry sink, where I usually served snacks during parties. "Or should I say, a category six *human hurricane?*"

"I thought hurricanes only went up to five," Astrid noted, shaking out her poncho, which featured elaborate zodiac-inspired designs. I suspected the garment came from the clearance rack at her quirky shop, Astrid's Astral Emporium, located in a narrow purple storefront on the bustling Main Street of our eclectic, artsy hometown of Zephyr Hollow, Pennsylvania.

Without waiting for instruction, because my friends often helped with my gatherings, Astrid grabbed a matchbox from a shelf near the door and began to light the many candles I kept tucked around the barn. The power at my property had been unpredictable lately—handyman George Van Buskirk was somewhere working on the problem at that very moment—and as the studio shook from floor to rafters, I thought the nonelectric light might come in handy.

"Can a storm really be worse than five?" Astrid asked again, striking a match and lighting a sage-scented candle I'd placed on a windowsill. She shook out her hand, extinguishing the flame. "And who is this terrible person who's about to blow us away?"

As if on cue, the wind howled angrily, and a petite gray cat with a white crescent-shaped mark on her chest—one of the inspirations for my studio's name—yowled in protest and jumped up onto the long farmhouse table where I planned to create the still life.

I smiled at the sleepy feline, who didn't like her naps to be interrupted, even by forces of nature. "It's time you woke up for a few minutes, Luna," I reminded her, setting the basket on the table. "You've probably been sleeping all day."

Luna flicked her tail and blinked her yellow eyes, seeming to ask why that might be a bad thing.

Over by the dry sink, where she was arranging a tempting display of treats, Pepper grinned wickedly and waggled her fingers, which were heavy with silver rings. "You know I could probably calm this tempest so poor Luna can get her beauty rest."

"Please, no messing with the weather," I begged, smoothing my white spaghetti-strap blouse back into place. "Put those fingers away!"

Pepper laughed and waved off my concerns. "Oh, I can't really banish a storm."

I wasn't so sure about that. Of me, Astrid, and Pepper—the sole members of the world's least organized coven—Pepper was by far the most powerful witch. Female members of her family could trace their interest in magic and divination back to the *Mayflower*'s arrival, and I suspected the Armbrusters' ancestral fortune was tied to the women's special abilities more than to the men's business acumen.

Meanwhile, most of what I, Willow Bellamy, knew about witchcraft came from a tattered family journal that contained a mishmash of recipes for everything from healing herbal teas to less-than-mystical Jell-O salads; handwritten "spells" with margin notes explaining when they had—and often hadn't—worked; and descriptions of rituals that seemed to enjoy roughly the same success rate as the spells, all collected by the last four or five generations of aspiring Bellamy witches.

My grandmother, Anna—quite the brewer of powerful, sometimes misfiring, teas herself—had given me the *Bellamy Book of Spells, Lore & Miscellany* when, at age eighteen, I happened to rest a hand on a painting and found myself accidentally *sucked into the artist's soul*, making me, apparently, a witch of the arts-and-crafts variety, just like Pepper was an elemental.

I could vividly recall how Grandma Anna, who'd also handed down the genes for my thick, black hair and unusual green eyes, had pulled me aside and said, *"Your mother hates what she calls 'hocus pocus.' But, given that you obviously have gifts, I'd take a gander at the stuff in these pages before you get yourself killed."*

I'd taken that advice and come to embrace a world that my mother, Mayor Celeste Bellamy Dinsmore Crockett Bellamy—who had a winding history of divorce and remarriage—did consider suspect.

In spite of lacking maternal support, I still had a stronger background than Astrid, who came from a family of determinedly mundane accountants, and who learned most of what she knew about her chosen path—astrological—from questionable Internet sites. However, what Astrid lacked in knowledge and experience, she made up for with clothing and jewelry.

Every so often, Pepper and I had to tactfully let her know that she looked a bit too much like a cartoon version of Merlin. In fact, we'd secretly taken away Astrid's purple velvet pointed hat, the ashes of which would forever rest at the bottom of my backyard fire pit, surrounded by a cozy circle of Adirondack chairs that overlooked a bubbling stream called Peddler's Creek.

To quote a questionably wise axiom my Great Aunt Edith had added to the *Book of Miscellany*, "It's not a crime if it's a favor."

"Is anyone going to tell me who the hurricane is?" Astrid repeated, while I began to unpack the basket.

Glancing over, I saw that she was eating one of the watermelon-and-feta skewers Pepper had just arranged on a white platter. Pepper had also supplied bruschetta, topped with basil and heirloom tomatoes from my garden, and a pasta salad with grilled vegetables. I'd baked plum tarts finished with a drizzle of honey, the fruit and nectar gathered from my own trees and beehives. I was probably a borderline garden witch, if there was such a thing as borderline witchcraft.

As thunder rumbled in the distance, Astrid reached for a tart. "Should I be worried about more than getting struck by lightning on the way home?"

"I would never let you get struck, Astrid," Pepper promised, uncorking a bottle of wine. I had no idea if she was joking. I didn't see a twinkle in her blue eyes as she poured three tumblers full of the award-winning Pinot Grigio that was adding to the Armbruster fortune. Joining me at the table, Pepper slid a glass toward me, then gave Luna a quick scratch behind the ears. Luna tipped her head, practically grinning. "Unfortunately, I *can't* protect you from Evangeline Fletcher's lightning-sharp tongue tonight," Pepper added. "She is a force beyond my control!"

At the sound of my cantankerous next-door neighbor's name, Luna yowled and ran off. Astrid was also clearly stunned. Her brown eyes grew wide, and she thumped her chest, like she was choking. "No!" she cried, when she could finally speak. Her worried gaze darted between me and Pepper. "She's not really coming here, is she?"

Before I could respond, I heard a loud rustle of feathers above us, and I looked up to the exposed beams to discover that the Owl & Crescent's other namesake—a majestic, suitably wise barn owl named Rembrandt—also seemed displeased to learn that our surly neighbor planned to join the gathering, which was sponsored by the Zephyr Hollow Small Business Alliance.

Narrowing his dark, intelligent eyes, Remi rattled his wings again, letting us all know that he'd be keeping an eye on the woman who'd once called a wildlife officer to trap the "pet" I was "illegally keeping" at my place of business.

Given that Rembrandt had lived in the barn before I'd renovated it, and came and went as he pleased, the accusation had, of course, been ridiculous. Just like Evangeline's claim that the *pig who lived in a pink playhouse*, complete with flower boxes, was "livestock," and therefore also suitable for seizure and relocation.

Evangeline had even called the authorities on Luna,

insisting that my feline companion was feral because she sometimes napped on top of my potting shed.

And then there were the shadier rumors she'd spread about me . . .

"I can't believe Ms. Fletcher has the nerve to show up here," Astrid said, interrupting my thoughts and puffing her poncho indignantly. "I know she's responsible for that crazy tale about 'blood ceremonies' being held at the Owl & Crescent!"

Pepper shook her head. "Such a shame that you had to spill red paint all over yourself, Willow. If only it had been blue!"

Astrid's cheeks were pink with outrage on my behalf. "And such a shame that Evangeline was, as always, spying when you went to the cottage to clean up, because that rumor cost you business for a good six months. I swear, Evangeline Fletcher wants to get rid of all your poor animals and force you to move, too!"

While Astrid was speaking, the door had opened, ushering in a gust of wind and Mr. Van Buskirk. "Don't mean to eavesdrop, ladies, but Astrid's right," he said, stomping his work boots on the rug just inside the door. He set down a box of tools. "But I suppose you knew that already, Willow."

Of course, I was well aware that Evangeline wanted to buy my house and paint the pink, yellow, and aqua Victorian cottage some dull shade, like brown. She also hated Mortimer's playhouse and wanted to raze the barn, too. My small colony of bees were another source of aggravation, although they mainly just buzzed around my own gardens—which, if Evangeline ever did succeed in wresting my home away from me, would probably be replaced with the uniform, short grass that surrounded her much larger home, known locally as "Fletcher Mansion."

"Well, I'll never sell," I told everyone, as I continued arranging my scene, adding a rustic trowel, a hand rake, and an ancient, but wickedly sharp, pair of pruners. Then I looked up at Rembrandt. "No one's going to throw a net over you again," I promised him, turning to Luna. "And no one's sending you to the pound, either, or—heaven forbid—turning poor Mortimer into pork."

Glancing out one of the barn's windows, I saw that the black-and-white pig in question had ventured out of his house, which was like a miniature version of my cottage. He trotted around his enclosure, his snout raised as he watched the weather vane spin in the wind. I made a mental note to bring him inside the barn if the storm got too bad.

"I'd keep an eye on that piggy," Mr. Van Buskirk said, looking out the window, too. "Poor little guy is in Evangeline's sights. Who knows what she might do."

I rested one hand on my chest. "You don't think she'd really harm him . . . ?"

"I don't know, Willow," Astrid fretted. "She is unpredictable."

"Yes," Pepper agreed, giving Mr. Van Buskirk a sympathetic look. "I'm so sorry she let you go, after so many years!"

Of course, everyone in Zephyr Hollow knew that Evangeline had recently fired Mr. Van Buskirk, after decades of loyal service to the Fletcher family. Having known him since my childhood, I was trying to find odd jobs for him—which wasn't difficult, given my home's age. Everything needed tweaks, from my roof to the fence around Mortimer's enclosure.

Pepper had mentioned offering Mr. Van Buskirk some work at the Crooked Chimneys, too, but she didn't have a spot for a full-time employee. I didn't think she had any extra rooms at the inn, either, but she asked, "How long can you stay in the caretaker's cottage? I'd like to help, if you need a temporary place."

"Thanks, Pepper, but I don't have to move off the property for another week." Mr. Van Buskirk was around my grandmother's age, and vital and kindly, like her. But he sounded more gruff than usual, and his blue eyes, set in a weathered face, hardened when he spoke about being tossed out of the charming outbuilding, just across the creek, that he'd occupied for as long as I could remember. "And I think I have a place to go, if things go as planned," he added.

I was going to ask where he intended to move, but he changed the subject, addressing me again. "I don't know if I've found the real problem with the power, Willow. We'll see how things go during the storm. In the meantime, I noticed some boards are loose on the bridge. I'll nail 'em down before the wind tears one away. Just as a favor."

The wooden footbridge that connected my property to the Fletchers' was technically my responsibility. "I'll pay you—"

"No," he interrupted me, bending to pick up the battered, metal tool box. "It won't take long."

"Well, thanks," I told him.

He tipped his worn bucket hat to us as he exited the barn. "Good night, ladies!"

"Poor Mr. Van Buskirk," Astrid said, when he was gone. "I still think you should tell Evangeline she's not welcome here."

Part of me wished I could do that, but I didn't want

to start discriminating against customers who had been invited by outside organizations. "We need to remember that, as a member of the Small Business Alliance, Evangeline has every right to join this gathering," I reminded everyone. "She *does* own one of Zephyr Hollow's most successful restaurants."

Pepper rolled her eyes. "I swear, she gets half her business by leaving fake reviews—both good ones for the Silver Spoon and bad ones for every other place in town—all over the Internet. The Crooked Chimneys has received several *one-star* ratings in the last few months."

Astrid frowned. "Everybody knows your inn is the best, not to mention most romantic, restaurant around, and that there are lots of other good spots in Zephyr Hollow, too."

"*Locals* might know that," Pepper pointed out. "But tourists go by what they read online. And, I swear, lately somebody has been planting nasty reviews everywhere. Linh Tran, from Typhoon, has noticed it, too. Her business is way down at the height of the tourist season. She only has twelve reservations for the night of the Gallery Walk."

I'd been adjusting the garden tools one last time, but I paused, surprised by that news.

"That is worrisome," I agreed as the barn creaked loudly, shaken again by the wind. The ten paintings I'd created for Zephyr Hollow's most popular summer event rattled against the wall, and for a moment, I thought one of them was about to crash to the floor.

The watercolor, depicting a tall, dark-haired man walking a boxerlike dog down Main Street, had its own energy and always seemed restless to me. Thankfully, the piece, which I planned to price at three hundred dollars, stayed put and wouldn't need an expensive new frame before its sale. At least, I hoped the scene would find a buyer during the Gallery Walk. I counted on selling all my works, which would be displayed at a shop called the Well-Dressed Wall, to boost my income, and I knew local restaurant owners factored the weekend's profits into their yearly budgets, too.

"You and Typhoon should be *over*booked by now," I added, growing more concerned for the owner, who was a friend. "Linh should be turning people away."

Pepper smiled, but wryly. "I hear the Silver Spoon, which is averaging *five stars* on every review site, is packing them in."

Astrid wandered over to the sideboard, where she helped herself to another tart. "Well, at least you don't have to worry, Pepper," she noted, taking a bite and talking through the crumbs. "I'm sure the Crooked Chimneys is booked solid, right?"

"Our dinner reservations are down a bit, but, yes, our rooms are filled for the weekend of the walk and gala," Pepper said, referencing a party she always threw in conjunction with the community-wide art show. Ever the hostess, even at my establishment, she rose and moved about the studio, plugging in fairy lights that were strung along the shiplap walls and draped from the rafters. The soft glow, like fireflies, made the always festive space, which was cluttered with painted antique furniture, vintage Turkish rugs, and knickknacks I collected at the Penny For Your Stuff flea market, even more cozy. As Pepper passed by the wall that held my Gallery Walk paintings, she paused, studying the watercolor of the dark-haired man and his dog. Then she turned to me. "Who is *that* guy?"

I shrugged. "Someone from my imagination."

Pepper grinned. "Do you have a spell in your 'book of miscellany' to bring him to life? You *do* have some power with art."

"First of all, you can barely see his face," I pointed out, although I also thought there was something undeniably attractive about the man. Then I glanced at the painting and felt a prickle in the pit of my stomach. "And I'm honestly not sure if summoning him from that canvas would be a good idea."

My words sounded more ominous than I'd intended, against the backdrop of thunder that again rumbled in the distance. The light in the barn dimmed, too, as clouds rolled closer, and I wondered, briefly, if Pepper had anticipated the darkness, or if her decision to plug in the lights had been coincidental. Then, still feeling uneasy, I stepped back from the table and pulled a folded piece of paper from the back pocket of my jeans.

"I hope my guests don't cancel tonight," I added, consulting a handwritten list of people who had RSVP'd positively. "This gathering isn't big to begin with. It would be a shame if the weather kept people away."

Pepper and Astrid didn't reply. Astrid was rearranging the snacks, to fill the gaps she'd created, and Pepper began to set canvases, brushes, and tubes of oil paint on the table.

"Thanks for all your help," I told my friends, as I scanned the roster of about twenty local business owners. I knew everyone, at least to some degree, but a few names and notes I'd made popped out at me.

Evangeline Fletcher

Myrna Crickle—Owner of the Well-Dressed Wall

Linh Tran—Chef and owner, Typhoon

Penelope Dandridge—Penny For Your Stuff

*Benedict Blodgett—Independent filmmaker
(horror) and proprietor, Take 666 Studio*

"Do either of you know anything about Benedict Blod-gett and his little film school?" I inquired. "Because I'm not even sure where that's located."

"Umm, Willow?"

Astrid answered my questions with a question, and I looked up to see that she and Pepper were both watching me with something like concern. "What?" I asked warily. I folded the paper and shoved it back into my pocket. "What's wrong? And spit it out, please. Because people are going to arrive any minute now."

"Speaking of that," Pepper said, sharing a funny, almost guilty, look with Astrid. "There's something we've been meaning to tell you."

"Yes," Astrid agreed nervously. Her cheeks flushed, and in spite of my reminder about the need to speak quickly, she took a moment to clear her throat before failing to get to the point. "We do have *possible* news."

Luna crept closer, seeming curious, too, while I looked between my friends. To my surprise, Pepper, who was nor-mally very straightforward, averted her gaze. "Seriously," I said. "Someone please spill, ASAP."

"We've . . . we've both heard another rumor," Astrid stammered. "One that I tried to confirm, using a tracking spell from a website that I now fear might have been less than reliable, along with a plastic 'crystal ball' made by the HappyTime toy company."

I made a rolling motion with my hand, urging her to get to the point.

"It seems that someone's coming back to town, maybe as early as this evening, appropriately in conjunction with the storm," Pepper finally chimed in. "Someone who might make Evangeline even more disagreeable than usual—"

I was dying to learn who the heck they were talking about, but our conversation was interrupted, first by Rembrandt, who swooped down from the rafters to make a quick, warning circle around the barn, and next by a loud, insistent, staccato rap on the door.

For better or for worse, at least one of my guests had arrived.

Chapter 2

"Oh, Willow, these paintings are lovely," Myrna Crickle said, resting one hand, laden with chunky, glittering rings, onto her equally sparkly sweater as she studied the watercolors I'd sell in her gallery the weekend of the walk and gala. Myrna's black top was covered with multicolored crystals that twinkled like her blue eyes, which were magnified by the lenses of oversized, round, black plastic eyeglasses. She had to be at least seventy, and her hair was snow white, but she dressed with admirable abandon and had the energy of someone half her age.

In fact, although the party was just getting under way, Myrna had already completed her painting, an abstract spattering of bright colors that barely suggested the scene I'd set up. Maybe that's why she'd finished early, too.

Regardless, she was the first to abandon her easel and wander around my studio, followed closely by Luna, who liked baubles. "These will all sell quickly, I'm sure," she added, stepping closer to the piece that had caught Pepper's eye, too. "I predict this moody one, in particular, will go fast."

"Funny you should say that," I said, studying the image,

too. I'd painted the man with his collar turned up against an imagined chilly, wet wind, so his face was partially concealed, but he had a strangely compelling energy. The dog, muscular with a white spot on its forehead, looked worshipfully, or worriedly, up at its human. "I've felt like that painting has been ready to go, even before it was framed."

Myrna smiled at me. "I always believe that each work of art has its own sort of life force, too."

For a split second, I debated telling her just how much "life" I could sometimes sense in a painting, then I changed my mind. "Well, thanks so much for displaying my work."

"My pleasure, dear!" Myrna held out her empty wineglass so I could refill it with the bottle I was carrying around in my role as hostess. Although lightning was flickering outside, most of the guests who'd promised to attend had braved the weather. The Owl & Crescent was crowded, and the barn was filled with happy chatter as people painted, ate snacks, and mingled, checking out each other's progress.

Even Evangeline Fletcher's presence didn't seem to be dampening the mood, although I was keeping a watchful eye on her.

Shifting slightly, I looked up at Rembrandt, who seemed to be focused on our neighbor, too, like she was a vole he'd like to carry off and dump outside.

Then I gave Astrid and Pepper, who were dabbing at their canvases, a thumbs up to let them know that, in spite of Evangeline, I thought the event was a success so far.

I didn't think they noticed me. Pepper was staring at Astrid's painting, a quizzical expression on her face.

I watched them for a moment, wishing they'd had a chance to share their secret before a flurry of guests had arrived. Then I checked on Evangeline again, only to discover that she'd left the easel where she'd been painting, usually alone. Hoping she'd taken a restroom break, as opposed to, say, sneaking out and pig-napping Mortimer, I turned back to Myrna. "I feel like my works are quite humble, compared to those you usually sell. It's very nice of you to host me during such an important event."

Myrna patted my arm, nearly causing me to spill the wine. "It's my pleasure, dear."

"Maybe Myrna will sell one of *your* paintings for a million dollars or so, Willow."

The raspy voice, coming from right behind me, sent Luna darting off, and my heart plummeting to my sandals. I had to force a smile as I stepped back to reluctantly include Evangeline, who'd appeared out of nowhere, in the conversation.

If my welcome was lukewarm, Myrna's was frosty. Her normally animated face had frozen into a mask, her lips set in a thin line, and her cheeks ashen. I read her expression as a strange mixture of dismay and fury.

Meeting Evangeline's nearly black eyes, which matched her unnaturally jet-black hair, I continued to grin weakly. "I'm afraid my paintings don't sell for quite that much. I'm not exactly a familiar name to most people."

"No, you're certainly not famous," Evangeline agreed, too heartily. She had a funny gleam in her eyes and addressed Myrna, who continued to seem locked in place. "But that wouldn't necessarily stop you from passing Willow off as Picasso at the Well-Dressed Wall, would it, Myrna?"

I was caught in some sort of crossfire I didn't understand, and I waited tensely while Myrna opened her mouth to defend herself against what I sensed was an accusation. Then she seemed to change her mind and smiled graciously, if only at me. "I'm going to mingle, Willow," she said, patting my arm again. "It's lovely of you to host this gathering at your charming studio."

"It's my pleasure," I said. But she was already walking away, and I turned back to Evangeline, my smile getting thinner, and my voice sounding less genuine. Still, I attempted to make her feel welcome. "It was nice of you to come, Evangeline. I hope you're enjoying yourself."

My crotchety neighbor wore a cardigan that was an insult to kindly Mr. Rogers's memory, and she pulled the sweater more tightly around her ample bosom, jutting her chin. "I will admit that I have always been curious about the goings on in this place." Her gaze flicked to the ceiling. "I see that you still keep an exotic, wild bird as a pet."

I looked up, too, silently begging Remi not to swoop down and undo Evangeline's tight bun with his talons. He puffed up for a moment, then deflated to normal size, letting me know that his temper was, of course, in check.

"'Wild' is the operative word," I reminded Evangeline, who was absently rubbing her wrist, where she had a dark bruise. If she hadn't been so antagonistic, I would've asked what had happened. Instead, I said, "Rembrandt comes and goes as he pleases."

"Yet, he has a name," she pointed out, as a burst of lightning lit up the windows, causing a few guests to gasp before laughing at their own jumpiness. I, meanwhile, was starting to feel as thunderous as the rumbles that shook the rafters, my mood darkening more when Evangeline added, "And I see . . . or should I say smell . . . the *pig* that continues to be penned in our *residential neighborhood*."

I wanted to bite my tongue and not even respond. I

really did. But I was already upset on Mr. Van Buskirk's behalf—and worried about his warning related to Mortimer, who did *not* stink—and I found myself taking Evangeline's bait to get into an argument. "I keep Mortimer's pen very clean," I informed her. "There's no way you smell anything but flowers on this property, where at least there's life and growth and *heart*."

I didn't mean to snap, or sound cruel by implying that Evangeline's home was sterile and lonely, and as soon as the words came rushing out, I regretted them. Yet they didn't seem to hurt Evangeline's feelings. On the contrary, she seemed amused by my comment. Or maybe my anger.

"That sounds like the sort of mumbo jumbo you and your grandmother would say," Evangeline noted, her eyes cutting to a tall, tole-painted Swedish bookshelf, which stood between a moss-green velvet sofa and a red enamel wood stove that kept the Owl & Crescent warm in the winter. I displayed a lot of volumes on art and art history on the shelves, so guests could page through for inspiration. And the *Bellamy Book of Spells, Lore & Miscellany* was there, too, in a place of honor, on a shelf too high for anyone to reach without a stool.

No one but me, Pepper, Astrid, and my grandmother even knew that journal was there, but I swore that Evangeline stared right at it. Which didn't really matter. The book was locked, and accessible not with a key, but with a spell that only my grandmother and I knew. Even Pepper and Astrid weren't privy to the code, as per Grandma Anna's instructions.

"I know what *really* goes on here," Evangeline added. "I'm well aware of the happenings in this barn!"

If she meant that a lot of people stopped by to create art, celebrate things like birthdays and girls' nights out, and, in the case of my friends and I, cast the *occasional* harmless and hopefully helpful spell, she was correct. But Evangeline was implying that something dark and dangerous happened at the Owl & Crescent, which just wasn't the case.

"I really need to mingle, too," I said, with one last glance at the painting with the powerful energy. I held up my bottle of wine. "Can't let my guests go thirsty, you know!"

Evangeline didn't reply. She spun on her heel and made a beeline for her easel, while I stood quietly for a moment, composing myself.

"That was nearly as unpleasant as the weather, wasn't it?"

I felt Benedict Blodgett's warm breath against my ear and quickly stepped away—only to have the horror-film director grasp my bare arm in his clammy hand.

"Please," he said, with a funny smile. Like Myrna, he wore glasses, but they were small and reflective, so I had trouble seeing his eyes behind the lenses. "I'm having a little difficulty with the composition of my frame . . ." I assumed that was filmmaker talk for canvas. ". . . and I'd appreciate your opinion."

"What's wrong?" I asked, gently pulling free of his grasp. "I mean, how can I help?"

Benedict shrugged, a helpless, confused gesture. "It just seems as if some people think my painting is a bit . . . off."

"Oh, goodness." I cocked my head, which didn't make Benedict's painting any less "off," to me, either. I was all about creative expression, and I was actually a fan of Myrna Crickle's unique take on the scene I'd set out. But I had to admit that Benedict Blodgett's painting was difficult for me to appreciate. "That's very . . . intense," I told him, hoping he'd consider the critique as positive. "The rabbit is . . ."

"Terrified," Benedict noted, finishing the sentence for me. I realized he was quite pleased by my reaction to his canvas, where the ceramic bunny, looking admirably alive—maybe too alive—cowered, wide-eyed and nearly quaking, behind the daisies, which he'd rendered as shadowy, spiky, and almost *predatory*.

The gardening tools were featured prominently in the foreground. The edges of the trowel and shears glinted menacingly, and the small rake, which *used to* remind me of a child's toy, now resembled a clawed hand, perhaps emerging from a grave. I spied hints of red in the white highlights on the tools' sharper edges.

"I was going for a Peter Rabbit sort of thing," Benedict added, tilting his head, too, and continuing to smile in his strange way. "You know, the troublemaker bunny courting danger, but knowing that someday she'll . . . I mean, *he'll* . . . pay a price at Mr. McGregor's hand. Which is part of the thrill, of course, for both parties. Miscreant *and* punisher."

"Of course," I agreed quietly, thinking the tale hadn't seemed quite so grim to me as a child. But maybe I remembered it wrong. As lightning flared again, even closer, causing yet a few more gasps, I dared to pat Benedict's shoulder. "Well, keep up the *interesting* work."

"I will," he said, his eyes still obscured by his glittering lenses. "And you should stop by Take 666 some time. I'm offering classes on stop-action animation this summer. An artist like yourself might like to explore a new medium."

Film did interest me, so, although I was fairly busy, I said, "Sure. Sounds fun." Then I recalled that I had no idea where his school was located. "Are you in a building in town?"

Picking up one of his brushes, which held a clot of dark paint, he nodded. "Yes. I'm in the basement under the Silver Spoon." He must've seen the surprise I was trying to hide, because he explained, "I also develop film. A dark space is necessary."

"Yes, I'm sure it is."

"The entrance is behind the restaurant," he added. "There's a small sign, of course."

"Sounds . . . intriguing," I said, still processing the fact that he worked in a cellar, and that Evangeline was apparently his landlady. I was also less inclined to visit, now that I knew I'd be underground with the man who'd managed to make my garden tools look like murder weapons. Still, I told him, "Maybe I will stop by, someday."

Benedict seemed to accept that answer, or perhaps he was already lost in the act of painting, because he didn't respond. He just dabbed at his canvas, that half-smile still curling his lips.

Backing away, I edged through the crowd, making small talk, pouring more wine, and complimenting some of the merchants' paintings, most of which were quite good. Joining Astrid and Pepper for a moment, I briefly commented on Pepper's technically accurate oil, and praised the starry sky that Astrid had inexplicably painted, too.

I could tell that Astrid, especially, wanted to unburden herself of whatever news she'd been hiding, but the last thing I needed was another distraction, and I quickly moved on to greet Linh Tran, who was working side-by-side with Penny For Your Stuff flea market owner Penelope Dandridge.

I hadn't realized the two were friends, and I hoped to

learn more about the connection between Linh, who looked elegant in a not-suitable-for-painting silk top and white linen slacks, and Penny, who looked like a middle-aged hippie throwback in a pair of bell-bottom jeans, a flowing tunic, and Birkenstocks.

As I approached the women, I continued to compare, or more accurately, contrast them. Linh's sleek, dark hair was pulled into a classic chignon, and her slender hands moved with elegant grace as she painted, imparting to her scene an airy, slightly Asian sensibility.

Penelope, meanwhile, had rough hands and ruddy cheeks, and her curly red hair was barely contained by a flowing scarf she'd tied around her head. Her painting was a chaotic, colorful echo of her jumbled market, which was located at an old fairground on the edge of town.

Yet, as I drew closer, I realized Linh and Penny had something in common, beyond the fact that they were both entrepreneurs. And that something was Evangeline. Or, more specifically, anger at my neighbor.

I didn't mean to eavesdrop, but when I stepped up behind Linh and Penny, whom I also knew pretty well, I heard Linh say, in a hushed but vehement tone, "Evangeline . . . leaving terrible reviews . . . destroying my business . . ."

Then, as I took a step backward, I heard Penelope reply, with bitterness bordering on *pain*, "Someone will destroy *her*."

"Oh, goodness," I whispered to myself, just as lightning ripped through the night, causing nearly *everyone* to yelp, including me. In the wake of the flash, the studio was plunged into near darkness. And while my guests all fumbled to get their bearings by the weak light of the candles, the studio's door abruptly and unexpectedly swung open, letting in a blast of hot, damp, highly charged air.

For a moment, I blamed the wind for the intrusion. Then lightning flashed again, and I realized that someone was standing outside in the darkness.

I had just a split second to see the person's face, but I knew him so well that, although I hadn't seen him in years, I found myself struck speechless, while behind me, something clattered to the ground.

I spun on my heel, and, although the studio was dim, I was pretty sure that Evangeline had knocked over her easel.

Then I swung back around as Derek Fletcher, the first love of my life—and Evangeline's nephew—stepped into the Owl & Crescent, looked around and grinned, seeming oblivious to the blackout and the tempest. And I could imagine the familiar gleam of mischief that I was sure twinkled in his blue eyes when he said, "I don't suppose the *pig* that keeps butting his head against my door belongs to you, does he, Willow?"

Chapter 3

"I can't believe you're here," I told Derek, for at least the tenth time. He moved with the ease of familiarity around my cottage's cheerful yellow-and-white, candlelit kitchen, pulling mugs from the cabinets while I gingerly tried to light a gas burner with a match, since the electric ignition doohickey wasn't working, due to the continued power outage.

Thankfully, Pepper and Astrid had been nice enough to help my guests gather their things and say their farewells, so I could run to Fletcher Mansion and retrieve Mortimer. Derek and I had then tried to fix the fence around the pig's enclosure, which had blown down in the storm, only to give up when the rain had become torrential and the lightning far too dangerous.

In an effort to apologize for Mortimer's unannounced visit, and the fact that Derek had gotten drenched while helping me, I'd invited my ex-boyfriend in for a cup of "storm tamer" tea, made with chamomile, lemon balm, and thyme from my garden.

I was pretty sure my Great Aunt Abigail, who had added the recipe to our family book, had been referring to *emotional* storms. However, I thought the drink was doubly appropriate as the rain battered the windows in my breakfast nook, which was tucked in the cottage's semi-circular turret, and I tried to adjust to the sudden reappearance of a guy I'd last seen at an airport, shouldering a duffel bag and waving good-bye after a tearful, inevitable breakup that still gave me twinges of heartache, three years later.

"Have I mentioned your arrival is quite a surprise?" I asked, continuing to struggle with the burner.

Derek grinned. "Have *I* mentioned that I am *not* surprised you added a pig to your menagerie of plants and animals?"

As if he'd understood the comment, Mortimer, who was settling down under the table for a nap, snorted happily. At least, the black-and-white swine with the permanently upturned mouth always seemed cheerful since I'd rescued him from a family who hadn't expected their adorable "teacup" piglet to grow into a "big gulp"-sized pig. Fortunately, my property had plenty of room for Mortimer to meet his full potential, whatever that might be.

"He's a good addition," I told Derek, lighting yet another match. I didn't like explosions, and I knew, from anecdotes in the *singed* family journal, that I came from a long line of women who shouldn't play with fire. To make matters worse, my hands were a little shaky, much to my frustration. I glanced at the fridge, where Luna was perched, watching me with sympathy in her yellow eyes. She was very tuned into matters of the heart. "Mortimer is normally well behaved," I added, blowing out the flame right before it reached my fingers. "I think the storm must've scared him."

"I can understand why." Derek winced at thunder that boomed across the valley. Then he gestured for me to hand over the matches. "Here, let me do that. It seems like I'm always in places where the power's out. I've learned to adapt, and I haven't blown anyone up yet."

"Thanks." I gratefully pressed the matchbook into his open palm. It felt strange to touch him, and I stepped back, finally taking a moment to really study him by the dim, flickering firelight.

Dr. Derek Fletcher, whom I'd known since our school days, hadn't changed much since joining the international aid organization Physicians for Peace. He still had thick, dirty-blond hair, an athletic build, and gorgeous blue eyes. But I thought his job, which kept him on the move around Africa, had altered him to some degree. I'd only been around him for about a half hour, but I could tell that he'd added layers of maturity and gravity to his once purely happy-go-lucky, positive personality, which had first led him to choose changing the world over settling in Zephyr Hollow, where he could've been a surgeon with the local hospital.

I'd admired his choice, although it had taken him away from me. Even if I'd wanted to uproot my life, as we'd discussed, the doctors in his organization often traveled solo to remote and sometimes war-torn areas, by necessity. We'd mutually decided that me giving up my family, friends, and home to tag along on his adventure, only to be stuck alone for long periods of time, probably wasn't a good idea.

"It's okay to stare," Derek joked, setting the kettle on the flame he'd lit. He turned to me, resting against the butcher block countertop, and grew more serious. "I've been eager to see you, too. To know if you've changed. Which hasn't happened. You're as beautiful as ever, if not more so."

The compliment was nice, especially since, like Derek, I had a towel draped around my neck and my hair was damp. I'd also pulled a warm sweatshirt over my summery top, so I knew I wasn't looking my best. However, I wasn't going to let him off the hook with a few sweet words. I moved another step away from him and crossed my arms over my chest. "Why didn't you tell me you were coming home? Why did I *nearly* have to get that news via a rumor that Astrid and Pepper somehow heard?"

"Aah, your coven." The corners of Derek's mouth twitched. "I'm happy the trio is still united."

He was gently mocking me, because he was a rational scientist. But I knew that he was fond of Pepper and Astrid, who—like pretty much everyone—liked Derek, too. "Seriously," I prompted him again. "Why didn't you give me a heads up?"

Derek cringed a second time, and not because what sounded like sleet suddenly clattered against the windows and tin roof. "I am sorry about that," he said. "I thought about contacting you. But I didn't know if that was a good idea. For all I knew, by now you couldn't care less if I came back to Zephyr Hollow. And I thought there's a good chance you might be seeing someone . . . ?"

His voice trailed off, and he arched an eyebrow, so I realized the statement had turned into a question. One that I didn't intend to answer.

I wasn't seeing anyone, right then. But I wasn't sure how long Derek would be in town, let alone whether we should consider dating again, even if he was back permanently.

Fortunately, the kettle whistled loudly, and I used the interruption to change the subject.

"So, you haven't explained what brings you back here,"

I noted, pouring two cups of tea. The fragrance of lemon and fresh herbs filled the kitchen, and I whispered a quick incantation about peaceful hearts before handing one mug to Derek. It would've been more hospitable to invite him to sit down, but I wasn't even certain we should settle in for more than a quick chat. "It's quite a long trip, and you haven't made it for several years."

A shadow darkened his eyes. "Yes, I feel terrible about missing my parents' funeral. But I was in a remote location, and I didn't even get the news about their accident until it was too late."

"I'm so sorry," I said, for two reasons. I was expressing my condolences, and I hadn't meant to make him feel badly about his failure to attend his mother and father's memorial service. "I didn't mean anything, and your parents were so proud of you. They would've understood."

Derek managed a smile. "I know. That was just my guilt talking."

"Well, the service was lovely," I assured him, wrapping my hands more tightly around my mug. "Everyone adored your mom and dad."

Derek grunted. "Except for my Grandfather Fletcher. He never gave Mom credit for everything she did to make the Silver Spoon such a thriving, well-respected restaurant. And he hated the fact that my father chose to be a novelist. Even when Dad had some modest success, Grandfather complained that he was wasting his time 'playing make believe.'"

I could never understand why rich, imperious Grantland Fletcher, long deceased himself, hadn't been more pleased by his daughter-in-law's business acumen, not to mention his son's success as a writer, which Derek was downplaying. Instead, old Mr. Fletcher had clearly favored

Evangeline, and had supposedly left the entire estate to her on his passing.

The topic made me uncomfortable, so I shifted the subject back to Derek's visit. "You still haven't explained what brings you to town."

"I'm being reassigned," he said, sipping his tea and making a face. He wasn't always a fan of my herbal concoctions, and apparently "storm tamer" wasn't one of his favorites. He set the mug on the counter. "I have a few weeks while the program administrators decide where I might go next, and I thought I'd return here. Recharge a little."

"Well, welcome back to Zephyr Hollow for however long you stay," I said, smiling. To my surprise, it felt pretty genuine. Maybe the fact that his visit would be brief was almost a relief. Then I glanced out the window, noting that the lightning seemed less intense, and the wind was dying down. "Not to rush you off, but the storm seems to be waning, at least temporarily. This might be a good time to make a break for it."

"Yes, probably so." Derek moved toward the back door, pulling the towel from around his neck and hanging it on a hook meant for coats. "I'm sure my aunt is worried about me!"

The comment was jokingly sarcastic, and I frowned as I set down my own mug and followed him to the door. "I take it Evangeline isn't happy to see you?"

"That is an understatement," he said, although he was clearly amused by his aunt's displeasure. His eyes twinkled merrily.

"Why not?" I spoke loudly, over Mortimer's dream snorts and Luna's meow of objection to the pig's noises. I got the sense the nosy feline didn't want to miss anything that might be happening between the two humans. "Even Evangeline must like to have company now and then," I added. "And the house is certainly big enough for two— or twenty—people."

"The house is part of the issue," Derek said, grinning. "Although I've assured her that I have no interest in up- rooting her, or stealing her half of our inheritance, Aunt Evangeline is afraid I'm going to make a claim on the whole estate, from the mansion to the restaurant to the stocks, bonds, and cash assets."

I pulled back, not sure I'd heard him correctly, although Mortimer had stopped snoring, and Luna was silent, too. Then I carefully watched the man who'd given up a lucra- tive career as a surgeon to work humbly with the poor, wanting to see if he was teasing me when I asked, "Are you telling me that you . . . you're the heir to at least half the *Fletcher fortune*?"

Chapter 4

I lay awake in my high, four-poster bed for a long time that night, sorting out the evening's events as the tail end of the storm swirled around my cottage, causing the candles I'd lit in my bedroom fireplace to flicker erratically and cast strange shadows on the faded cabbage-rose wallpaper and crisp, white moldings. The tall, narrow windows in the upper part of the turret, which I used as a reading nook, rattled in the wind, too, and more sleet clattered against the tin roof as the temperature dropped. But my thoughts, more than the noise, kept sleep at bay.

Giving up on drifting off, I slipped out from under my coverlet, earning a soft mew of complaint from Luna, who was dozing at the foot of the bed. Then she yawned and wrapped her white-tipped paws around her pink nose, promptly returning to sleep. Mortimer was also sound asleep on a cushion by the hearth, snorting again in his dreams. Doing my best to be quiet, I went to the turret, taking a seat on my overstuffed chair and pulling a throw over my knees.

Gazing out the windows, I noted that a light glowed in

the Owl & Crescent, meaning the power had come back on at some point.

I also realized that I hadn't returned to the barn after Derek had left. I knew Astrid would have taken any left-overs, so I didn't need to worry about food spoiling, but I assumed I'd still have some cleanup to do in the morning.

"I wonder if I should go now," I said, even as I yawned and snuggled deeper into the chair, my thoughts drifting back to the night's events.

Needless to say, Derek's unexpected return weighed heavily on my mind. I kept picturing his smile—and re-calling his explanation, when I'd asked how he'd come to be the potential heir to a fortune.

"My grandfather changed his mind on his deathbed," Derek had revealed. *"In a hasty revision to his will, he di-vided the estate in complicated, if well-intentioned, ways. And when my parents died, their share of the property went to me."* At the second mention of his mother and father, his eyes had darkened again. *"The legal situation is complex. But, as I've told Aunt Evan, I have no need of a house or fortune—although that money could build more than one hospital in Africa."*

All at once, my thoughts were interrupted by a shadow that flitted past the windows. For a moment, I was startled, then I smiled as Rembrandt glided above the yard, heading toward the small patch of woods that separated my prop-erty from the Fletchers' land. The storm had obviously waned enough to send him looking for dinner in one of his favorite spots.

"Happy hunting," I told him quietly, rising to return to bed, where I began to replay other snippets of conver-sation from the party. Things that struck me as odd, or even worrisome.

"*. . . Myrna will sell one of your paintings for a
million dollars . . .*"

"*Miscreant and punisher . . .*"

"*Evangeline . . . destroying my business . . .*"

"*Destroy her . . .*"

My eyelids were getting heavy, fluttering closed, but I
flinched at that final pronouncement, right before I dozed
off, slipping into a series of increasingly troubled dreams.

Twisting under my sheets, I saw flashes of silvery rain
pelting Zephyr Hollow's Main Street, a shadowy figure,
his collar turned up against the elements—and a woodpecker that tapped insistently against a bare and gnarled
tree in a nearly pitch-black forest. Then I stepped into the
woods, where the man was waiting, one hand extended.

Jolting awake, I bolted upright, trapped for a moment
between the sphere of dreams and reality. Resting one
hand against my chest, I willed my heart to slow down
and blinked a few times, quickly realizing it was still very
late. The candles were guttering out, but the sky beyond
my windows was dark—and someone was knocking at
my door.

Mortimer and Luna had woken up, too. Mortimer
quickly jumped to his hooves, while Luna's wide eyes
looked almost black with alarm.

I felt uneasy, too, when my visitor rapped more insistently, like the bird in my dream. My waking self knew
that the woodpecker was the symbol of opportunity. Yet I
hadn't been sure the chance I was being offered was one
that I should take. And I wasn't certain if I should answer
the real rapping. But I couldn't exactly ignore it, either.

"You both stay here," I told Mortimer and Luna, tossing off the coverlet and pulling on my flannel robe before tip-toeing downstairs.

Of course, Luna and Mortimer ignored my order to stay in the bedroom. Luna slipped past me, a shadow on the steps, while Mortimer trotted in my wake, his legs moving swiftly and stiffly as we crossed the living room.

"At least stay back if I open the door," I urged, pausing at a window with a view of the porch. Pushing aside the curtain, I peeked outside. Then I hurried to the door and opened it wide.

"Derek?" I asked, confused to find him again on my doorstep. And this time, he wasn't grinning. "Are you okay? It's kind of late—"

"I need to know when you last saw Evangeline," he interrupted, dragging one hand through his hair. I realized, then, that he was dripping wet again, as if he'd been wandering in the dying storm. "Did you see her leave the barn tonight?"

"No, I don't think so." I wrapped my robe more tightly around myself and stepped back, gesturing for him to come inside. "What's going on?"

He didn't accept my invitation and remained on the porch, telling me with genuine concern, "I don't think she made it home tonight."

"How do you know Evangeline's not home?" I asked Derek, who stood with me outside the barn where I'd last seen my neighbor. He'd refused to take the time to change out of his wet clothes, but had given me a minute to pull on some jeans, boots, and my slicker, then grab my phone and a flashlight before we'd both headed to the studio. As

I'd expected, there'd been no trace of Evangeline inside the small space. "Are you sure she's not somewhere in your house?" I asked, thinking Fletcher Mansion would have lots of rooms in which an individual could disappear. "Maybe she decided to sleep in a spare bedroom."

Derek shook his head. "No. I checked the house thoroughly."

I still wasn't convinced he should be worried, let alone wandering around wet in the chilly wake of a storm. "What made you think to even look for her?"

His voice was tight, almost *guilty*, for some reason. "I fell asleep reading by the fire, and when I woke up, I realized I hadn't seen nor heard anyone else in the house all evening. I thought maybe Aunt Evan didn't come directly home after leaving your studio. But I never heard a door open or close the whole night." The clouds had finally parted, and by the light of the pale moon, I saw a muscle twitch in his jaw. "I've become a remarkably light sleeper. I wake at every sound. If Evangeline had come in late, I would've heard her."

I wanted to ask why he was always alert. But it wasn't the right time.

"Trust me," he said. "The house is empty. And she's not answering her cell phone. I just felt—and feel—in my gut, that something is wrong."

I had to admit that Evangeline's failure to answer her phone was worrisome. But, more than anything, it was Derek's faith in an intangible instinct that convinced me something really might be amiss, because I always trusted my gut.

Rembrandt must've sensed something was awry, too. He'd been silently circling for the last few minutes. I'd kept him in my peripheral vision, and I didn't think Derek had noticed him at all. But as the intelligent bird flew off toward the woods, I pointed upward, and, with a sinking feeling in the pit of my stomach, rested my other hand on Derek's sleeve. "Would you think I'm crazy if I tell you that I believe we should follow that shadow in the sky?"

"Aunt Evangeline?" Derek called softly, bending to scan the ground. We picked our way through the trees at the edge of our properties, and he turned back to me, his face nearly obscured by the darkness. "The *owl*'s advice aside . . . You're sure there's a chance she came this way?"

Ignoring his skeptical comment about Rembrandt, I nodded, although I doubted that he could see me. My flashlight was almost dead, the beam weak and flickering. "If she was trying to stay dry, she might've chosen the path under the canopy of trees," I said. "And ever since I built the bridge over the creek"—I pointed to the structure that lay just ahead of us—"this is really the quickest way between our houses."

Derek didn't respond. He dug into his pocket and found his cell phone. Tapping the screen, he used the flashlight app to illuminate the woods and bridge. I'd forgotten that my own phone had a similar capability and mentally kicked myself for not using it.

Stepping onto the arched, wooden bridge, I shined my weaker light on the boards, where shiny new nails winked. I realized, then, that we should probably enlist Mr. Van Buskirk's help. "Do you want me to run to the caretaker's cottage?" I asked.

Derek was halfway across the bridge, and he glanced over his shoulder. "I tried to find George before I knocked on your door. He wasn't home."

That was strange. I couldn't imagine where a man in his seventies would be so late at night.

Were he and Evangeline *together*?

That certainly seemed unlikely.

"Willow!"

I'd been staring into the rippling water, while Derek had moved ahead. At the sound of his sharp cry, I hurried after him, my flashlight flickering out. But as I grabbed his sleeve, stopping myself on the slippery path, I saw something he'd illuminated in the woods.

A pale arm, sticking out of the heavy carpet of wet, fallen leaves under a canopy of oaks and maples.

"Stay here," Derek urged, grabbing my wrist. His voice was low and deadly serious. Then he released me, left the trail, and picked his way through the trees, while I dug into my pockets, searching for my phone. I was already lightly touching the receiver icon when Derek said, "She's dead, Willow. Please call 911."

"Yes, I'm doing it," I promised, forcing my fingers not to shake.

It seemed like hours crawled by until flashing red and blue lights split the night, but, in truth, only a few minutes passed, during which Derek joined me, shrugging out of his coat and placing it around my shoulders, over my slicker. The jacket was wet, so it wasn't very helpful, but I appreciated the gesture.

"Derek?" I finally whispered. Car doors were slamming and heavy footsteps came crashing through the woods. I'd told the dispatcher exactly where to find us. "What do you think happened?"

"I'm pretty sure she was murdered," he said softly, staring in the direction of his aunt's body. I sensed that, although they hadn't always seen eye-to-eye, like me, he wished he could've moved Evangeline's body to someplace warmer, more dignified. But, of course, we hadn't been able to do that. "It looks like a homicide, to me."

"I'd like to hear more about your theories," someone said, stepping up behind us.

The deep, very serious—perhaps suspicious—voice startled me, and I spun around to discover that we'd been joined not by a uniformed officer, like I'd expected, but by a tall, dark-haired man in a white dress shirt and slightly askew necktie.

Crossing his arms over his chest, he cocked his head. "Go ahead, either one of you. I'm very intrigued to learn why you suspect homicide." His tone was almost languid, but there was an underlying authority to his request. "And if you'd like to explain why you're both wandering in the woods in the middle of the night, I'd be interested to hear that story, too."

It was that single word—"story"—or rather the skeptical emphasis the stranger placed on it, that let me know Derek and I were *both* in trouble with a man I'd never seen before . . . not counting the day I'd painted him into a rainy street scene, and the time, just about an hour before, when he'd shown up in my dreams.

Chapter 5

Needless to say, I got very little sleep the night of Evangeline Fletcher's murder, and I yawned as I cut into the French toast I'd ordered at a coffee shop called Morning Buzz, located on Zephyr Hollow's bustling Main Street. Jabbing my fork into the buttery, syrupy treat, my thoughts again drifted back to Derek's and my interrogation by the police officer who'd caught us off-guard in the woods, then marched us back to my cottage, where we'd sat on the couch like guilty schoolchildren while he'd paced the room.

"It sounds as though you've been at odds with your neighbor for quite a while," Detective Lucien Turner had said, after I'd been perhaps too honest about my contentious relationship with Evangeline. But I'd known the truth would come out. Then, before I could even respond, he'd turned his dark, intelligent, strangely familiar eyes on Derek. *"Tell me, one more time, about how you came to realize your aunt was missing."*

"He didn't trust either of us," I muttered, setting down my fork. "Me! Who might've conjured him to life!"

I didn't really believe that, and I wished I hadn't used

the word "conjure" in front of my mother, Mayor Celeste Bellamy, who'd summoned me and Grandma Anna to breakfast, so she could get all the details on the murder. I knew Mom was worried about me, but she was also concerned about her town's reputation. And she wasn't happy to hear a witch-y verb come out of my mouth.

"What did you just say, Willow?" she asked, her hazel eyes, quite different from mine, wide with alarm. "Please tell me you didn't just say you brought someone to—"

"Willow did no such thing," my grandmother interrupted. Smiling, so the lines around her twinkling green eyes—very reminiscent of mine—crinkled even more, she winked at me. "We don't have *that* kind of power, do we, dear?"

Mom wasn't convinced. She leaned over her mug of black coffee and spoke softly but vehemently. "Please, don't even joke about 'powers' and 'spells,' you two. Evangeline Fletcher is dead." She glanced around to make sure no one could hear. The shop was busy, but everyone seemed to be involved in their own conversations. "And, to be honest, I, for one, immediately feared that some ritual, inspired by that old book, had gone awry. I imagine the police might wonder the same thing. Which is why you must never, I beg you, speak of your *hobby*."

"Celeste, enough." Grandma Anna spoke quietly, too, but firmly. "If Willow is under suspicion—"

"Which I believe I am," I admitted. "And the detective who arrived on the scene also seemed skeptical about Derek's story."

My grandmother, who wore an old pair of jeans and bright pink Wellies, rested one hand over my arm. Her fingers were rough from gardening and tending to chickens and alpacas at her farm, Gooseberry Hill, but her touch was comforting. "Are you all right, dear?"

She was asking how I was coping with finding a body *and* with Derek Fletcher's return. "Yes," I assured her, smiling, too. "I'm okay, Grandma."

"How can you be, when things are such a mess?" Mom shook her head, seeming more agitated than usual. She used one manicured finger to push a copy of the Zephyr Hollow *Weekly Whisper* toward me. "Have you seen the newspaper? You are featured very prominently. There's even a picture of your pig pen!"

Taking another bite of toast, I reluctantly pulled the paper, which I hadn't seen, closer.

Not surprisingly, the entire front page was devoted to coverage of the murder, which was huge news in our normally peaceful village.

And, sure enough, Mortimer's house was inexplicably featured in a photo, above the caption, *Swine's swanky domicile sits close to site of killing.* There was a picture of the Owl & Crescent, too, including an interior shot by a photographer who must've sneaked inside.

Thankfully, someone—probably Pepper or Astrid—had cleaned up nearly everything from the party while I'd been preoccupied with Derek and Mortimer. The studio was even tidier than usual.

In fact, when I'd visited the barn early that morning, I'd almost felt like the place had been *too* orderly.

"Willow, are you reading or daydreaming?" Mom inquired, snapping me back to the present. "I'm very worried about you. You look more glazed than your pottery!"

"Oh, you have made some lovely bowls, Willow," Grandma said, deflecting the admittedly funny, if cutting, joke with a compliment. She'd pulled her gorgeous gray hair into a low ponytail, and she absently smoothed some strands that had escaped from the elastic band. "You should come out to Gooseberry Hill tomorrow. The alpacas miss you, and we haven't fired up the kiln in ages!"

"I'd like that—"

"Willow!" Mom interrupted again, before my grandmother and I could set a time. "We're talking about murder here, not making plans to play with llamas and clay."

I started to protest that *casting* clay was different than "playing with" clay. And llamas were a completely different species from alpacas. Then, seeing my grandmother subtly shake her head, to let me know those weren't battles worth fighting, I gave up and returned my attention to the newspaper. Checking the written part of the story, I discovered that it was, indeed, peppered with my name, although I'd declined to be interviewed by legendarily inaccurate local journalist Hugh Fitzhugh.

Mr. Fitzhugh *had* convinced Derek to talk, if only briefly, and I skimmed his quotes.

"I haven't been told much. Don't want to say more."

Then, jumping lower in the article, I saw that someone else on the scene had been even less forthcoming. A person whose name I'd never heard before the wee hours of the previous night, but who was certainly familiar to me now.

Detective Lucien Turner refused comment.

"Do you see how many times you're mentioned?" Mom asked, snapping me back to reality again. As I folded and placed the newspaper on the table—noting, for the first time, the horrible subhead, *Prominent Restaurant Owner Stabbed After Merchants' Gathering*—Mom watched me closely. "It really does appear that you and Derek are suspects."

"We *did* find the body, right on the line separating our properties," I reminded Mom and my grandmother. "There's no way we could be ruled out until the *real* killer is found. Which will happen soon, I'm sure."

I was trying to reassure my mother, since Grandma Anna tended to think things would work out for the best, especially if nudged along by a little magic. However, judging by Mom's dismayed expression, she was very concerned that her daughter's tangential involvement in a homicide was going to hurt tourism and tank her next mayoral campaign.

"This is just a mess, Willow," she repeated, shaking her head. "For you and the whole community."

"I am well aware of that," I agreed, eating the last bite of my breakfast. Then I looked around the crowded bistro and lowered my voice, like Mom had just done. "However, as I told the police, I was probably in bed when the murder happened. Derek woke me up when he knocked on my door."

"Why did he come to you for help?" Mom asked. "Why not George Van Buskirk? He's still living on the property, right? He can't have moved already."

"Mr. Van Buskirk wasn't around," I whispered. "To be honest, I think he might be a suspect, too—although I can't imagine him committing murder."

"Has he shown up since the killing?" Mom noted, sounding suspicious. Perhaps strangely *hopeful*. "Been questioned?"

"Now, now . . ." My grandmother spoke soothingly. "Let's not start speculating too much. That's the detective's job."

"And shouldn't we be focused more on the victim than on any bad publicity for the town?" I added.

"Yes, Celeste," Grandma agreed. "A woman has been murdered. That's the real tragedy here."

"Of course, I feel terrible about Evangeline." Mom sat back and tapped her manicured nails against the table. Then she immediately turned the conversation back to her village, which, in her defense, was like a living, breathing entity to her, as important as any real person.

I was fond of Zephyr Hollow, too. Glancing out the café's large front window, I took a moment to watch the many locals and tourists who were strolling through the picturesque town, which inspired so much of my artwork. Across the street, red lanterns swung by the black-lacquered door to Typhoon, which was housed in a charming Victorian storefront. There was a line outside the door for fresh bread from a bakery called Baguettes & Beignets, which was tucked in a pink-and-white structure that was like a confection, itself. And, of course, my attention was drawn to Astrid's always eye-catching, purple Astral Emporium, where an A-frame chalkboard sign announced a big sale on the crystal balls that had failed to help Astrid track down Derek the other day. The whole scene warmed my heart. Still, I thought my mother's next comment was a little insensitive.

"Who knows what will happen to the Silver Spoon, now that Evangeline's gone?" she mused. "It's prime property, right in the heart of town. And right now it's closed—with the Gallery Walk just days away. It's going to be another black eye for Zephyr Hollow. Customers are going to be *turned away*."

And make a beeline for Typhoon and the Crooked Chimneys.

That thought crossed my mind, but I didn't speak it out loud. I was learning the importance of being circumspect after being questioned by Detective Turner, who had an almost languid façade that masked the same intense, but harnessed energy that radiated from the canvas upon which I'd *somehow* painted him. Energy that I hadn't been sure should be released.

Why hadn't I told Astrid and Pepper about the guy who maybe, just maybe, a tiny part of me feared I really had summoned to life, just like Pepper had joked I should do . . . ?

"Honestly, Willow, it's difficult to talk with you when you keep entering these fugue states," Mom complained, catching me drifting again. Then she addressed *her* mother. "I don't care what you two say. I'm not convinced that this whole disaster isn't somehow rooted in the book you insist upon using." She smoothed her short, red hair. "Even the Jell-O recipes make me nervous."

"The Jell-O recipes always work," Grandma objected. "They're foolproof!"

"And some of them are pretty good," I added, wiping my fingers with a napkin. I'd somehow gotten sticky syrup on myself. "I really like the one with the pretzel crust and cream cheese."

My mother hesitated, then conceded, "Yes. That's not bad." She quickly narrowed her eyes at me and Grandma. "But the rest of that book is nothing but trouble."

I reared back, surprised by Mom's vehement tone. Normally, she was dismissive, and at most mildly aggravated, when it came to the *Bellamy Book of Spells, Lore & Miscellany.*

"Celeste . . ." My grandmother was shaking her head.

"Did you ever try to cast a spell?" I interrupted, the corners of my mouth twitching with ill-concealed amusement. I could tell by the way Mom's eyes widened, just slightly, that I'd struck a nerve. "What did you do, Mom? Burn something down? Because it seems like we do have trouble with fire-related spells."

"You're talking nonsense, Willow," my mother said firmly. Draining her mug in one quick gulp, she stood up and grabbed her purse, slipping it over her shoulder. "I don't want you to speculate like that again—"

"You did use the book!" I said, laughing. I looked to my grandmother, not sure why she wasn't amused, too. "I can tell!"

"I don't see what's so funny," Mom snapped, snatching her copy of the *Whisper* off the table. If she hoped that jamming the paper into her oversized bag, as she was doing, would stop anyone from reading my name in an article about a homicide, she was sadly mistaken. "And don't try to divert attention from the real issue at hand, which you, Willow, need to face."

She was right to question my laughter. It was partly stress-induced, but nevertheless inappropriate. No wonder my grandmother hadn't joined in.

"Sorry." I apologized to both of them. Then I asked Mom, with sincere curiosity, "But what, in your opinion, is the issue I have to face? Because I can't undo last night's tragedy, much as I wish I could."

Mom gave me a level stare. "You need to determine what, exactly, you plan to do about this murder on your property," she informed me. "Both to keep yourself safe— and to make sure you don't end up in jail. It's really quite simple, Willow."

With that, Mayor Celeste Bellamy swept out of the Morning Buzz, leaving a cloud of Chanel No. 5 in her wake.

"Well, Willow?" Grandma prompted, when her daughter was out of earshot. "What, if anything, *do* you plan to do about the murder?"

I knew my grandmother was asking if I intended to cast some sort of spell to find the killer, in which case, she'd probably like to be involved.

I opened my mouth to tell Grandma that I didn't plan to do anything about the homicide, except wait for Detective Turner to solve it. He seemed quite capable. However, as I dug into the pocket of my jeans, searching for cash to pay for my mother's coffee, and treat Grandma, too, I realized that I might actually be able to help catch a murderer.

In fact, I was already devising a course of action and knew exactly what I needed to do first. Yet, I couldn't tell even my grandmother, who was one of my closest confidantes, because there was a *teeny* chance my plan might kill *me*.

Chapter 6

As darkness fell the evening after Evangeline Fletcher's murder, I moved around the Owl & Crescent, gathering the candles, pouches of herbs, and vials of oil—along with one feather from Rembrandt—that I'd need to perform a ritual that intrigued and kind of terrified me.

Luna and Remi seemed to sense my conflicting emotions. The soft-hearted cat hopped up onto the couch near the tall bookshelf, watching me closely. And Rembrandt left his usual perch in the rafters, gliding silently down to rest on the back of the dry sink.

A moment later, I heard a thud at the door. The unanticipated sound caused my heart to leap, because I wasn't expecting a visitor, and I was awfully close to the scene of a homicide.

Then I realized the knock hadn't been delivered by a human hand, and I opened the door for Mortimer, who trotted inside like he owned the place.

Leaning outside, I saw that he'd walked right through the fence, where Derek and I had made the hasty, makeshift repair.

"I take it you'd like to be an indoor-outdoor pig," I

noted, closing the door and smiling when he made himself at home on the rug near the woodstove.

I swore, Mortimer grinned in reply.

"Thanks for joining me, everybody," I said, my smile fading away. "It's nice of you to watch over me."

Luna purred, a sound of quiet concern, and Remi stretched his wings to their full, impressive span, as if to let me know that he had my back. Mortimer was already asleep.

Glancing at the windows, I realized it was growing quite dark, and a full moon was visible in the clear sky.

Working more quickly, I created a ring of deep purple candles on the floor near the easels used at the previous night's party. Not surprisingly, no one had stopped by to pick up their paintings, most of which were still drying.

Lighting the candles, which were meant to strengthen my connection to another realm, I next found the easel that held Evangeline's painting and carried it to the center of the flickering ring, where I set the frame and canvas down.

Then I stepped back, finally taking a moment to carefully study my neighbor's rendering of the garden scene, which featured layers of thick paint, applied with erratic brushstrokes.

While not as creepy as Benedict Blodgett's rabbit, Evangeline's bunny had deep-black, lifeless eyes, and her flowers were basically smears of clotted blue and pink. In the foreground, the trowel and pruning shears were silvery blurs, the color of steel punctuated, now and then, by jarring glints of pure cadmium white.

"This doesn't bode well for what happens next," I noted softly, stealing a quick glance at Benedict's spooky painting. The rabbit seemed to be begging me for help, and I honestly considered tweaking the eyes before Benedict claimed the piece. Then my gaze flicked to Luna and Rembrandt, who continued to observe me. "I suppose I should be grateful I don't have to visit *Benedict's* world."

Remi hooted softly, and I got the sense that he thought I should forgo visiting any realm but that of my own dreams, in my bed. Luna's worried eyes conveyed the same message.

"How about this," I said, grabbing my phone off the table and tapping the screen. "I'll send Pepper a text, letting her know I'm doing a *slightly* dangerous spell. She's not panicky and won't rush over like Astrid would. But at least she'll know to check on me, if I'm out of touch tomorrow."

Neither cat nor owl seemed reassured, but I texted anyway, letting Pepper know that I was using the spell book in a somewhat risky way, without sharing the exact incantation. I was pretty sure even she would rush over to help, if I told the truth—and there was nothing she could do except worry, whether she was at the Owl & Crescent or the Crooked Chimneys.

Pepper's response was immediate. Need me?

Nope, good, I replied.

Be safe, she texted back.

Of course! I assured her. Talk to you tomorrow!

"There, we're all set," I told Rembrandt and Luna, putting away the phone and climbing a rickety stool near the bookshelf, so I could reach the *Bellamy Book of Spells, Lore & Miscellany*—which Luna must have nudged at some point. The book, which I always aligned carefully, was slightly askew.

I looked over my shoulder at the cat, who often prowled

around the shelves. "Please be careful not to knock this down," I told her. "It's my family legacy!"

Luna twitched her tail and meowed in protest. And she was probably right about the odds of her knocking the book to the floor. I was surprised she'd even managed to move it. The heft of the huge, dog-eared volume nearly caused me to topple backward when I pulled it down before climbing carefully off the stool.

Setting the book on the table, I hesitated, thinking something else seemed out of place. However, I couldn't put my finger on what seemed amiss, so I lit one last candle, to read by, before casting the simple spell that would unseal the *Book of Miscellany*.

Tracing my hand across the familiar cover, I wondered, as I often did, why Grandma Anna had placed a locking spell on a volume that, let's face it, didn't hold a lot of power or secrets. But all my grandmother would ever say was, "Better safe than sorry."

Lacking a better answer that evening, I closed my eyes, rested both hands on the book, and whispered a few words—*"periculosum opibus"*—that sounded like nonsense to me. But I supposed that was deliberate on my grandmother's part. The strongest passwords didn't make sense, and she certainly wouldn't have chosen "open sesame."

Opening my eyes, I discovered that I'd successfully unsealed the book, and the yellowed, sometimes suspiciously smudged pages crackled as I gently turned them, enjoying looking at the oldest notes and illustrations while I moved toward newer entries, including my own.

Okay, maybe I was stalling, too, when I paused at the recipe for orange gelatin with pretzel crust and cream-cheese filling.

"I should make that tomorrow, and take some to Mom and Grandma Anna," I whispered to Remi, Luna, and Mortimer, who'd opened one sleepy eye.

All three animals seemed to watch me critically, and I turned the pages more quickly, telling them, "Fine, fine. I'll get this over with."

No one gave so much as a hoot, and the studio grew quiet until I located the page I sought.

It was one of the few inscribed in my own handwriting, my words crossed out and rewritten as I'd tried to find a way to control the gift that had first sucked me into another realm, back when I'd been a teenager.

I was fairly certain I'd developed a ritual that would keep me safe, and my hand was steady when I pulled a tarnished silver bowl closer to myself, following one of the few "recipes" I'd added to the journal.

Add three drops of camphor (for psychic power)

Six drops carnation oil (to restore energy)

A scant half-teaspoon of bladderwrack (enhances camphor's power—SCANT!!)

Three petals of honeysuckle (protection)

Two pinches agrimony (to ensure safe return)

When I read the last note, and added the final herb, my hand *did* tremble, and the studio grew deathly quiet.

Reaching for the feather, which I'd found on the table one day and saved for the ritual, I dipped the beautiful, brown-and-black plume into the potion and stirred the mixture clockwise seven times. Then I spread the bitter-smelling, infused oil onto my right palm.

Outside, crickets chirped in the sultry, summer night, and my collection of wind chimes tinkled loudly in a rising breeze, the notes a peaceful accompaniment to the gentle rush of Peddler's Creek. Yet, in the distance, thunder rumbled, as if another storm was approaching.

The sound was ominous, and I wished I hadn't heard it, right before entering the forbidding world of a murder victim's grim painting. But I suspected I might find something of value there, and I was determined to go.

Looking to Luna, Remi, and Mortimer one last time, for reassurance, I stepped into the circle of candles and closed my eyes, first picturing my neighbor as I'd last seen her, with her black hair pulled into a severe bun and a disapproving look on her lined face. Then I lightly rested my hand against Evangeline Fletcher's canvas.

"Art and soul, uniquely combined," I whispered, already feeling a surge of energy leaving my fingertips. Still, I forged ahead. *"From brush to canvas, a story unwinds. Hidden dreams within each work. Show me where the TRUE soul lurks."*

The words had barely slipped from my lips when a profound and oppressively dark shadow seemed to loom within me, and I barely heard myself crying out softly, "No . . ."

"Ms. Bellamy? Are you all right?"

Someone was holding my wrist. I could feel strong, cool fingers around my arm, right at the point where my pulse beat closest to the skin. And a masculine, somewhat familiar voice was trying to break through to rouse me from a deep, deep slumber.

"Do you need me to get a doctor?"

The man spoke again, and I reluctantly opened one eye. Then the person who was *checking to see if I was alive* must've felt my heart race like crazy when I abruptly sat up, pulling away from him and asking, in a voice thick with lack of use, but high with alarm, "Detective Turner? What are *you* doing here?"

Chapter 7

"I think a better question might be, what in the world have you been doing here?" Lucien Turner asked, straightening and perusing the room with his perceptive, dark eyes.

I followed his gaze to the table, wondering what he must think of the silver bowl, surrounded by drying herbs and vials of oil; the owl feather; the book I needed to put away before he looked too closely at it; and the canvas in the circle of guttered-out candles.

Although I doubted he'd noticed Rembrandt, who was perched in a high, dark corner, and there wasn't anything odd about Luna—discounting her insistence upon twining worshipfully around our visitor's legs—I imagined that he also found the presence of a pig unusual. Mortimer was trotting happily around the barn, literally sticking his nose into everything.

Then the tall law enforcement officer returned his attention to me, his eyebrows arched. "Are you sure you're okay?"

I smoothed some hair, which had gotten caught in my mouth, off my face. "I promise you, I'm fine." I vaguely recalled waking to the sound of rain on the barn roof at one point before basically passing out again. "I was just sleeping. Hard."

Detective Turner appeared skeptical, and I wondered just how far my pulse had dropped while my body had tried to recover from performing the spell. However, he didn't press to call for help, asking instead, "Would you care to explain what's going on here?"

I was very tired after an incredibly frightening journey, details of which, unfortunately, I could barely recall, but I suddenly realized that Detective Turner was technically trespassing on my private property. And his question was completely out of line.

"I'm sorry, but I don't think I'm obligated to explain anything," I said, speaking firmly, but not unkindly. Then I swung my legs to the floor, sitting up.

The rapid motion was a mistake. The studio spun around me, and the next thing I knew, Detective Turner had grabbed me again, by the elbow. "Are you *sure* you feel all right?" he asked, squeezing my arm.

He sounded genuinely concerned, and as the barn drifted to a slow halt, like a carousel when the song ends, I finally took a moment to study him in the sunlight streaming through the windows and open door.

Of course, I'd noticed that he was good-looking the night before, but during our tense exchange, in the wake of a shocking tragedy, I hadn't fully appreciated his thick, dark hair, cut short in the back and a bit longer in the front. His eyes were even darker than I'd recalled, making them difficult to read—which, I had to admit, was somewhat intriguing. And, as he continued to steady me, I also again felt the energy I'd captured in the painting that, like the book, I somehow needed to hide, before he saw it. His touch exuded confidence, but restlessness and intensity that were at odds with his leisurely movements and laconic, unusual speech, with an accent I couldn't quite place.

Detective Turner was studying me, too, staring into my eyes, and I wondered what he saw, or sensed, in me.

Our connection lasted maybe a moment too long, and, feeling warmth creeping into my cheeks, I pulled away, rubbing my head and clearing the cobwebs. "I'm honestly fine," I assured him. "Just a little groggy."

Detective Turner was lean, muscular, and tall, maybe six-foot-three, and he'd bent over me. Before he straightened, he scratched Luna under the chin, and the fickle feline made a sound like a deep, happy sigh. Then my *still uninvited* guest nodded toward the table.

"You wouldn't be shaking off the aftereffects of whatever's in that bowl, would you?" he asked. "Because that's going to add a layer of difficulty to an already complicated visit."

It took me a second to figure out what he was implying, then I gasped. "No! Those herbs are all legal, from my garden. And I haven't smoked or ingested any of them—because I don't do that." I finally rose on surprisingly steady legs and impulsively held out my hand. "I just smeared the infused oil on my palm. You can sniff, if you want to." I realized that would make no sense to him, and I quickly added, "It's like a . . . a beauty treatment."

Detective Turner lowered a skeptical eyebrow. "For your palm? One single palm?"

I didn't like to lie, but I didn't always reveal everything about myself to people right away. Especially detectives who were investigating a homicide and who might have old-fashioned views about witchcraft. "Something like that," I said cagily, skirting the far, far edges of the truth. "Do you want a sniff, or not?"

He struggled to contain a smile. "No, thanks. I'm good," he assured me, nevertheless moving to the table, where he contradicted himself—and let me know that he thought I might be lying—by picking up the silver bowl and inhaling. Apparently, my herbs passed muster, because he set the vessel down and said, "Now that we've determined that I don't need to make a drug-related arrest, I really would like to know what's been going on here." He cocked his head, watching me. "So, if you'd care to explain the candles around the easel, the 'beauty treatment,' and the fact that for a moment I feared you were Evangeline Fletcher's killer's second victim—"

I felt my eyes grow wide. "You caught the killer?"

He finally did grin, but wryly. "No. Not *yet*."

Detective Turner clearly believed he would solve the case.

"So," he prompted, gesturing to the table and the circle of candles again. "If you don't mind?"

I was wearing a T-shirt that advertised Astrid's shop—I liked to be comfortable when traveling amid astral planes—and I tugged at the hem, jutting my chin. "I'm afraid I do mind. And I still don't think you have any right to barge into my studio, let alone ask me questions about my personal business. I've already told you what little I know. So, if *you* will please explain why you're here, that would be much appreciated."

While I was speaking, Detective Turner had reached into the back pocket of a pair of faded jeans that would've made Pepper very glad *someone* had summoned him to life, and he shook out a piece of paper. "I have a warrant to be here, Ms. Bellamy—"

"Please, call me Willow," I said, immediately wondering why I'd invited him to use my first name, especially when he didn't reciprocate.

He merely nodded, a shock of his dark hair falling over his forehead. "Fine," he agreed, offering me the paper for inspection. I didn't bother taking it. It was obvious that the document was official, and the words SEARCH WARRANT were printed in huge letters across the top. I also recognized the name of the judge who'd issued it. Malcolm Magee had once nearly been my mother's third, or maybe fourth, husband. "As I started to say," Detective Turner continued, "I have a warrant to search this property."

My empty stomach churned, and I wished I'd had breakfast. Or maybe that I hadn't visited another realm, depleting all my energy without much result. Forcing myself to focus on something other than my desire for a blueberry muffin, I asked, "Why is that?"

Detective Turner folded the paper again and tucked it back into his pocket. I noted that, along with the jeans, he again wore a crisp white shirt and slightly undone necktie, which I thought was some sort of self-imposed uniform, or maybe a cursory nod to a superior's insistence that he appear professional. Not that Lucien Turner struck me as someone who would have much regard for authority.

"Why do you have a warrant to search the barn?" I repeated, speaking above Rembrandt's wings, which flapped loudly.

I thought the gesture was meant to let our visitor know that I had one of nature's most effective predators on my side, and Detective Turner did give the bird a respectful, and surprisingly unsurprised, glance that told me he'd already spotted my avian bodyguard.

I folded my arms over my chest while Luna finally took my side, too, jumping onto the seat I'd just vacated. Mortimer, who had a smear of yellow paint on his snout, was also watching us.

"Well?" I challenged the frustratingly unforthcoming officer. "What are you looking for?"

Detective Turner took his time answering. I could hear my old Bakelite clock ticking on the bookshelf. Then he said, "How about we strike a bargain?" Before I could respond in the negative, which was my first instinct, he added, "I'll tell you what I'm looking for, if you tell me what *you* were seeking, by *casting the spell* in that book you wish I hadn't noticed?"

"You seem awfully comfortable with the idea of witch-craft," I noted, right before cramming my third blueberry muffin into my mouth. Once my ill-concealed secret had been revealed, and Detective Turner had admitted that he was searching for potential murder weapons, the tension between us had relaxed enough for me to suggest that we have some breakfast. He'd waited in the Owl & Crescent with Mortimer, Luna, and a still dubious owl while I'd re-trieved the muffins and a big pitcher of iced tea with mint and honey. Covering my mouth, I added, "Some people get very nervous around witches."

"I grew up in New Orleans," he said, paging through the *Bellamy Book of Spells, Lore & Miscellany*, with one arm braced on the table. He'd refused my offer to take a seat and hadn't touched the muffins, either, although, like a good Southerner, he'd finished his tea and was on his second glass. As Luna, who'd jumped onto the table, edged closer on her dainty paws, he glanced at me. "A little hoodoo, Voodoo, and witchcraft don't phase me."

That tidbit of information made him even more intriguing, especially since his accent didn't quite match his city of origin, and I wanted to learn more. However, he'd flipped another page and glanced at me, frowning. "Your spell book contains a recipe for *pudding pops*?"

I felt my cheeks flush again, and not just because the day was getting hot. "Although we Bellamy women are honestly wonderful bakers and cooks, as you'd learn if you'd *try a muffin*, we have an unfortunate, perhaps genetic, weakness for gelatin-based desserts."

"Interesting." Detective Turner closed the book and stepped back from the table, crossing his arms. "So, what were you trying to achieve with the spell titled 'Art and Souls'?"

As Mortimer trotted by, still exploring, I sat up straighter. "You're really interested?"

"I'm investigating a murder," he reminded me, pulling a pair of thin, latex gloves from his back pocket, where he'd stashed the warrant. He slipped them over his hands with the ease of experience and snapped them against his wrists. "I'm curious about anything out of the ordinary that happens on this property. And, clearly, a lot of extraordinary things happen here."

Not sure if that was a compliment, a criticism, or neither, I stood up, wiping my hands on my shorts and glancing at Evangeline's artwork. I wasn't certain how much I planned to share, but I did tell him, "The canvas in the circle is Evangeline Fletcher's."

I could tell that Detective Turner was immediately interested. He stepped over the ring of candles, inspecting the painting, and I followed him, while Rembrandt hooted softly, warning me to tread carefully, and not just over the candles. I sensed that my avian advisor didn't think it was wise to reveal too many secrets to a stranger, let alone one conducting an investigation. Still, I told Detective Turner, "Sometimes I can read things in people's paintings."

He'd been studying Evangeline's scene, his gaze roving around the strange piece, but he stopped and looked at me. "What kind of 'things'?"

I'd said enough, and I shrugged. "I don't know. I just hoped that I might see something that would serve as a clue to help find her killer."

Detective Turner studied me for another moment, and the air seemed to chill slightly. "You went to all that trouble for someone who lodged complaints about your pig and hoped to steal your home away? That seems odd."

I hadn't revealed anything about Evangeline's grievances nor her desire to buy my property during my brief interrogation the night before, and I looked up at him, watching him warily. "Who told you that?"

He shrugged. "I have, of course, been asking around. Which also accounts, in part, for my lack of surprise over your interest in witchcraft." He studied me more closely. "There's a rumor that you once ran across your yard, covered with blood."

Above me, Rembrandt flew in a tight circle. He clearly didn't like the turn the conversation had taken. Luna didn't seem pleased, either. Still on the table, she flattened her ears, finally expressing disapproval of our guest. Only Mortimer seemed oblivious to the change in mood. He'd found a collection of baskets, which I kept tucked all around the Owl & Crescent, and he was happily rooting in them, no doubt looking for something to munch on.

"That's all that was," I said evenly. "A rumor. And the

'blood' was paint, which I needed to clean off my clothes as quickly as possible. Hence my messy dash to the cottage and my washing machine."

Detective Turner didn't respond. He continued to observe me with a cool gaze, so I added, "And, while Evangeline and I didn't get along—which I *did* admit—I would never have harmed her." I made sure to meet his dark, dispassionate eyes, even when I heard Mortimer knock something over behind us. "You can ask anyone in Zephyr Hollow whether that's in my nature."

Detective Turner was the first to break our gaze. He resumed his evaluation of Evangeline's painting, and he sounded distracted when he spoke to me. "Believe me, I'm doing my best to get a complete picture of you and everyone who attended your event last night."

I felt a twinge of sickness, combined with a prickle of interest, deep in my stomach. "So, you're convinced the killer was at the party?"

Detective Turner returned his attention to me. "I didn't say that. But do *you* have reason to suspect that's the case?"

I thought back to the cryptic conversation between gallery owner Myrna Crickle and Evangeline, which had caused Myrna to walk away, clearly upset. And Linh Tran and Penelope Dandridge had almost certainly been complaining about my neighbor. Last but not least, I'd learned that Evangeline was . . . had been . . . Benjamin Blodgett's landlady, right before he'd made that ominous comment about predator and prey.

If I were a detective, I might consider any of them suspects—along with George Van Buskirk, who hadn't been a guest, but who certainly had motive.

"Well, Ms. Bellamy?" Detective Turner prompted. "Is there anything you'd like to share?"

I paused, considering how *I* had clashed with Evangeline at the gathering. But I certainly hadn't killed her, and I wouldn't want anyone raising suspicions about *me*. "I don't have anything more to say right now," I finally told him.

Detective Turner knew I was withholding information, but he didn't press the issue. He stepped out of the ring of candles, while I finally turned to see what the heck Mortimer had gotten himself into. "In that case," Detective Turner said, "I really should take a look around."

I was hardly paying attention to him. I was too busy watching a pig who stood near an overturned basket, a guilty look on his face because he'd broken a ceramic rabbit that someone had kindly packed away for me after the storm had ended the party.

As I stared at the swine and the mess, I suddenly realized what had seemed strange to me when I'd first reentered the Owl & Crescent the morning after Evangeline's murder, and right before I'd cast the previous night's spell. Not only was the place straightened up, but somebody had broken down the still-life scene and packed everything away, in the basket Mortimer had discovered tucked in with other containers that concealed practical supplies, like paper towels and drop cloths.

While Detective Turner was opening cupboards and poking in drawers, and Mortimer beat a hasty retreat through the still open door, I ran a mental checklist of the items now strewn on the floor.

The ceramic bunny was there, if now broken.

The terra cotta pot was also accounted for, as were the trowel and rake.

Even the now-wilted flowers had been crammed into the basket. I couldn't imagine Pepper being so careless. She would've found a vase and put the blooms in water.

And Astrid probably would've taken them home, along with the leftover snacks I knew she'd claimed.

That was odd.

And something was missing, too. Something that had been in the foreground of most people's paintings.

All at once, as I pictured the AWOL item, I also recalled Hugh Fitzhugh's article about the murder in the *Weekly Whisper*. Or, more specifically, the story's subheading: *Prominent Restaurant Owner Stabbed After Merchants' Gathering.*

"Detective Turner?" I asked, my heart sinking to my toes and my gaze fixed on the *two* garden tools that lay on the floor. "I'm afraid I know what you *should be* looking for."

Chapter 8

"So, you had tea with Derek Fletcher, found poor Evangeline's body in the forest, painted a handsome detective to life—and learned that Mortimer is actually a crime-solving pig, who likely unearthed a clue, like it was a truffle in a French forest!" Astrid exclaimed, summing up everything I'd blurted out after rushing into the Astral Emporium, where she was stacking boxes full of crystal balls, which apparently weren't selling well, in spite of the even deeper discount advertised on the sign outside. Stepping away from the display, she fanned herself, causing the bell sleeves of her embroidered purple tunic to flutter. "It's all quite a bit to take in!"

"Yes," Pepper agreed, joining me at a glass display counter, where she slid gracefully onto one of two high seats that optimistically waited for customers who might want to try on Astrid's personal line of handcrafted silver rings, necklaces, and bracelets. "I hardly know where to begin, with all the questions I have."

That wasn't surprising, given the rushed, random way I'd told my friends about my recent activities, after gathering them at the Astral Emporium, which was dim on that sunny day. The shop always had a suitably saturnine atmosphere, and it smelled of patchouli, although I couldn't ever recall Astrid burning incense.

"I'd like to hear more about this detective," Astrid said, slipping behind the counter and bending to pick up her huge, fluffy white shop cat, Gandalf. Straightening with a grunt, she hoisted him onto the countertop, where he curled into a dust-mop-like ball, watching us with his deep blue eyes. "I can't ever recall you summoning someone from a canvas," she added. "Is there a spell for that in your book? Because that would be quite a power to have. I might order up somebody, myself!"

I shook my head. "I'm afraid I can't do that, Astrid. And I don't think anything like that happened. Maybe I just saw him somewhere, and his image stuck in my subconscious. He's quite memorable."

"Then you probably would've remembered him," Pepper noted dryly, crossing her arms on the counter. Diamonds in a tennis bracelet that probably cost more than Astrid's entire inventory twinkled on her bare, tanned arm. Pepper also wore a pale pink sheath dress that reminded me of something Jackie Kennedy would've worn to a summer party in Hyannis Port, while I was comfortable, if slightly mismatched, in a knee-length, yellow sundress and Converse. "I think Astrid is right, and something strange is going on."

"That's an understatement," I said, reaching for one of the mass market mood rings Astrid had dumped into a small basket. I jammed the ring, which retailed for five dollars, onto my finger. "Someone was murdered, practically in my backyard."

"And I can only assume that you, Derek, and George Van Buskirk are under suspicion," Pepper added.

"I don't know about Mr. Van Buskirk, but, yes, Derek and I are suspects." I twisted the ring on my finger. "My own mother asked if I committed the crime." Seeing my friends' shock, I added, "By accident, using a spell that went awry."

Pepper sighed. "Well, there is precedent for spells in that recipe book to misfire."

Before I could defend my family legacy, Astrid waved a hand. "You couldn't hurt a flea, even by accident, Willow. And Mr. Van Buskirk has such a nice aura—while Derek's a *healer*!"

"I agree with all that," I said. "But . . ." I looked between Pepper and Astrid, then lowered my voice. "Can you keep a secret, about Derek?"

Pepper rolled her eyes. "Honestly, Willow? Did you really just ask that?"

I'd insulted her, and probably Astrid, too. "Sorry." Then I leaned closer, telling them, "Derek told me that Evangeline was afraid he'd come home to steal her half of the Fletcher fortune." Both my friends' eyes widened, and I explained, "Apparently, his grandfather's will was complicated, and I think there's a chance he's now the sole heir."

"Ooh!" Astrid sounded almost like Rembrandt, on the rare occasions he hooted. "That's not good."

"No," I agreed. "And Derek was questioned extensively the night of the murder. I know, because the interrogation took place at my cottage. I didn't hear much, but the discussion went on for a long time."

We all took a moment to consider the secret I'd just revealed about the will. I wasn't sure how much Derek had told Detective Turner. But if he had mentioned his potential inheritance . . .

"Willow?" Astrid's concerned voice broke the silence.

"Yes?" I asked, distracted. I was tugging at the mood ring, which was stuck. It had also turned orange, which meant "stressed," according to a hand-lettered chart Astrid had tucked into the basket.

"You say the detective—"

"Turner." I reminded both my friends of his name. "Lucien Turner."

"You're sure that Detective Turner is okay with spells and such?" Astrid continued, exchanging a worried glance with Pepper. I'd already told them that he'd seen the *Bellamy Book of Spells, Lore & Miscellany* and the circle of candles around Evangeline's painting. "Because some people might be inclined to suspect one of our . . ."

Astrid couldn't seem to find the right word, so Pepper supplied one. "Ilk."

Astrid nodded. "Yes. Aren't you worried that he might be more inclined to consider you a suspect, given your lifestyle?"

"I don't think so." I gave up trying to remove the ring, which I was apparently going to have to buy. "He said he's from New Orleans, and that Voodoo and magic aren't that strange to him."

"What if Voodoo and magic aren't strange to him *at all*?" Pepper noted, lowering her voice, although there were, unfortunately, no customers that afternoon.

I glanced at Astrid, who also appeared confused.

"What do you mean?" I asked Pepper.

She leaned even closer. "You said you felt a certain energy

in his painting. You mentioned that maybe it shouldn't be released, which obviously means it made you nervous."

I had said that. And, as I recalled the underlying current of restless intensity I'd felt in Detective Turner's actual touch, I started getting edgy, right then. My new mood ring was glowing red, and I was glad I hadn't mentioned the strange dream I'd had about the town's new sleuth. A dream that had also occurred before I'd met him, and in which a woodpecker had been knocking on a tree, indicating opportunity. Yet I hadn't been sure I should jump at whatever chance was being offered.

"What if this Lucien Turner is a practitioner, himself?" Pepper whispered. She sounded so ominous that Gandalf rose and slipped off the counter, plopped loudly to the floor, and darted into the shadows. "What if he's involved in *dark* magic—and here in Zephyr Hollow for more than just a job?"

"What are you saying?" Astrid demanded, even as she accessorized, reaching for a countertop rack of floaty scarves. Selecting one with spangles, she tied it around her head, fortune-teller style. "I'm confused."

"I'm saying that we should all be careful." Pepper leaned back and spoke more normally. "My family endured the Salem witch trials, and my ancestors have crossed paths with a lot of different types of witches and warlocks. I'm worried that, if Willow had a premonition, or vision, as seems to have happened, and Detective Turner isn't phased by a spell book and a potion for divining through art work, he might know even more about the craft than he's letting on. And people usually keep those kinds of secrets for a reason."

Although I had felt that strong, unsettled energy in

Lucien Turner, I had also seen the warmth and concern in his eyes when he'd thought I was ill, and I wasn't yet convinced that we had serious cause to be suspicious. Still, I nodded. "Okay. I'll be careful."

"You weren't careful when you cast that spell alone." Astrid shifted the conversation to an exploit I wished I hadn't mentioned. "You should've asked us to come over if you felt you needed to read Evangeline's painting."

"Yes, you weren't *quite* forthcoming in your text," Pepper reminded me.

"Sorry." I cringed. "But, in my defense, I had Mortimer, Rembrandt, and Luna with me. I wasn't exactly alone."

Pepper arched an expertly plucked eyebrow. "Really, Willow? The pig, while adorable, was going to call 911? Or the cat is trained in CPR?"

"No," I conceded, twisting the mood ring, which was still a telltale, agitated red. "But Remi is calm and resourceful. He could've flown for help."

Even as I said that, I knew what Pepper and Astrid were thinking.

Who, besides them, would've understood if an owl had flown up to them, seeking assistance?

"Okay, maybe I should've waited for you two," I admitted. I was glad I hadn't told them Detective Turner had been trying to find my pulse when I'd woken up, and I apologized again. "Sorry."

"Well, it's too late to turn back now," Pepper reminded us in her practical way. She turned to me. "So, what did you see?"

I again tried to recall details from the time I'd been under the spell, and, failing, told my friends, "The weird thing is, I barely remember anything, except a feeling of overwhelming darkness, which seemed to loom from deep inside of me." The mood ring turned *black*, and I thought it might be worth more than five dollars. "It was almost like the experience was too intense, and my mind blocked out the details."

"What a waste," Astrid said softly and sadly. She knew that casting the spell took a lot out of me, and that I feared a portion of the lost energy never came back. She reached across the counter and squeezed my wrist. "I'm so sorry, Willow."

Of course, Pepper didn't dwell on regrets. "Maybe you'll recall something later." She continued to watch me closely. Above us, celestial-themed wind chimes, strung from the inky-black ceiling, tinkled in a breeze that drifted in through the open windows. "What, exactly, did you *hope* to see?"

I hesitated, reluctant to tell the truth, for fear of alarming my friends with what seemed, even to me, like a morbid motive. Then I took a deep breath and confessed, "In the interest of catching a killer, I'd sort of hoped to see Evangeline's . . . *murder*."

To their credit, Astrid and Pepper didn't act like that comment was odd. They just took a moment to process my remark. Then Pepper said, "Maybe you *did*."

That thought had crossed my mind, too. I'd wondered, more than once, if my brain was blocking out an actual homicide.

Astrid blanched and rested one hand against her ample chest. "Oh, goodness, Willow."

Hesitating another moment, I added, "Detective Turner—"

"Who knows too much, the more I think about it," Pepper interrupted, frowning.

"Please, don't get ahead of yourself," I told her, in spite of my own doubts. "I don't think we have any evidence to suggest that he's some kind of warlock, let alone an evil one."

"Just be careful, Willow," Pepper repeated gravely. "I'm serious."

Her tone made me uneasy again, because normally, Pepper would've been teasing me about Detective Turner, joking that I should try to get a date with him, or suggesting that she might swoop in and flirt, herself.

"I am being circumspect," I promised. "I overheard some things at the painting party. Things I kept from Detective Turner."

Pepper's blue eyes glittered with curiosity. "Such as . . . ?"

I bit my lip, then decided I could confide in my coven. "A strange conversation between Myrna Crickle and Evangeline, in which Evangeline seemed to accuse Myrna of fraud." I could tell that Pepper and Astrid were doubtful, just like me. "I'm pretty sure Linh Tran and Penny Dandridge were complaining about Evangeline, too," I added. "And Penny said something about 'destroying' her."

Astrid sucked in a sharp breath. "That's incriminating!"

"Perhaps," I agreed. "And Benjamin Blodgett was just . . ."

"Creepy." Pepper again supplied a word.

"Yes." I nodded. "He was talking about punishing people. And he mentioned that his studio-slash-school is located under the Silver Spoon, which made Evangeline his landlady." I grimaced at the thought of Evangeline waiting to pounce if the rent was a minute overdue. "I can't imagine that it was nice to be under her thumb, month after month."

"I think you were right to keep all that to yourself, for now." Pepper again crossed her arms on the counter, the diamonds in her bracelet scraping against the glass. "We need to do a little investigating before we tell the police anything."

"Investigating?" Astrid sounded borderline alarmed. "And . . . *we*?"

I pretended I didn't hear the concern in her voice and looked hopefully to my friends. "You'll both help me? Because I feel like I have to look into the murder, to protect myself and Derek. Which is why I used the spell on Evangeline's painting in the first place."

Pepper shot Astrid, whose round cheeks were still pale, a warning glance. Then she smiled at me. "Of course, we'll help."

My ring lightened to a more hopeful shade of blue. "Thanks. I should've known you two wouldn't let me down. You certainly went above and beyond, cleaning up after the party while Derek and I corralled Mortimer."

"No problem." Astrid patted her stomach. "I'm still eating leftovers!"

"Yes, it was our pleasure," Pepper agreed. "We wanted you to have time to get over the shock of seeing Derek, who we honestly didn't expect to arrive right at that moment, in the middle of a party and a power outage."

"Yes, it was a surprise." I hopped off the chair, thinking I should head home to feed Mortimer and Luna their afternoon snacks. Pepper, who probably had lots of business to take care of at the Crooked Chimneys, stood up, too.

Leading the way to the door, I rested one hand on the dragon-shaped handle, then turned back. "By the way, I meant to ask you both a really important question. I can't believe it almost slipped my mind."

"What's that?" Pepper asked, nearly bumping into me.

Astrid was close on her heels, so we narrowly avoided a chain reaction.

"What's up?" Astrid echoed Pepper.

"When you packed away the scene with the bunny and flowers and gardening tools . . ." I could tell they were already confused, but I continued, anyhow. "Were the shears on the table, or did they disappear later?"

Astrid and Pepper were both clearly baffled, and they exchanged funny looks before telling me, in unison, "We didn't touch that scene!"

Chapter 9

"I hope I did the right thing, leaving a message for Detective Turner," I told Mortimer and Luna, who were both in my kitchen, watching me assemble a towering pan of lasagna for Derek, who probably had enough casseroles to last a single man several months, when chances were he'd only stay in town a week or so.

At least, I assumed my temporary neighbor was being bombarded with food. The evening was balmy, and I'd opened all the windows and the back door, and I could hear a seemingly endless stream of vehicles coming and going from Fletcher Mansion. Knowing how my small town operated, I was pretty sure that every visitor who came to offer condolences bore a covered dish, too. Yet I still felt as if I should contribute something.

"I'm not a professional solver of crimes," I added, scattering some fresh basil over the top layer of sauce, which I'd brewed up using garlic and heirloom tomatoes from my garden. "But the fact that someone likely returned after Pepper and Astrid left, and hid away the flowers and other tools—discounting the shears—seems important to me."

Mortimer snorted agreement, while Luna licked a paw

and scraped it over her ear. I got the sense that she wasn't particularly interested in finding Evangeline's killer.

"I know you prefer love stories to mysteries," I said, smiling at the gentle cat, and Mortimer, who might've had a bristly exterior, but who also had a soft heart. "Who doesn't like romance?"

"Who, indeed?"

The deep voice, coming from outside the screen door, startled me, and I nearly jumped out of my grandmother's old apron. Then I opened the door, telling Derek, "You scared the bejeepers out of me."

"Sorry." He apologized, but with a grin that said he wasn't too remorseful. Stepping into the kitchen, he bent to scratch Mortimer's head. Then he straightened, looking more serious. "Am I interrupting?"

"No, it's fine." I wiped my hands on the apron. "I was actually about to come see you."

He quirked an eyebrow. "Really?"

I nodded, but before I could tell him about the lasagna, he added, "To be honest, I'm glad I got here first. I needed to get away from the house. I think everyone within a three-county radius has come to pay their respects."

"Yes. I've heard the traffic."

"It's nice that so many people want to express their condolences. But I'm up to my eyeballs in casseroles now. I'll be eating macaroni and cheese for months."

I gestured to the blue casserole dish on my counter. "I don't suppose you'd like a lasagna, would you?"

He laughed, an infectious sound, and his blue eyes glimmered with amusement. "You know, I was hoping someone would bring a lasagna. It'll give me a break from five mac 'n cheeses I've received, including 'buffalo-style' and 'ham and pea.'"

Mortimer squealed, and I realized Derek's mistake. "He's sorry, Mortimer!" I assured the pig. "He didn't mean anything!" I addressed Derek. "If you don't mind, please try not to say h-a-m around you-know-who. I'm starting to think he has a decent vocabulary—which is not uncommon for pigs. They're very smart."

"Oh, my apologizes," Derek told Mortimer, more, I sensed, to appease me than the offended swine. "I didn't mean to upset you."

Mortimer still seemed miffed. Lifting his snout, he marched past us and waited by the screen door until I let him out. Then he trotted across the yard to his enclosure, where I'd left the gate open for him, because he seemed to like coming and going on his own and hadn't wandered off again. A moment later, his curly tail disappeared into the playhouse. Closing the door, I turned back to Derek, who seemed both amused and chastened.

"Do you think he'll ever forgive me?"

"I have no idea." I pulled my apron over my head and hung it on a peg near the door. "I've never been on his bad side."

"Well, since I can't do much to placate him, can I atone for my error with you—by taking you to dinner?"

The suggestion caught me by surprise. "But I thought you had way too many casseroles."

"I do, in spite of sharing quite a few with George."

I hadn't seen Fletcher Mansion's fired caretaker all day, and I'd been wondering about his whereabouts. "So, Mr. Van Buskirk has shown up?"

"Yes. In fact, he's been helping me with the funeral arrangements, in spite of the bad blood between him and Evangeline."

"That's nice of him."

"Well, George doesn't blame me for his dismissal, and he recalls my parents so fondly that he's been happy to be of assistance."

"Has Mr. Van Buskirk been questioned?" I asked, quickly raising a hand. "Not that I really suspect him of murder."

"I don't believe he's a killer, either," Derek agreed. "But the detective might disagree. He has interrogated George, who, like me, has been advised to stick around town."

It really was nearly impossible for me to believe the older man with the twinkling eyes committed murder, but I had to ask, "Did he tell you where he was, the night of Evangeline's death?"

Derek shook his head. "No. And I didn't ask. I'm not investigating the crime, and a grown man's activities, at whatever hour, are none of my business."

"I guess I'm nosier than you," I said, smiling.

"How about hungry? Because I'd still like to take you out to dinner—at a restaurant I want to visit for more than the food. A place that, at the risk of sounding like a wimp, I'd rather not go alone."

I realized where he was probably headed, and I had to admit, I was intrigued. "Just let me close Mortimer's gate for the night," I said. Then I hesitated, because there was a flaw in his dinner plans. "Um, isn't the Silver Spoon *closed* since Evangeline's death?"

Derek dug into the pocket of his jeans, and I realized that his attire should've been my first clue that we weren't going to his family's fancy restaurant for a normal meal. Then he held up a shiny, silver key, telling me, "Yes. As a matter of fact, it is closed, at least for the next few days. Which is precisely why I want to go *tonight*."

Chapter 10

"Wow, this place brings back a lot of memories," Derek said softly, as we both moved around the Silver Spoon's dining room, which was lit only by moonlight streaming through large, twelve-paned windows, which were original to the eighteenth-century, clapboard building.

We'd decided not to turn on the lights, because Zephyr Hollow was busy that evening, and we'd already seen a few people peek hopefully inside, ignoring a sign that said the place was closed. "Why don't you light a few of the votives on the tables, while I find something to eat," Derek added, nodding to the podium where the hostess usually stood. "There are always matches near the reservation book."

"Sounds good." I headed for the station, while Derek disappeared through a concealed swinging door at the far end of the room.

Bending, I pulled the restaurant's reservation book out of a shelf, so it would be easier to feel for matches amid the scattered pens, paper clips, and other items that were also tucked away.

However, as I set the binder on top of the podium, in a

shaft of moonlight, I realized it was more than just a place to prepare for the flow of customers. It also appeared to be a catch-all planner, presumably for Evangeline, who'd pasted sticky notes all over the place. I recognized her distinctive, bold script from notes of complaint—*One of your creatures left a rat on my doorstep! Your wind chimes are breaking noise ordinances!*—that she used to slap onto my front door.

Forgetting good manners for a moment, I flipped a few pages, reading Evangeline's shorthand on the bright slips of paper, each affixed to a specific date.

July 3—Meeting Typhoon 2 p.m.

July 7—Meeting Martin Beswick 8 a.m.

I recognized the name of a local attorney, known for being litigious. Then I checked another note.

July 8—Place Whisper ad—New TNT!

Not sure what to make of what appeared to be a note about *dynamite*, I flipped one more page and discovered that three weeks in August were crossed out entirely, as if the Silver Spoon would be closed, which I could never recall happening.

Peering more closely, I saw that someone had scribbled over a notation in the margins. I could barely make out *MN* and *vac*.

"Did Evangeline schedule, or maybe cancel, a vacation to Minnesota—or Montana?" I muttered aloud, unable to remember which state was abbreviated "MN." "I can't remember her ever being gone for long. . . ."

My musings were cut short by the sound of the swinging door, which opened at the far end of the dining room. Feeling guilty, I quickly shut the book and tucked it away.

I didn't think Derek noticed I'd been snooping, or that I'd failed to find the matches. He'd obviously discovered something of interest, too.

"Willow." He waved a hand, urging me to join him. I could just make out the gesture in the dark room, but I could hear the unhappiness in his voice. "You really need to see this."

"Even the eggs are cheap," Derek noted, setting an omelet in front of me. He put an identical plate full of cheese-and-onion stuffed eggs, and a bottle of wine he'd tucked under his arm, on the other side of the table I'd set with utensils I'd found in the kitchen. Pulling a corkscrew from his shirt pocket, he uncorked the wine, shaking his head while he poured us each a glass. "I don't understand."

"Me, neither," I agreed, picking up my fork and slicing into the eggs. A gooey river of cheese flowed out. However, I was skeptical about how things would taste, after Derek had shown me a walk-in refrigerator and pantry that were vastly different, in terms of content, from the storage spaces he'd last seen several years before, when his mother had still been co-manager of the Silver Spoon.

Gone were the imported Irish butter, *fleur de sel* from France, and house-baked baguettes. In their place had been butter with a big-box-store label, plain old table salt, and *heat-and-serve rolls*. Although Derek wasn't a serious food snob, the presence of that last item had made him turn a little green, mainly, I thought, because his mother would've been horrified.

"Why would Evangeline compromise your family's decades-old reputation?" I mused, taking a bite of the eggs, which were okay. Derek had spent a decent amount of time working at his family's business when he was a kid, and it was hard to mess up breakfast-for-dinner too badly.

I thought the food was also enhanced by the novelty of eating a makeshift, picnic-like meal in a restaurant known for its authentic French cuisine, usually served by impeccably trained staff against a backdrop of soft classical music. To sit in one of the private, candlelit booths and chow down on a simple plate of eggs, while drinking wine from tumblers instead of long-stemmed glasses, seemed like a mini-adventure to me.

I reached for my glass, adding, "Evangeline's decision to cut corners seems especially strange when there are more and more amazing locally sourced foods available— like eggs from my grandmother's farm, which are, no offense to your omelet, much better than these."

"No offense taken." Derek lifted his glass, too, and clinked it against mine. "I have no idea what she was thinking," he noted, before taking a sip.

I took a drink, too, and was surprised to discover that the wine, at least, didn't taste cheap. Checking the label, I saw that we were drinking an expensive merlot from Pepper's family vineyard, and I nearly wondered aloud why Evangeline wouldn't compromise on the contents of the wine cellar. Then I quickly realized that a lot of customers would order full bottles, which would have to be delivered, uncorked, to the table. Unlike butter or salt, which could be concealed in recipes, wine would often be visible.

However, that didn't solve the greater mystery about the overall decline in the quality of the Silver Spoon's once proudly persnickety ingredients.

"Do you think the restaurant is in financial trouble?" I asked, immediately thinking the question was stupid. What other explanation could there be?

Derek leaned back, sighing. "Either that, or Evangeline was just trying to maximize profits. Banking on the restaurant's reputation, she could've passed off cheap food without changing the prices. At least for a while. But I think your guess is correct." He looked past me and frowned. "Especially since something else is missing."

I twisted in my seat to follow his gaze. "What's not here?"

"A painting." He pointed his fork at an empty spot on the wall. "An expensive oil, which my mother hung a few years ago."

I spun back around. "I remember that piece. It was an actual Duvalier." The artist wasn't a household name, but his works commanded impressive sums. "It was a French pastoral scene, right?"

Derek nodded, his mouth a grim line. "I'm starting to wonder if Evangeline sold it—without permission."

"What do you mean?"

"It was expensive enough to be itemized in my mother's will. I should've been alerted if Aunt Evan planned to do *anything* with it."

"Derek, I'm so sorry."

Dropping his fork, he rubbed the back of his neck. "This is a lot to take in. I'm sorry I dragged you here."

"It's okay." I suddenly felt badly for considering our dinner an amusing adventure, and I almost reached out to squeeze his arm, only to stop myself at the last second.

Me, touching Derek Fletcher—who looked even more handsome than usual by candlelight—probably wasn't wise. Especially in an atmospheric and otherwise empty restaurant. I didn't think he'd leap across the table to kiss me, given his unsettled mood. I just thought, over-all, it would be a bad idea as I tried to protect my recently healed heart.

"I'm sorry about how Evangeline undermined every-thing your mom did to make this place amazing," I added, setting down my fork, too. I'd also lost my appetite. "And the negative reviews she was supposedly leaving every-where, harming other local restaurants, make the whole situation worse."

Derek had been looking down at his plate, but his head jerked up, and the color drained from his face, which was fair to begin with. "She was doing what?"

I wished I'd kept my big mouth shut. "It's just a theory Pepper has," I clarified. "She, and apparently some other local chefs . . ." I nearly named Linh Tran, then did manage to edit myself. "They think Evangeline was behind a bunch of terrible online reviews that seem to be cutting into tourist trade at some places. Bookings for the weekend of the Gallery Walk, even, are down dramatically."

Derek looked horrified, and that urge to reach out struck again. I once more fought it off. "Are you okay?" I asked.

"Yes, I'm fine," he promised, immediately contradicting himself. "I'm just stunned and angry to realize that, while I was away, Evangeline didn't just risk the restaurant's reputation. She seems to have damaged our family name. Because undercutting competitors with bad reviews . . . That's fraud, in my opinion. And a court of law might agree."

Looking back at my recent dealings with Derek's aunt, I realized that Derek was right about his family's tarnished reputation. Living next to the Fletchers when the house had been full of life had always been fun. But since Derek had moved away, and his parents had died, the name "Fletcher" had started to leave a sour taste in my mouth. I knew the same was true for other people in Zephyr Hollow, and I didn't quite know what to say.

"You honestly didn't know about any of this, did you, Derek?" I asked, reluctantly. "The changes Evangeline was making at the restaurant, or the—possible—attempt to undercut her competitors?"

He shook his head. "No, trust me. I didn't know anything until tonight. I've been so divorced from this place, for years. And I certainly didn't know about some scheme to badmouth our own neighbors."

I believed him. But I hoped he could prove that he'd been unaware of activities that he'd just admitted made him angry at his recently murdered aunt.

Derek seemed to follow my line of thought. And he must've read the concern on my face. "Willow, there's no reason to worry," he said. "I didn't know anything. There's nothing for Detective Turner to dig up."

I felt relieved, but neither one of us seemed inclined to finish the meals that had grown cold on our plates. On some wordless cue, we both rose and cleaned up, hardly speaking as we worked, or on the ride home. He dropped me off in front of my house before driving a little farther to the mansion that had once seemed like a happy castle to me, then a forbidding fortress when Evangeline had taken control, and which now just seemed sad and way too big for one guy who'd lost his whole family, and who would soon return to a meaningful, but distant, exile.

I watched until the taillights on Evangeline's Lexus, which he'd borrowed, disappeared around the back of the mansion, where the old carriage house had been converted into a four-bay garage.

Then I walked slowly to my cottage, which was very dark, since clouds, seeming to match the evening's mood, had rolled in, obscuring the moon—and a man who sat on the porch swing, waiting for me.

Chapter 11

"You're the second person to scare me at my own house today," I told Detective Turner, who'd stood up and apologized after I'd yelped. Reaching into my mailbox, I pulled out a mix of flyers and bills, and one manila envelope. The package was large but light, and I hoped it contained some paintbrushes I'd ordered. "Why are you even here?"

The question sounded ruder than I'd anticipated, but I saw a flash of white teeth in the darkness when Detective Turner smiled. "You called me, remember? You said you needed to tell me something about the night of Ms. Fletcher's murder. I thought that might be worth a visit."

I wasn't sure if he'd needed to stop by. And, as I dug awkwardly into my bag for my keys, I wasn't positive that I wanted to invite him inside my home. I supposed Pepper had gotten to me with her lecture about trusting a man who might know more about magic than he was letting on. Yet part of me thought Pepper was being paranoid, and I didn't want to chase him off or stand on the porch in the dark, either.

Hesitating, I considered my options while my stomach, which wasn't happy about my decision to pass on the omelet, rumbled. Then I looked up at the tall police officer who was waiting for me to say something and asked, "Would you like a s'more?"

"I'll admit, I haven't done this in a long time," Detective Turner said, leaning forward on one of the Adirondack chairs that ringed my fire pit, located right next to Peddler's Creek. He'd built an impressive fire while I'd assembled a tray with homemade graham crackers and vanilla marshmallows, along with chocolate made at a Zephyr Hollow shop called Loco for Cocoa.

While I'd arranged everything on a folk art table that stood between our chairs, I'd explained how I'd figured out that *someone* had returned to the Owl & Crescent and put away the still-life scene. However, to my surprise, Detective Turner hadn't hurried off after I'd delivered that news.

Holding a marshmallow-topped stick over the fire, he looked over at me, a glimmer of curiosity, tinged with amusement, in his eyes. "Why do you have gourmet ingredients on hand? Is s'more making a hobby of yours?"

"Kind of," I said, smiling. "I host a lot of kids' art parties here. In the summer, we usually make s'mores." I shrugged, then pulled back my own stick. My marshmallow had caught on fire, and I quickly blew it out. "If you're going to eat something, why not make it as delicious as possible?"

When I said that, I thought about the Silver Spoon, and Evangeline's switch to cheap ingredients. I was still trying to figure out how cutting food costs would've helped her bottom line in the long run—unless she really was planting a lot of inflated reviews to lure unsuspecting out-of-towners.

Detective Turner was oblivious to my line of thought, focused instead on smooshing his perfectly toasted marshmallow between two graham crackers, one of which he'd topped with chocolate. I followed suit, and we were temporarily silent, the only noise the gentle rush of the creek and the crackling fire. Even the animals were quiet that night. Mortimer was asleep in his playhouse, and Luna was hiding in the garden, probably pretending she was a jungle cat.

Sitting back, I caught a glimpse of Rembrandt, who coasted in a circle above us before settling onto a low branch in a nearby apple tree.

Detective Turner leaned back, and, although I hadn't seen his gaze so much as flick in the direction of the sky, he asked, "Do you always have an avian bodyguard?"

"Rembrandt keeps an eye on me," I said, winking at the owl, who was watching us with his intelligent eyes, set in his snowy white, serious face. Then, just in case Pepper was right, and I should be suspicious of the enigmatic detective who was wiping marshmallow from his appealingly full lower lip, I added, "I think he'd be surprisingly helpful if anyone ever threatened me."

Detective Turner's gaze finally did shift noticeably to Remi, who plumped his feathers, making himself larger.

"Those are some impressive claws," Detective Turner noted. "And I have great respect for, and interest in, owls." He looked at me again, making a motion to indicate that I also had something on my face. I swiped at my chin, which felt sticky. He didn't laugh at me, though. In fact, he spoke more softly and seriously. "Still, in spite of your impressive familiar . . ."

My eyes widened at his use of that word, which wasn't completely obscure, but which was particular to witch-craft. However, he didn't seem to notice my surprise.

". . . I really think you should be careful until I figure out who killed your neighbor. I wouldn't sit out here alone at night for the time being." He raised a hand. "And I'm not being sexist. I wouldn't walk alone in the woods here right now, either."

I was pretty sure Pepper, and maybe Astrid, would've cautioned me against spending time in a dark, isolated yard at the edge of the trees with *Detective Turner*.

I shook off that thought. "I'm being careful, within reason," I told him. "Meaning I can't hide inside my cottage." I'd finished my s'more, and I reached for another marshmallow, which I jabbed onto my crude skewer. Hovering it over the flames, I looked sideways at my guest, who was apparently done eating. He sat back, his long legs stretched out before himself and his off-duty sneakers close to the ring of stones. Detective Turner was dressed more casually than usual, too, in worn jeans and a gray T-shirt that showed off his biceps and hinted at a muscular chest.

The fact that Pepper had stopped joking about the hot new guy in town made me wary again. "You must've thought it was necessary to come here when you're obviously off duty," I noted. "I'm sorry if the information I had wasn't important enough to merit a trip."

Detective Turner stared into the fire, which cast shadows on the planes of his face. "I actually think what you told me might be incredibly important. Especially since the shears continue to be missing, after a thorough second search of the woods near where the body was found. And someone obviously returned to your studio and tampered with the scene, hiding the other objects away, after your friends—"

"Pepper and Astrid." I supplied their names in case he'd forgotten them. Skipping the graham crackers and chocolate, I slipped the gooey marshmallow off the stick and popped it directly into my mouth. Then I spoke through the sticky bite, my voice muffled. "Who, I guess, will be questioned now, since you know they stayed late and cleaned up the rest of the barn."

I was pretty sure that had already been common knowledge, since he would've pieced together a timeline based upon interviews with other guests, but the moment the words left my mouth, I felt like I'd just betrayed my two closest friends.

My concern must've been obvious. "Ms. Armbruster and Ms. Applebee were already on my list," Detective Turner said. "Although, talking to them hasn't been a priority, because I can't find any motive for them to have committed the murder—unlike someone else who has admitted to having access to the barn."

"Mr. Van Buskirk."

Detective Turner nodded. "Yes. He said he's been working on projects around your property." Detective Turner's tone was almost too neutral. "Did you give him a key, Willow? Maybe to the barn?"

"No, but to be honest, I hardly ever locked any of my doors before the murder. *Anyone* could've entered the studio." I doubted Detective Turner would answer my next question, but I asked it, anyway. "Did Mr. Van Buskirk ever say where he was, the night Evangeline was killed?"

"We did discuss that, of course. But I'm not sure his

alibi holds up. Nor can I give you more details." He looked me hard in the eyes. "I'm only telling you *any* of this so you'll be on guard."

"Okay, thanks. But it's hard for me to believe a man who lived just across the creek, practically my whole life, killed anyone."

"You have no idea how many times I've heard that, right before I arrested someone's neighbor or friend." The hint of a grin played at the corners of his lips. "Well, not everyone mentions a creek."

I ignored the joke. "Pepper and Astrid didn't kill anyone. I'm *sure* of that."

I was deadly serious, but Detective Turner smiled more broadly. "I have to admit, I'm inclined to agree that Astrid Applebee, at least, is innocent. I see her now and then, hanging spinny, shiny things outside of her 'Astral Emporium' when I'm walking my dog—"

I got a funny prickle in the pit of my stomach. "You have a dog?"

He nodded. "Yes. A boxer mix who's as protective as your owl." He used his thumb to lightly touch his forehead in a gesture that reminded me of a blessing. "She has an unusual white mark, like a diamond, right here."

"Interesting," I muttered, sliding lower in my seat.

Had the keen-eyed detective who'd spotted the stealthy bird in the apple tree really failed to see a painting of himself when he'd searched the Owl & Crescent?

And if he had noticed his image, why wasn't he saying anything?

Last but not least, *how the heck had I painted his dog, too?*

"Are you okay?" Detective Turner sat up straighter, like

he was ready to take my pulse again. "You look pale. You're not going to pass out again, are you?" He made that sound like another joke, but I could tell he wasn't kidding. "Because I should get you inside, if that's the case."

I pulled myself upright, too. "I'm fine. Just suffering a little bit of marshmallow overload." I studied his eyes by the flickering light. "The fact that you're telling me so much . . . Does that mean I'm *not* a suspect?"

Detective Turner's gaze cut, just for a split second, in the direction of Fletcher Mansion, and the gesture was enough to let me know that, while I'd had motive, I wasn't ranked highest on his list of suspects, either. I was ahead of Pepper and Astrid, but lower than Derek and Mr. Van Buskirk. My position was probably improved by the fact that I was going out of my way to share information, even though the possible weapon I was trying to help him find belonged to me.

"How long have you known Derek Fletcher?" Detective Turner asked, as if reading my mind. "He grew up here, like you." Of course, he'd looked into Derek's past, just like he'd asked around about me. "Were you friends?"

"I'm not going to answer that," I said, bristling a little. "In part, because I think you already know the answer."

If I'd guessed right, and Detective Turner knew that Derek and I had once been a couple, he didn't react. His expression was impassive, and I missed the more approachable man who'd just been joking around and expressing concern for me.

"I'll only say that Derek is a good guy—whom I *have* known for a long time," I added. "I was raised here, with my mother and grandmother, who sold me the property when she bought the farm."

Detective Turner's expression softened. "I'm so sorry."

It took me a second to realize why he seemed so sympathetic, but when I figured it out, I laughed, even though I'd just been mildly irritated with him. "No! She bought *a* farm. A real, working agricultural establishment, where she raises goats, chickens, and alpacas."

Detective Turner grinned, too, and rubbed his jaw, which was shadowed with a hint of stubble. "Oh. Sorry, I misunderstood. I'm glad she's all right."

The tension that had briefly formed between us dissipated, to the degree that was possible, given that he was investigating a bunch of people I knew, including Derek, who might not have been my boyfriend anymore, but who was still important to me. Detective Turner seemed to realize it was a good time for him to leave, and he stood up. As I rose, too, he bent and picked up the tray with the leftover s'mores fixings. "Thanks for taking me back to my childhood."

"Near New Orleans, right?" I asked, still curious about his accent. We began to walk across the grass, toward my cottage. Luna appeared out of nowhere and joined us, trying to rub up against Detective Turner's legs while he was in motion. Rembrandt lifted off, too, and flew above, still watchful on my behalf. I looked up at Detective Turner. "That *is* what you said, correct?"

He smiled at me. "You can't place the accent, can you? Because it's unique to me, I'm afraid. Or unique to my upbringing, with a Creole mother and British father."

I stopped in my tracks. "Oh, I totally hear it now. And you're right. I never would've guessed that."

"No one does." He grew more serious, and it seemed

like the sweetly perfumed air around us grew heavier, too. "And they are . . . were . . . an odd pair."

I wasn't sure if he meant that his parents were divorced, or if one or both of them had died, and I couldn't figure out how to tactfully ask. Instead, I ventured, "How so? Why were they odd?"

He looked into the distance. "My father is an Oxford-educated Tulane professor, while my mother was a high-school-educated—and an incredibly talented—folk artist from the edge of the Honey Island swamp. It was a strange pairing, by most standards."

So, his mother had passed away. "I'm sorry about your loss."

"Thanks. Me, too." Detective Turner continued walking, and, like Luna, who resumed trotting worshipfully in his wake, I followed. I wanted to ask more questions about his mom, and what sounded like an unusual upbringing, but we'd reached the cottage. Stepping up onto the porch, he set the tray on a table near the door. "Thanks again for the s'mores."

"You're welcome," I said, keenly aware that we were suddenly very close on the narrow, wraparound porch.

Then he held out his hand, and for a second, I thought I was supposed to shake it. Or *hold* it. Fortunately, before I could make an embarrassing mistake, he asked, "Do you have your phone?"

"What?" I had no idea why he was asking.

"Your phone." He gestured for me to hand it over. "I'll add my direct number in case those shears ever turn up."

"Oh, yes. Of course." I dug into the back pocket of my jeans, where I had tucked my phone, and handed over the device. "Here."

That word was barely out of my mouth when I realized I'd stupidly just relinquished my safety net, and I tensed. But Detective Turner wasn't even looking, let alone lunging, at me. He tapped the screen, then handed the phone back. "Please call if you find, or learn, anything else, okay?"

Slipping the phone back into my pocket, I nodded, but didn't say anything more. I just kept looking up at Detective Turner, who was still inches away from me.

Although it was dark, I could make out his strong jawline. I could also smell his cologne, mingled with the scent of the fire, and sense his unique energy, which was becoming less frightening and more compelling.

Detective Turner was observing me, too, and I absently tucked some of my hair behind my ear, again wondering how he viewed me, with my messy ponytail; my jeans, which were smeared with some marshmallow; and the mood ring I still couldn't get off my hand, and which was glowing a strange shade of violet.

My cheeks also felt like they were changing color, turning pink, and I slid my left hand, with the ring, behind my back just as the strange, sort of charged moment was interrupted by a pig who trotted noisily up the steps, headed directly for the door, like he wanted to go inside for the night.

Glancing across the yard, to the west, I saw that clouds were gathering. "You might want to get going," I told Detective Turner. "Mortimer seems to think there's a storm coming, and I have to agree."

At that moment, lightning flickered, and I saw something in Detective Turner's eyes. Something that unsettled me all the way to my core. Then that moment passed, too, and he said, "Yes. I should get home to Marinette."

The possibility that someone might be waiting for him

hadn't even crossed my mind. "Marinette?" I asked, with surprise. "What an unusual name."

Detective Turner was already walking away, toward the front steps, but I saw a flash of white teeth again when he spoke over his shoulder, smiling. "If you knew my dog, you'd realize it's actually very appropriate."

His *dog*.

"Good night," I said, as he stepped off the porch and into the night. I doubted he heard me. He was already crossing Wending Way. I finally spotted his car, a black SUV, parked under some trees. I hadn't noticed that when Derek had dropped me off.

I continued watching Detective Turner, noting that Rembrandt was swooping overhead, as if escorting our guest to his vehicle. Then lightning flickered again, and I let Mortimer and Luna into the cottage.

I knew I should go inside, too, and lock the doors, because Detective Turner was right. It probably wasn't wise for anyone to be outside alone, near the scene of a homicide, until that murder was solved.

And yet, after I heard his SUV start up and pull away, I ignored that advice and hurried back across the yard, jogging past the dying fire and into the darkness.

Chapter 12

The storm that arrived shortly after Detective Turner left wasn't nearly as powerful as the one that had blown through Zephyr Hollow the night of Evangeline's murder, but the atmosphere was still eerie as I padded quietly around my bedroom, being careful not to wake Mortimer, who slept on his pillow, and Luna, who dozed at the foot of my bed.

Stepping around the pig, I bent to light five candles I'd set in the fireplace, then shook out the match. I'd already lit several other candles on the mantel and in the bookshelves that lined part of the turret, where my unreliable spell book, which I'd brought in from the studio, lay unsealed and open on a small table.

The white, wooden stand also held a sketch pad, a soft charcoal pencil, and a mug of tea I'd brewed from pennywort, sage, and rosemary.

Sitting down on the overstuffed chair, I took a deep breath as lightning flickered outside, echoing the candles. A moment later, the rumble of thunder caused Mortimer to shift and grunt in his sleep.

"Are you behind this weather, Pepper?" I said quietly,

with a quick glance out the window, just as a gust of wind rocked the cottage and rattled the shutters.

I swore, it seemed like my friend had replied to me, although I knew she wasn't *that* powerful, and certainly didn't have super hearing. We were modestly skilled witches, not characters from Marvel comics.

Shaking off the crazy thought, I returned my attention to the book, where one page, on the left, featured a hand-written recipe for piccalilli. While I was fond of my great-grandmother's relish recipe, I was more interested in the page on the right, where I'd inked a spell I'd created through trial and error.

Bending close, I tried to figure out my own hand-writing, because I'd done quite a bit of erasing and revising. However, I was pretty sure I'd gotten the measurements for the tea right, and I quickly deciphered the words to the small rhyme, too.

Committing the script to memory, I lifted the teacup and closed my eyes, hesitating for just a moment. The spell wasn't as powerful as the one that had caused Detective Turner to check my pulse. However, it might unleash some frightening images, if I was, indeed, able to summon mem-ories I was almost certain I was repressing, related to my unsettling interaction with Evangeline's painting.

Reminding myself yet again that recollections of the experience wouldn't be nearly as intense as the original journey "into" the canvas, I took a deep breath and whis-pered, *"Pennywort, sage, and rosemary, draw my memo-ries back to me. Take me to a forgotten land, and show me its secrets, through my hand."*

Then I drank the tea in one big, pungent gulp.

Grimacing, I opened my eyes, picked up the sketchbook and pencil, and walked to my bed, where I crawled under the covers, momentarily waking Luna, who yawned, stretched, and curled up even more tightly.

Then, as the storm continued to batter the house, and the wind sneaked down the chimney, causing the candles to flicker and wink, I waited for sleep to come and the spell to *hopefully* work its magic.

I woke up at dawn, my arms and legs tangled in my sheets and my hair a knotted mess.

My restlessness overnight must've chased off Mortimer and Luna, both of whom had disappeared from the room, which was now lit by the first rays of sunshine on what I guessed was going to be a hot and humid day.

I wanted to open the windows I'd closed the night before to keep out the rain, but first I was eager to see what, if anything, I'd drawn while sleeping under the veil of the spell.

Digging around in my disheveled bed, I first found the pencil, which had left some marks on the sheets. Then I dug out the sketchbook, too, and flipped to a page that was also covered with charcoal.

My heart started racing with excitement, tinged with fear related to what I might discover.

Then, as I began to recognize the images I'd managed to draw, if poorly, during my troubled slumber, I cocked my head and frowned.

What the heck?

Chapter 13

"I'm not sure what to make of any of these things," Pepper admitted, turning my sketchbook every which way. I'd brought my spell-inspired drawings to the Crooked Chimneys, where she, Astrid, and I were gathered in the shade near a swimming pool that looked almost like a natural pond, tucked behind the white-clapboard inn, which did indeed have two slightly askew brick chimneys.

I'd called our quick coven meeting during one of Pepper's few breaks in the day, after she'd served breakfast and most of the guests had left to explore Zephyr Hollow and the surrounding region, which was full of lovely hamlets, including a unique pet-friendly town called Sylvan Creek. While her cleaning staff fixed up the rooms and prepared the dining room for lunch, Pepper could usually steal a moment to chat.

Astrid should've been minding her shop, but she'd placed a sign on the door telling potential customers she'd be back soon—although the tote she'd brought along, stuffed with a bathing suit and beach towel, told me she wasn't in any hurry to return to the Emporium.

"Am I even seeing what you both see?" Pepper added, continuing to scrutinize my drawings. She sat next to me in a chaise longue, her legs stretched out and ankles crossed. "The snake, the dog house, and the playing-card spade?"

"Yes, I also see *most* of those things," I said, scooching forward on my own chair. "But I'm not certain about any of them. Everything is too vague."

"And messy," added Astrid, who was standing. She leaned over me and Pepper, the better to see the book. "It looks like you were using the wrong hand or something!"

"Well, she *was* asleep," Pepper noted, handing me the sketchbook. "Tell me again what you hoped to achieve with this spell?"

"Yes, I'm a bit confused," Astrid added, gesturing for me to move my legs, so she could sit at the end of my chair.

I edged over, giving her some room. "It might sound crazy, but I was trying to remember what I saw when I rested my hand on Evangeline's canvas."

My friends exchanged concerned looks.

"I *didn't* plan to repeat the entire awful experience," I clarified. "I just wanted to recall *something*, so the whole first, more taxing spell wasn't a waste. Because, the more I think about it, the more I'm convinced that I witnessed Evangeline's murder—essentially *suffered through it* with her—and my brain just won't let me access the traumatic memories."

Pepper was wearing sunglasses, and she lowered them to the tip of her nose. "Willow. Maybe you *shouldn't* access those memories. Maybe it would be too much. I know you, Astrid and I talked about solving this crime. But you have to protect yourself."

"I also need to protect Derek," I said. "Detective Turner made it pretty clear that he considers Derek the chief suspect in the crime."

Pepper pulled off her glasses and narrowed her eyes. "When? When did he make that clear?"

I realized I'd made a mistake, and I decided to be honest with my friends. "He stopped by last night because I called him after you both told me you didn't clean up the scene with the missing shears. I thought that was important." I could tell that I was in for a lecture, so I kept speaking quickly. "I didn't let him inside the cottage or barn. We talked outside, over some s'mores—"

"You made s'mores with him?" Astrid sounded worried for me, but also betrayed, like she wished she'd been invited.

"Sorry," I told her and Pepper. "I didn't expect him to come over when I called. I thought he'd call or text back. And I did the best I could to keep myself safe when he showed up out of the blue."

"I'm sure you did, Willow," Astrid said, with a sympathetic pout.

"Yes, I'm sorry if I snapped at you," Pepper added. "Please know that I'm merely concerned."

I smiled at my fellow witches. "I know, and I'm grateful to you both."

Pepper slipped on her sunglasses again. "Since you survived the encounter, I suppose there's no sense dwelling on what could have happened. I'd rather hear about anything you might've learned, either about the investigation, or the detective conducting it."

"Especially the detective." Astrid requested.

"I did learn a few things that might be of interest," I told them. "Such as, his father is a professor from England, and his mother is a deceased artist and cook, whose education ended at high school."

"Sad, and a tiny bit unusual, but not exactly informative," Pepper said.

She had a point, so I moved on to something that I thought might interest her and Astrid more. "He also has a dog named Marinette."

Pepper visibly jolted. "Like the loa associated with Voodoo?"

I nodded. "Yes. I believe so."

Astrid was obviously confused. "Can someone please explain what a loa is? I know very little about Voodoo, although I do carry a book called, *Who Do Voodoo? You Do Voodoo!* at the Emporium." She sighed. "It has terrible reviews, though, and probably isn't very reliable or comprehensive."

I started to mention that maybe she should stop selling what did sound like a poor reference, then reconsidered. Instead, I told her, "I don't know much about that practice, either. But, from what I understand, a loa is a spirit, and Marinette is a particularly powerful, sometimes contradictory one."

"A spirit who can be protective, but who can get out of control, too," Pepper added.

I shot her a funny look. "How do you know so much?"

"I keep trying to tell you," she said. "There's a potentially dangerous man—or entity—in our midst. I am doing my research."

"I could loan you a book . . ." Astrid started to offer Pepper a copy of *Who Do Voodoo*, then thought the better of it. "Never mind."

"Detective Turner also referred to Rembrandt as my familiar, and mentioned having an interest in owls, himself," I noted.

"I'm still lost," Astrid complained. "Familiar is a pretty

common term, and I don't understand why caring about owls is pertinent."

"Owls are strongly associated with the spirit, Marinette," I said, with another glance at Pepper. "I'm doing some research, too."

"Can we all agree that, at the very least, Detective Turner is *very* familiar with at least one paranormal practice?" Pepper requested. "If not a practitioner, as I suspect?"

"Yes, but let's keep in mind that we're paranormal practitioners, too," I reminded my coven. "And we don't plan to do anyone any harm."

Astrid stood up and grabbed her tote. "I'm still suspicious, like Pepper. But since there's nothing more to do right now, and it's getting hot, I believe I'll take a swim, if that's okay with you, Pepper?"

"Yes, of course," Pepper said. "You can change inside."

Astrid pointed across the cool water, which was tempting me, too. "I'll just use the cabana."

Pepper shook her head. "Sorry, but that's a disaster right now. I hired George Van Buskirk to spruce the place up before the gala. But then the whole mess with Evangeline happened, and he's been too preoccupied to come back and finish the work. I've locked the place up."

Astrid headed for the inn. "In that case, I'll be back in a few minutes."

"It's not like Mr. Van Buskirk to leave a mess, even when he's busy," I said, when Astrid had gone inside. "I'm sure he'll finish the job before the party."

Pepper always decorated the Crooked Chimneys' adorable pool house for the gala, using the little building to serve snacks and drinks. But it looked like the current year might be an exception.

"Even if George does offer to come back, I might leave the cabana closed this year," Pepper said. "I'm thinking of renovating it entirely, for use as a guest room."

"Oh, that would be a great job for Mr. Van Buskirk. It would pay more than the odd jobs I'm able to offer him."

"Willow, I'm not sure about that idea."

"Why not?"

Pepper seemed unwilling to answer. Then she confided, "To be honest, George has been acting a bit erratically lately. I don't know that I want him to oversee this project. I may hire a professional contractor."

I furrowed my brow. "Erratic . . . how?"

"He's just saying strange things."

"Such as?"

"Oh, I don't know." Pepper smiled, but it seemed forced. "He's just rambling sometimes, lately. You really haven't noticed?"

"No, I haven't."

"Well, it's nothing *too* alarming. I suppose he's just getting on in years, and has been under some strain, even before he became a murder suspect, poor thing." It was obvious that Pepper didn't think the kindly ex-caretaker was a killer. She pointed to the sketchbook, changing the subject. "Now, back to the reason you called this meeting."

I'd nearly forgotten the book that was sitting on my lap, full of the nonsense I'd drawn. "I don't think we'll be able to learn anything worthwhile," I said. "The spell was obviously weak. It didn't do any harm. Or, I think, much good."

"*Luckily*, it did no harm," Pepper noted. Then she pushed her sunglasses up into her blond hair, the better to scrutinize me. "So, did it work at all? Do you remember anything?"

"No." I suffered a twinge of disappointment when I again looked down at the sketch pad. "None of this makes any sense to me." I angled the pad so we could both see it, then pointed to the objects I'd drawn. "Like you, I see a dog house. And there's definitely a snake, who seems to be lying on a jagged stick."

Pepper leaned sideways, frowning. "It kind of reminds me of the old medical symbol, you know? The snake twined around a stick?"

My mind immediately went to a doctor who'd recently arrived back in town, and Pepper must've thought the same thing.

We both shook our heads, and I said, "No. Derek's not a killer."

Tapping the pad again, my finger hit a smudgy shape. "Moving on. What you identify as a spade looks more like a fleur-de-lis to me."

Pepper didn't say anything, and I looked over to see that her mouth was set in a firm, unhappy line.

"What's wrong?" I asked warily. "You don't see another connection to Derek, do you?"

"No, not Derek." Pepper's voice was low and serious.

"Then what's the matter?"

"I'm telling you," she said. "Something is *not right*."

"You mean, about the murder? Which, of course, is very wrong . . ."

Pepper was shaking her head. "No. I'm talking about what you drew—as you tried to summon fragments of memory, related to Evangeline's death."

I glanced at the sketches. "Which thing? The dog house, the snake, or the French symbol?"

"The fleur-de-lis," she said quietly, although we were alone on the patio. "A symbol related not just to France, but to *New Orleans*."

It took me a moment to connect the dots, during which Pepper noted, "That's *Detective Lucien Turner's hometown*, correct?"

Chapter 14

I was still mulling over Pepper's revelation about the fleur-de-lis—and questioning whether that was even what I'd drawn—while I puttered around the Owl & Crescent later that day.

The studio wasn't air conditioned, and Luna was keeping cool by stretching out under the work table, along with Mortimer, who seemed to be getting chummy with the cat. Rembrandt, who normally would've been sleeping, was making himself useful by occasionally swooping past me to create a breeze.

"Thanks," I told him, when he dipped over my shoulder before landing on his new favorite spot, Evangeline's easel, which I'd moved to a corner while I figured out what to do with the painting.

In the meantime, I was packing up the works created by the other members of the Small Business Alliance, having resigned myself to dropping them off, since nobody seemed inclined to stop by the Owl & Crescent in the wake of the murder.

"What if Evangeline achieves in death what she couldn't do in life?" I mused to Remi. "What if she actually

112   *Bethany Blake*

manages to ruin my business and derail my life by *getting killed*?"

Rembrandt hooted softly, maybe to remind me that only one planned party had been canceled since the homicide. I'd also booked a new gathering for Sylvan Creek resident Daphne Templeton, who was bringing her sister Piper, a bunch of bridesmaids—and possibly a basset hound and poodle "couple"—for a last-minute bachelorette party.

In a burst of complete honesty, I'd warned Ms. Templeton about the recent murder, which, to my surprise, she'd waved off as tragic, but not exactly shocking. In fact, she'd offered to help solve the case—a gesture I'd appreciated, but ultimately turned down.

Regardless, although my business wasn't suffering so far, I felt a bit concerned as I carefully placed Linh Tran's delicate, Asian-inspired garden scene in a box with Penelope Dandridge's chaotic rendering of the display. Then I added Benjamin Blodgett's terrified rabbit, which still disturbed me, and Myrna Crickle's abstract interpretation.

"I guess I should take my own canvases to the Well-Dressed Wall, so Myrna can hang them before the Gallery Walk," I added, looking across the barn at my framed works.

Not surprisingly, my attention was first drawn to the watercolor that featured Lucien Turner and his pet with the strange name, Marinette, walking in the rain.

Moving closer, I first noted how I'd captured Detective Turner's *aura*, for lack of a better word, more than his features. His quiet confidence, the way he carried himself, even the hint of mystery that surrounded him, all came through.

"If only I could see that expression in his eyes again, when the lightning lit up his face," I told Rembrandt, who continued to observe me from his perch. I glanced at the owl. "What compelled you to follow him last night?"

Not surprisingly, Remi didn't respond, and I returned my attention to the painting, looking more closely at the dog. Although I couldn't recall adding a white diamond on the animal's forehead, sure enough, the mark was there, almost like my brush had missed a spot by accident.

Yet I didn't think I'd made a mistake.

So how had I known about Marinette's marking?

And was there a connection between the symbol I'd drawn and Detective Turner's supposed hometown of New Orleans?

Finally, why hadn't I asked him what brought him to Zephyr Hollow?

"Ho-o-o."

It almost sounded like Rembrandt was also asking who the heck Lucien Turner really was, and I pulled my phone from my pocket. "Let's find out, shall we?"

Remi hopped closer while I typed "Lucien Turner New Orleans" into a search engine.

Then I waited. And waited. And waited some more, until the connection timed out.

I tried again with the same result.

"Weird," I told Remi, moving to put away my phone just as a text popped up on the screen.

The person wasn't in my contacts, so for a second, I feared that Detective Turner had used some sort of magic—or technology—to figure out I'd been cyber-stalking him, and he was texting to warn me against that activity.

Then I read the message, and it still took me a moment to realize who'd asked, out of the blue, **Do you have a date for the gala?**

* * *

I didn't answer Derek's question right away, because I was ninety-eight percent positive he'd follow up by inviting me to be his date for the party, and I wasn't sure if attending together was a wise idea.

"Probably not," I thought, as I parked my old Subaru near the Well-Dressed Wall.

Hopping out of the car, I went around to the hatch, keeping an eye out for people I knew among the tourists who were already strolling around in advance of the big weekend.

Normally, I recognized at least a few locals, but the only familiar person I spied was Linh Tran, who was opening Typhoon for the dinner crowd. If there would, indeed, be a crowd.

Spotting me, Linh paused in hanging a red silk Vietnamese lantern outside of her storefront, where the glossy black woodwork was gleaming in the setting sun. Smiling, she waved.

"Linh, wait," I called, waving back at her. "I have something for you!"

She hesitated, then said, "Sorry, Willow. Not right now."

I only needed a few seconds of her time, and I quickly opened the hatch and grabbed her painting, hurrying across the street.

She was about to go inside, but she waited for me. "I've got your painting," I told her, holding up the canvas.

Linh smiled, but halfheartedly. "Oh, goodness, Willow. I've been reluctant to claim my reminder of that night." She nevertheless accepted the painting from me. "I'm sorry I didn't stop by."

"It's okay," I said. "No one claimed their artwork."

The late afternoon sun cast Linh's pretty face in a warm glow. She was probably about forty-five, but she looked younger. And she was always polished, usually wearing silk and linen, like she was doing that day. Her outfit—a taupe shirt paired with wide-legged black pants—looked expensive to me.

"I didn't mean the party was bad," she said. "That came out wrong. I only meant that Evangeline's death was upsetting."

I knew I didn't have much time to talk with her, so I cut right to the chase. "Linh, did you know Evangeline well? Because I heard you talking with Penelope at the Owl & Crescent, and you seemed unhappy with my neighbor. Maybe related to some bad reviews she was giving your restaurant?"

Linh's body stiffened, and I knew I'd struck a nerve. "I don't know what you mean."

I thought of the note in Evangeline's planner, about a meeting at Typhoon. "Or maybe you had some sort of business dealing with her?"

Linh was normally friendly, but her expression hardened like cement. "I don't like what you're implying—"

"I don't mean to imply anything," I said. "I'm just trying to piece together the last few hours before Evangeline's death. Because Derek Fletcher, George Van Buskirk, and I are all suspects. If you knew about something she was doing that was making people angry—other people, aside from you—maybe that would be helpful."

"I have nothing to say, Willow," Linh insisted. Her tone softened slightly. "I'm sorry about your predicament. But there's nothing I can tell you right now."

With that, she turned on her heel and ducked into her restaurant. I had no choice but to return to my car, where the hatch was still open. Grabbing the box that held my own paintings, I lumbered awkwardly to the Well-Dressed Wall's arched wooden doors. However, when I managed to jiggle the brass knob, I discovered that the gallery was locked.

Knocking lightly—with my foot—I waited a moment, because I was certain Myrna would be inside, since the town's biggest celebration of the arts was just days away.

No one came to open up for me, though, so I decided to try the back door. Adjusting my box, which was getting heavy, I made my way down a narrow corridor between the gallery and the Silver Spoon, which was, of course, still closed. The passageway was short but claustrophobic, and I was glad when I emerged behind the buildings, in a small parking lot that faced an alley.

Sure enough, Myrna's Mercedes Benz was parked in a spot marked with her name.

I also noted a hand-painted sign on the back of the Silver Spoon, indicating the entrance to Take 666 Studio. An arrow pointed down a dark flight of stairs.

The sign wasn't exactly welcoming.

Then, because my arms were getting very tired, I hurried to the gallery's back door, which was, as I'd expected, unlocked.

"Hello?" I called, struggling to open the door and get through. No one answered, and I tried again. "Hello?"

There was still no response, so I decided to leave my paintings in a third-floor storage area, where I'd been directed to leave my artwork in years past. Climbing a back staircase, I passed by a second floor of airy, art-filled rooms before reaching the cramped upper story.

Setting my box just inside the door, I couldn't resist looking around at the treasure trove of oils and watercolors that were waiting their turn to be sold. Myrna had wonderful taste, and she was a savvy and well-respected broker, so there were quite a few pieces I recognized.

Walking around the room, which featured a sharply pitched ceiling and dormers, I paused before works by several artists I admired.

Then a gilt frame, propped in a shadowed corner, caught my attention, and I stopped short, blinking to make sure I wasn't imagining things. Even when I was almost certain I'd identified the painting correctly, I heard the confusion in my voice when I spoke aloud, asking nobody in particular, "Is that the *Duvalier* from the Silver Spoon?"

At least, I thought I'd been talking to myself, until Myrna Crickle said, from just inside the door she was suddenly blocking, "Oh, goodness, dear. I *really* wish you hadn't seen that."

"Why do you have the Fletchers' painting?" I asked, backing up a step when Myrna approached me, a hefty-looking claw hammer clutched in one hand—hopefully because she planned to hang some artwork. I wasn't paranoid, but Myrna Crickle was giving me a very funny look, and the attic was awfully isolated. Then I glanced at the French pastoral scene, which I'd last seen at the Silver Spoon, before again meeting Myrna's surprisingly cool gaze, magnified by her big, round eyeglasses. "Did Evangeline loan you the Duvalier or something?"

I could tell from the strange expression on Myrna's face that my admittedly wild guess was incorrect.

"No, Willow," she said, shaking her head. Then, much to my surprise, all the color drained from her face, and she confided, in a shaky voice, "I *took* that painting from Evangeline—on an evening that went very wrong!"

Chapter 15

"What happened?" I asked warily, backing up another step in the cramped space. Myrna Crickle was quite a bit older than me, but she carried heavy paintings all the time, and I had a feeling she was pretty strong. Plus, she was holding a hammer, while I didn't even have my car keys. I'd left them in the Subaru, because my hands had been full, and—one murder aside—Zephyr Hollow was remarkably crime free. My mother wouldn't have it any other way. At least I hoped my community was still safe. I was getting a little worried as Myrna stepped closer, still holding the hammer, and I swallowed thickly before inquiring, "And when, exactly, did 'things go wrong'?"

I was half terrified, half excited—and, at the risk of going over one hundred percent, in terms of emotions, also horrified and saddened—while I waited for a woman I respected and liked to confess to committing a murder. Therefore, my feelings were also mixed when Myrna, understanding what I was implying, appeared horrified, herself. Her free hand flew to cover her mouth. Then she pulled it away, telling me, "Oh, no! Willow! I didn't kill Evangeline! That's not what I meant!"

Before I could respond, Myrna's shoulders slumped with resignation, so the hammer hung lower, and I thought looser, in her fingers. "Although, I'm sure if the detective who's been nosing around ever hears my tale, I will be more of a suspect than I already am."

"Myrna, what's going on?" I asked, finally daring to edge closer. I debated suggesting that we go somewhere more comfortable and less remote, like her office, but I was afraid she might change her mind about sharing whatever she obviously needed to get off her chest. "Why would you be considered a suspect at all, beyond the fact that you were at the Owl & Crescent the night of the murder?"

Of course, I'd witnessed the tension between Myrna and my deceased neighbor, and I hadn't forgotten Evangeline's strange comment, which had made it seem like Myrna was involved in some shady dealings.

". . . That wouldn't necessarily stop you from passing Willow off as Picasso at the Well-Dressed Wall, would it, Myrna . . . ?"

"Seriously, Myrna," I prompted, when she didn't respond. She was clearly trying to decide how much to tell me, while I still wished she'd put down the hammer. I didn't feel nearly as threatened as before, but the sharp claw, especially, continued to make me edgy. "What's up?"

"If I tell you everything, you can't go running to the police," she said, tapping the tool against her palm. I *thought* the gesture was more absent than warning. "I told Detective Turner quite a bit, but he doesn't know, and doesn't need to know, the whole story of my feud with Evangeline."

"I noticed that you two weren't getting along at the Small Business Alliance party," I said. "And Evangeline made some cryptic remarks about you."

"Yes, I wondered what you thought when she again accused me of a fraud I never committed in the first place!"

My gaze shifted to the Duvalier, then back to Myrna, who looked not just angry, but *hurt* to have her integrity questioned. "It's something about that painting, right?"

She nodded. "Yes. Apparently, a few months ago, some so-called 'art expert' came into the Silver Spoon, and, when Evangeline started boasting about the Duvalier, the man 'sniffed with disdain.'" Myrna rolled her eyes. "That's how Evangeline *always* told the story."

I could imagine my neighbor repeating the same complaint over and over again in the same exasperating way.

"Anyhow," Myrna continued, stepping out of a shaft of sunlight streaming through one of the dormers and into a shadow. Her voice took on a darker aspect, too. "Evangeline insisted that this man was correct, and she claimed that I'd purposely defrauded the Fletcher family!"

"But she had no proof, beyond this 'expert's' opinion?"

"No," Myrna grumbled. "But that didn't stop her from disparaging my reputation." Her fingers clenched around the hammer, her knuckles growing white. "Do you know how devastating that is for an art dealer, in a town people visit to *buy art*? My reputation is everything!"

"I'm so sorry," I said softly. "Did you consider litigation?"

"Oh, I approached Martin Beswick, who told me that I didn't have a leg to stand on. Only later did I learn that he is—or was—in Evangeline's hip pocket."

I furrowed my brow, recalling the meeting reminder I'd seen in the Silver Spoon. "How so?"

"I'm not sure." Myrna sounded less angry and more thoughtful. "He might just be on her payroll. Or perhaps they were friends, or something more. I just learned through the grapevine that he probably hadn't tried very hard to help me sue Evangeline. And now . . ."

We both got quiet for a moment, while I looked around the storage room, which was filled with paintings Myrna had collected from around the world.

Was it possible that she'd failed to check the Duvalier's pedigree? And maybe even been duped, herself, by the previous seller?

Then I thought about Myrna's extensive travel, her Mercedes, and her home, which was rumored to be nearly as large as Fletcher Mansion—a lifestyle supported by a very popular, but, let's face it, small gallery.

Was there even a chance Evangeline had been *right*, and Myrna now and then tried to pass off the equivalent of a Bellamy as a Picasso?

It was difficult for me to believe. Then again, it was hard for me to accept that someone had just been murdered a few yards away from my peaceful home.

"Myrna?" I finally ventured. She'd been staring fixedly at the painting that might or might not have been painted by a noted French artist, but she dragged her attention back to me, a scowl still lingering on her face. She looked so profoundly unhappy that I almost didn't ask the question that she hadn't quite answered yet. "Why do you have the painting?"

Two spots of color formed on her otherwise ashen cheeks. "I went over to the Silver Spoon the night before Evangeline's murder," she confided, stepping deeper into the shadow, like she wanted to hide herself, which wouldn't be easy, since she wore a jewel-toned pink top with a ring of rhinestones around the neck. "And I told her I was getting that painting authenticated by a *real* expert, if it was the last thing I did."

I swallowed thickly. "And . . . ?"

"Evangeline said I'd take the Duvalier *over her dead body*."

That admission hung in the air for quite a few moments, while Myrna and I both looked at the painting. She was the first to say what we were both thinking about that lovely pastoral scene.

"And here it is!"

Chapter 16

Given the way the plants were bending under the weight of the biggest summer harvest I could remember, it was obvious that I needed to tend to my garden. But as I piled red, yellow, and deep-purple tomatoes into a basket the day after my discussion with Myrna Crickle, I also knew that I was stalling.

"I honestly don't know what to do about the Duvalier," I told Luna, who sat on a fence post. I was also addressing Mortimer, who was just outside the garden, eating some carrots I'd tossed him. Then I looked across the creek in the direction of Fletcher Mansion. "It seems like Derek deserves to know where his property is. Yet I don't want to make trouble for Myrna, who also deserves the chance to authenticate the piece and, if she's right about its legitimacy, restore her reputation—which was, let's face it, damaged by a Fletcher. And she swore she'd tell Derek, herself, the minute she gets an expert's report."

Luna, in particular, seemed unconcerned about a gallery owner's good name. Actually, Mortimer didn't seem to care, either. He was really enjoying his snack.

Still, I continued to talk to both of them. "I also promised Myrna that I wouldn't run to Detective Turner, and I want to honor that pledge. But I am a little shocked by what she told me."

As I began cutting cucumbers from a vine with a paring knife, I first wished I had my shears. Then my thoughts drifted back to Myrna's strange tale of what sounded like a serious altercation between two women who were far too old to exchange shoves.

And yet, that was exactly what had happened, according to Myrna, whose story was backed up by the bruise I'd seen on Evangeline's arm, the night of the painting party.

As I added more produce to my basket, I heard Myrna's voice echoing in my head.

"I told her, I am taking that painting tonight and having it evaluated by a REAL appraiser. Then she had the nerve to push me! So, I pushed her back, hard enough that she stumbled onto that wooden thing, where the hostess stands. And while she was rubbing her wrist, I snatched that painting off the wall—it was hung so poorly, I was practically saving the thing—and I stalked out into the night."

"I hope you're planning a response to my text—which you've completely ignored."

The teasing voice drew me out of my reverie, and I looked toward my cottage to see Derek making his way down the stepping-stone path, with a grin that told me he wasn't too upset that I'd avoided answering his question.

"Hey," I greeted him, picking my way across the rows of onions and peppers until I reached the gate, which I had sealed behind myself, so Mortimer couldn't sneak in. I nodded toward my cottage, indicating that Derek and I should talk on the porch, where it would be cooler. "What brings you over here?"

He took the heavy basket from me, and we fell into step, side by side. "I wanted to let you know that Evangeline's memorial service is scheduled for the day after tomorrow, at Wildwood Cemetery. I wasn't sure if you'd want to go, but I thought I'd at least tell you."

"Thanks," I said, not sure if I'd attend. We'd already reached the porch, and Luna, who'd followed us, darted past my legs and jumped onto the railing. Mortimer must've still been upset about the ham comment, because he'd trotted to his playhouse with his nose in the air, completely ignoring Derek. "I'll let Astrid and Pepper know, too."

"Only if you think they might come." Derek set the basket near the back door. "I won't blame any of you if you stay away."

I didn't know what to say, and before I could respond, Derek crossed his arms over his chest, a hint of laughter in his eyes. "So, are you ever going to answer my text?"

He might've been amused, but I got a little sweaty, even in the shade. "Sorry about that."

"I completely understand." He continued smiling. "Which isn't going to stop me from asking you, point blank, if you'd like to be my date for the gala."

I wiped my damp palms on my favorite gardening jeans. "I don't know, Derek."

He clearly grasped my concerns. "I just want to go as friends, Willow. I know that things are different between us, and they always will be. But we've been close since childhood, and I've missed having you in my life. I'd like to spend time with you again, and maybe keep in contact when I'm away."

His point-blank pronouncement regarding the future of our relationship was hard to hear, even though I knew it was true. No matter what happened between us, we probably couldn't recapture the past. I also missed Derek and wished we could find a way to renew our friendship. Still,

I told him, "I'm not sure about the gala. Let me think about it, okay?"

He backed away toward the front steps. "Fair enough. There's still a little time to decide."

I nodded. "Okay. I'll let you know."

"Great." Scratching Luna behind the ears, Derek took the whole set of steps in one easy stride and headed across the street, looking back once to wave.

I waved in reply, but the gesture was weak, because I was even more conflicted than before. And I'd completely forgotten about the Duvalier, and whether I should tell him the painting *hadn't* been sold.

I continued watching Derek's retreating back until he reached his family's . . . or *his* . . . property and disappeared inside the imposing house. Then I picked up the basket and went inside my own home, with Luna close on my heels.

Setting the veggies on the counter, I noticed the stack of mail I'd forgotten about, too, while I'd made s'mores with Detective Turner—an activity that seemed foolish, and perhaps dangerous, in retrospect.

Grabbing the manila envelope, I tore it open, looking forward to checking out the paintbrushes I'd ordered. But when I dumped the contents onto my counter, I discovered that I hadn't received new art supplies. In fact, the object that clattered onto the butcher block already belonged to me.

Except, when I'd last seen the garden shears, they hadn't been quite so clean, with the exception of what I thought might be a *smear of blood* on one of the blades.

Chapter 17

I probably should've used the direct number Detective Turner had punched into my phone and asked him to pick up what I greatly feared was a murder weapon. However, I'd basically assured my friends that I wouldn't be alone with him again until we learned more about his background and motives for coming to Zephyr Hollow. And I couldn't exactly ask, say, Derek to stop by while a police officer retrieved some potential evidence when he was a suspect.

Therefore, after much deliberation, I chose to carefully tuck the shears back into the envelope—while wearing makeshift gloves made out of plastic sandwich bags—then drive myself to the police station.

Unfortunately, that plan went slightly awry when my old Subaru refused to start, leaving me with the option of riding my single-gear Schwinn into town.

Parking the bike in front of the police station, I grabbed the envelope, not worried about fingerprints, since I'd already handled the paper at least twice. Then I bounded up to the large, wooden front door, which was thankfully open after five o'clock.

With the exception of one grade-school field trip and two visits to pay parking tickets, I didn't have any reason to visit the station, which retained its eighteenth-century character, right up to its glass-enclosed, four-sided cupola, which had always fascinated me as a kid. Stepping inside the station's tiled foyer, I located a modern sign that told me Detective Turner's office was on the highest floor.

I was tempted to follow other markers to a hidden elevator, then chose instead to climb a somewhat daunting spiral staircase that had to date back to the building's construction.

Unfortunately, halfway up, I regretted my decision. And by the time I reached the fourth floor, my legs were heavy, my lungs were wheezing, and the palm I was sliding up the walnut banister was slick with sweat.

I was relieved to open a door that led to an empty corridor, at the end of which waited a single, dark wooden door with a small plaque that read LUCIEN TURNER, DETECTIVE.

I assumed he had an assistant who would screen visitors, so I didn't even think to knock.

Opening the door, I stepped into the room, only to be surprised by the decor, the presence of the dog named Marinette, and Detective Turner, himself—who, I got the strange sense, wasn't at all surprised to see *me*.

"Your office is gorgeous," I told Detective Turner, admiring the spacious room, which was like a secluded— maybe too secluded—library one might find in a British mansion.

My footsteps were muffled by a massive, antique Persian rug that covered a good part of the gleaming, wide-plank floor, and the walls were lined with floor-to-ceiling bookshelves crammed full of volumes, many of them leather-bound. The shelves were interrupted here and there by large, arched windows that offered a bird's-eye view of Zephyr Hollow's pretty Main Street, and a fireplace with a curved, marble surround was at the ready for colder days. I presumed that another winding, iron staircase, visible through a narrow archway, led to the cupola, which would provide an even more amazing view of the town.

I loved working at my cottage, but I wouldn't have minded coming to Detective Turner's office every day. Especially since the building was apparently pet friendly.

I looked down at Marinette, who was trailing me around, seeming more curious than friendly. Her canine brow was furrowed under her white, diamond-shaped mark, and her eyes were guarded. I sensed warmth there, too, and I nearly moved to pet her. Then something told me to keep my hands to myself, and I glanced at Detective Turner, who was leaning over his massive, walnut desk, his head bent and his arms braced against the desktop as he studied the envelope and shears I'd offered him upon entering the room. Not sure if I should bother him, either, I nevertheless ventured, "Um, are you *supposed* to have a dog in here?"

"I've never asked permission," he said, without looking up at me. His attention remained fixed on the pruners, which he'd slipped into a plastic bag that he'd marked with a Sharpie, telling me he was documenting the "chain of custody," which obviously shouldn't have included me.

I waited for him to elaborate, but he didn't seem inclined, so I asked, "How in the world did you get this space, which seems like it should belong to a *governor*? You can't have that much seniority here."

Detective Turner still didn't look up, but his shoulders

shrugged under his white dress shirt. He'd rolled his sleeves up to his elbows, and his red-and-blue striped tie hung down, brushing the desk. "I simply liked the room, which is very private, since the elevator only reaches the floor below," he finally said, as if that explained how he'd managed to sweep into Zephyr Hollow and claim such prime territory. I didn't think most people would mind walking up one flight of stairs for the ambience and the views.

However, I could tell that Detective Turner didn't plan to say more, so I resumed strolling around the room, surveying the titles on his shelves. His tastes were eclectic, running from crime and law—of course—to travelogues and British fiction. He'd also collected a bunch of books on a subject that greatly interested *me*: art.

I immediately recognized a few foundational titles, including *Art in Theory, The Work of Art in the Age of Mechanical Reproduction*, and *Art as Experience*.

Then my eyes snapped wide when I spied a resource I'd never heard of, although it seemed like a book I should read.

The Conjured Canvas: Intersections of Art & Magic.

Moving a bit closer, I noted the author. *D. W. Turner.*

The last name was common, but was it possible that Lucien's scholarly father . . . ?

"Willow?"

I jerked at the sound of my name and turned to see that Detective Turner had straightened. Backlit by the room's biggest window, which was directly behind his desk, he looked quite imposing.

"What?" I asked, forgetting about the book and stepping closer, so I could see his eyes.

Marinette finally abandoned me and went to her person, lying down by the desk. I, meanwhile, wondered if I should've moved in the opposite direction. Maybe even bolted down the hallway and the spiral staircase. "What's wrong?"

"Tell me again how you found these." Detective Turner gestured with a sweep of his hand, taking in the envelope and the shears. Stepping around from behind the desk, he leaned back on it, crossing his arms and studying me closely. "One more time, please."

"The envelope actually arrived the night you were sitting on my porch."

"You've had it that long?"

I nodded and, although he seemed a bit frustrated by that news, I continued. "I assumed it contained some paintbrushes I'd ordered, and I stuck it on the counter with some other mail. I didn't notice it again until today, when I opened it and shook out the shears."

He tilted his head, studying me more closely. "And you're sure they're yours?"

"Yes." I glanced at the plastic bag that had my name scrawled on it, almost like an accusation. Then I met Detective Turner's eyes again, not sure if I was indicting myself or helping to clear my name when I said, honestly, "They're antique and easily recognizable by the worn green paint on the wooden handles. I use them all the time."

Detective Turner gave no sign that he believed or, on the other hand, distrusted me. His expression was completely neutral. Without speaking, he pushed off from the desk and stepped behind it again, his movements tracked by Marinette, who was either worried or protective. Or both those things.

I, meanwhile, was definitely starting to feel concerned as another silence descended on the room and shadows lengthened outside. In fact, without taking his eyes off the shears, which he was examining again, Detective Turner reached out and turned on a lamp, casting the desk in a soft puddle of light.

"Would you mind stepping closer, please, Willow?" he finally asked, his voice quiet and thoughtful. "I have one more question before you go."

I was relieved to learn that I was about to be dismissed— not that I'd been kept against my will up to that point. Moving closer to the desk, I looked down at the shears, too, only to be surprised when Detective Turner asked about the other item I'd brought to his office.

Pointing to the envelope, he posed a question I hadn't really thought about, in my surprise to discover the possibly bloodstained garden tool spinning across my countertop.

"Do you recognize this handwriting?"

I took a long moment to study the blocky lettering, which looked to me like someone had tried to conceal their writing style.

Then I raised my face to look at Detective Turner, who was practically nose-to-nose with me, and watching me like Rembrandt when he had a mouse in his sights. I could see unusual flecks of gold in Detective Turner's dark eyes—where, for one split second, during a flash of light-ning, I'd seen so much more—and smell the sandalwood and bergamot in his cologne.

Those two scents were common in men's fragrances, but I knew the essential oils were also used to protect against evil.

"Well, Ms. Bellamy?" Detective Turner's use of my formal name made his repeated question seem even more heavily weighted. "Do you have any idea who might've printed your name and address on this envelope?"

"No," I said, feeling a trickle of sweat run down my

back, although the room was actually rather cool. I also swore I could sense the cheap mood ring on my finger pulsing with colors. I was certain that if I checked my finger, I'd see the ring glowing red to reflect my tension, with maybe, just maybe, a traitorous tinge of purple, flickering deep in the heart of the plastic gem. But I didn't dare look down. "I don't think I can help you," I told Detective Turner. "Sorry."

He stared at me for a long time, and I stared back. "Fine," he finally said, evenly.

That simple word broke the tense moment, but the mood in the room didn't improve much. Detective Turner drew back, and I stepped away from the desk, too, following him to the door. It was quite obvious that I was being dismissed.

Neither one of us spoke as we crossed the large room, and I could hear the boards creaking under our feet, as well as the tapping of Marinette's toenails when we all stepped off the rug and onto the wooden floor again.

Clearly, the dog didn't plan to leave her person . . . or maybe her person's guest . . . out of her sights. Marinette's brown eyes remained watchful, and the white mark on her forehead stood out more prominently in the darkening room.

Reaching the door, Detective Turner opened it for me, and I crossed the threshold into the corridor, where he again broke the silence. "Willow?"

I'd been walking away, and I turned to see him standing in the doorway, his arms crossed again and Marinette at his side, watching me, too. "What?"

"I'm telling you again. Be careful."

I nodded, my mouth feeling strangely cottony. "Okay."

"And Willow?"

"Yes?"

"Are you going to the gala?"

The question caught me completely off guard.

Was I about to get another offer for a date?

"Um . . . yes," I stammered. "Of course. Nearly everyone in town goes."

I had no idea what I'd say if, for some odd reason, Detective Lucien Turner asked me to the party. It might be interesting to spend an evening learning more about, and dancing with, the handsome, mysterious man who stood before me.

Then I recalled my dream, in which Detective Turner—whom I hadn't even met, at that point—had offered me his hand, while a woodpecker had tapped out what had sounded like both an invitation and a warning in a dark and lonely forest. And I thought about Pepper and Astrid's concerns, too.

My friends would tell me that attending the gala with Lucien Turner might be the worst mistake of my life.

I needn't have worried about making a decision.

"Don't let your guard down at the party, even," he suggested, his voice low and deadly serious. "I imagine that everyone who was at the Owl & Crescent the night of your event will be there, too. And we both know how *that* evening ended."

I opened my mouth to respond, but Detective Turner was already stepping into his office and closing the door. The soft snick of the shutting latch echoed loudly in the otherwise silent building, as did my footsteps when I made my way to the staircase.

And while I carefully descended the tricky spiral steps, I couldn't help thinking that it wasn't clear if Detective Turner's advice about being careful had been born of concern, or if it had been a warning. Because it had kind of sounded like the latter.

I also wondered if he knew I'd been fibbing, to buy time to think, when I'd said I couldn't identify the handwriting on the envelope. Because a tiny part of me worried that I'd recognized a telltale flourish on one of the letters in my name.

Chapter 18

Just like on the night of the murder, I didn't sleep very well after I visited Detective Turner's office. A ton of questions kept swirling around in my brain. Most notably, should I have told him that I might've recognized part of the handwriting on the envelope? And as I drove to my grandmother's farm, Gooseberry Hill, early the next morning, I also questioned whether I should've at least dropped a hint about Myrna Crickle's argument with Evangeline Fletcher.

I'd promised Myrna that I wouldn't run to the police, but she *had* basically stolen a painting from the Silver Spoon—although Evangeline hadn't reported the incident to the police in the day between her altercation with Myrna and her death.

"I think, for now, I was right to stay quiet, don't you?" I asked Mortimer, who was riding in the very back of my Subaru, which I'd brought to life not with the help of a mechanic, but by employing my distant cousin Verna's spell for "calming cranky cars."

I'd never used that before and hadn't really expected it to work. And maybe it hadn't. Maybe I'd just been lucky, and the engine had turned over in spite of the tiny, plastic horse and piece of coal I'd placed in a velvet pouch, which I'd tucked in the glove compartment after uttering a non-sensical phrase that reminded me of the one that opened the *Book of Spells, Lore & Miscellany.*

Yes, it was likely I'd just gotten lucky.

"I probably *should* take this thing to a garage," I told Mortimer, who seemed to be enjoying his outing. It was a gorgeous morning, still early enough to be cool, although the day promised to be hot and sunny. My mood was already growing lighter as I turned onto the dirt lane that led to the farm. The twisting, shaded path was lined with oak trees, blueberry and blackberry bushes, and my grandmother's horticultural inside joke, a shrub called witch elder.

"Because she's an elder witch," I explained to Mortimer, who probably hadn't even noticed the plants. When I glanced in the rearview mirror, I saw that he was happily bouncing along, his cute snout twitching. "I'm glad I brought you," I told him, rounding the last bend in the road. Grandma Anna's white farmhouse came into view, but I drove past it, to park behind her barn. "I think you'll like the alpacas."

My one-sided conversation was interrupted when I pulled behind the barn and spied a familiar truck, sitting in the spot where I usually parked.

I shouldn't have been so surprised by my grandmother's visitor, yet I heard confusion in my voice when I said, "*Mr. Van Buskirk?*"

He's not a killer, and there's no reason to worry about Grandma Anna.

I kept telling myself that as I released Mortimer from the car. Yet I kept one wary eye on Mr. Van Buskirk's pickup.

I was pretty sure he was there to do odd jobs, because the old farm always needed work.

And yet, as I shut the Subaru's hatch, I noticed that the handyman's toolbox was in the exposed truck bed.

Mortimer ran off, while I took a step closer, eyeing the tools.

I was almost certain my pruners were the weapon someone had used to kill Evangeline.

But what if Mr. Van Buskirk, who had been working on the bridge the night of her death, had gotten into an altercation with the woman who'd fired him? A fight that led him to grab a *different* tool and, on impulse, commit an act of violence?

He could've returned to the Owl & Crescent, taken the pruners and smeared them with a little blood to muddle the investigation, casting suspicion away from himself.

Mr. Van Buskirk hadn't been to the party. But he could've seen the shears when he'd stopped by the studio to update me on the electricity. They'd been in plain sight, on the table.

Was there a chance I was wrong about the shears, and the real murder weapon was *in the truck*?

I stepped closer to the battered pickup, my brain spinning with theories. Then, looking around to make sure I was alone, I raised up on my tiptoes and reached into the truck bed, lifting the latch on the toolbox.

The squeak of the old hinges sounded like a scream in the quiet morning—but that noise wasn't as loud nor alarming as Mr. Van Buskirk's question, which came from right behind me.

"Willow! What are you doing?"

* * *

"Honestly, Willow, I can't believe you'd suspect George for one moment," my grandmother said, lightly patting Mr. Van Buskirk's arm. She leaned over him to set a heaping skillet full of scrambled eggs onto the round table in her cheerful, white farmhouse kitchen. Wiping her hands on her apron, she took a seat between me and Mr. Van Buskirk, whom she graced with a huge smile, even as she continued to scold me for snooping—a crime to which I'd admitted, sharing perhaps too many details about my suspicions. "We've known him for ages!"

"Now, now, Anna." Mr. Van Buskirk reached for a serving spoon and piled eggs onto my grandmother's plate. Then he filled up my plate, too, before serving himself. "Willow is just trying to look after you. And we all know there's cause to suspect me!"

"I'm still really sorry," I said. "Even if I did have some concerns, I had no right to open your toolbox. I don't know what I was thinking!"

"You were thinking of your grandmother's safety, which I appreciate."

His blue eyes twinkling, Mr. Van Buskirk handed me some homemade blackberry jam, which he'd retrieved from the pantry while my grandmother had whipped up the rest of our impromptu breakfast.

As I spread the jam on a thick slab of toast, it finally struck me that Mr. Van Buskirk seemed awfully comfortable in my grandmother's kitchen.

And, looking between the two older people, I noticed that they kept sharing glances, and Grandma Anna's cheeks had a rosy glow.

Plus, it was very early, and Mr. Van Buskirk hadn't

mentioned anything about what he planned to repair after breakfast. Nor had he taken his omnipresent toolbox from his truck.

Dropping my knife, I looked between my grandmother and the Fletchers' longtime employee, now murder suspect, and blurted, "I know what Mr. Van Buskirk's alibi is, and why Detective Turner thinks it's pretty flimsy!"

"Why didn't you tell me you and Mr. Van Buskirk were an item?" I asked, after my grandmother's new beau had hastily finished his breakfast, cleared the table, and departed for Fletcher Mansion, to continue helping Derek in the wake of Evangeline's death.

At least, that was his excuse. I suspected that he was being polite, giving Grandma Anna and me a chance to talk privately. Although I was relieved that he had what seemed like an airtight alibi, to me—who completely trusted my grandmother—it had been a little awkward, discussing how he'd spent the night of Evangeline's death at the farmhouse.

"Well, Grandma?" I said, pouring some dish soap into the deep sink and running the water. "Why keep your relationship secret?"

"It's very new, Willow," she reminded me, opening a drawer and retrieving a towel. Her cheeks still had an appealing flush. I credited happiness, and a tiny bit of embarrassment, to have been caught with a male visitor who'd obviously spent the night more than once. "Plus . . ."

"You don't want me to tell Mom," I guessed, grinning. Rinsing a plate, I offered it to my grandmother. "You think she'll overreact and get worried about you, thinking Mr. Van Buskirk is out to steal your retirement or farm."

I'd guessed right. My grandmother's eyes sparkled with amusement as she accepted the dripping dish. "Exactly."

"Okay," I promised. "I'll keep quiet." Then a worrisome thought crossed my mind, and I looked sidelong at my grandmother. "Grandma . . ." I hesitated, trying to choose my words carefully. "Does Mr. Van Buskirk ever seem *confused*?"

I'd clearly baffled Grandma Anna, who was sharp as a tack. She creased her brow. "Why would you ask that?"

Washing some forks, I shrugged. "Pepper noted that she was worried about him lately. She said he was saying strange things. Not making sense, at times."

My grandmother didn't seem concerned. In fact, she laughed. "Maybe he's been distracted by me." She took the forks from me to dry them. "I know I've been a bit day-dreamy, myself, since we started going out."

"You really like him, don't you?" I asked, happy for her. Still, before she answered—and the look on her face was response enough—I felt compelled to inquire, one more time, "You're sure he's acting normally?"

Grandma Anna still seemed amused. "Believe me, Willow. George Van Buskirk is doing just fine. Pepper needn't worry!"

I trusted my grandmother, because she obviously spent more time talking to Mr. Van Buskirk than Pepper did. Yet, as I washed the last two plates, I couldn't help wondering, why, if he really was fine, Pepper had a different impression. While my grandmother *was* captivating—I didn't know anyone else her age who could pull off pink Wellies—I doubted Mr. Van Buskirk was lovestruck enough to seem worrisomely confused.

"Speaking of people who are distracted!" Grandma Anna nudged me with her elbow. "What—or who—has got you staring off into the distance? And don't say the pig, because I don't think you've even noticed how nicely he's been playing with the alpacas."

I looked out the window above the sink to see that Mortimer was, indeed, romping happily with the herd in their paddock. Then I returned my attention to my grandmother, who was no longer smiling. "Well, Willow?" she prompted. "Is everything all right?"

"I have no idea," I admitted, pulling the drain plug. Soap and water swirled away. "In particular, the whole murder mystery plot continues to thicken."

Grandma Anna handed me the towel. "How so?"

"Someone anonymously mailed a pair of my own garden shears—which are probably the murder weapon—to my house." My grandmother registered both surprise and worry, but she let me keep talking while I dried my hands. "And when I took them to Detective Turner—"

"The handsome young man, from the newspaper," she interrupted.

I'd forgotten that, while Detective Turner hadn't been quoted in the *Weekly Whisper*, the paper had run a photo of him directing officers at my property. I nodded. "Yes. Him. And when I dropped off the shears, I could tell that Detective Turner half suspected that I'd had them all along, and I'd made up the story about the mailing. And he definitely didn't believe me when I said I couldn't identify the handwriting on the envelope." Cringing, I bit my lower lip. "Because I might've been fibbing, just a little."

Grandma Anna frowned. "Why would you do that?"

I opened my mouth to tell *her* the whole story, then thought the better of it. "I wanted to buy some time to think," I said, hanging the towel on a waiting rack. "And, although of course I trust you completely, I'm going to continue to stay quiet. Not because I think you'd ever mention our conversation to anyone, but because, if I'm wrong—which is possible—you might always have a tiny doubt in your mind about this person's character. And I wouldn't want to color your opinion."

Grandma Anna seemed to respect that response. Still, she told me, "Just be careful, Willow. Even a well-intentioned fib to the police can have serious consequences."

It was time for me to leave, and I led the way to the door. "I seem to be getting warnings quite a bit lately."

"From who else?"

"Pepper and Astrid," I said, opening the door and stepping onto Grandma's wide porch. My grandmother followed. "They think I should be concerned about Detective Turner, who seems to know quite a bit about the supernatural." I recalled the book in his office. The one about the intersections of art and magic, which had been *written* by a Turner. "And I think they might be right. And Detective Turner, in turn, warned me to be careful at the gala, for some reason."

Grandma Anna was heading to the pasture, but she shot me a concerned look over her shoulder. "Why the gala?"

I joined her at the gate. "He reminded me that everyone from the Small Business Alliance gathering will probably be there and noted how things had gone wrong after that."

My grandmother opened the gate so Mortimer could trot through. He looked tired but happy. Grandma Anna tugged the rope down over the post again, then faced me in the bright sunlight. "Interesting."

"Yes. I agree." I finally broached the subject I'd mainly come to discuss. "And speaking of the gala, Derek asked me to be his date."

I was sure that Grandma Anna had opinions about

that news, but she didn't let them show. "Are you going with him?"

"I haven't decided yet." I took my grandmother's arm as we strolled toward my car, where Mortimer was already waiting by the hatch. "It's been nice catching up with Derek again, even under the sad circumstances that have occurred since his homecoming. But I'm not sure if a date is a good idea."

"Perhaps Detective Turner was inadvertently right about you needing to be cautious," Grandma Anna noted. "Not because you need to fear falling victim to a crime at the party—which I think is unlikely—but because you might get a second broken heart." I was a bit taller than her, and she smiled up at me. "Then again, true love is worth some risks, and you don't really know what the future holds for you or Derek. Maybe fate has brought you together for a reason."

"Or, more likely, fate is about to pull us apart again, when Derek gets his next Physicians for Peace assignment." Releasing Grandma Anna, I opened the Subaru's hatch, bent down, and helped to hoist Mortimer inside, thinking we'd need to get a ramp if he kept gaining weight. Closing the hatch, I dusted off my hands. "To be honest, I'm not looking for a rekindled romance. Derek would need to understand that." Then I grinned, too. "I'll leave affairs of the heart to you and Mr. Van Buskirk."

I was joking, but Grandma Anna didn't laugh. Something other than true love was clearly on her mind.

"What's up?" I asked, stepping around her to get to the driver's side door. The silver handle was already hot to the touch, and it wasn't even noon. "Because I can tell something is bothering you."

"I was just thinking about that anonymous envelope."

My grandmother tilted her head, her gorgeous silver hair gleaming in the sunlight. "Where was the postmark from?"

I was embarrassed to realize that the question, so important, hadn't even crossed my mind.

"I . . . I didn't even notice," I admitted. "I was too surprised when I dumped the shears onto my counter to even look."

"But there was a postmark, right?"

"Yes." I tried to recall whether I'd seen a stamp on the envelope. "I think so. But I'm not positive."

Grandma Anna peered closely at me. "How did you come to find this envelope? Was it in your mailbox?"

"Yes. I pulled the envelope out with a bunch of other mail. But I didn't open it right away, because it was late, and Detective Turner was sitting on my porch, waiting for me."

Grandma Anna's eyes glimmered with interest. "So, he was alone? In the dark?"

I finally figured out what she was getting at. "You think *Detective Turner* might've planted the shears?" I wanted to tell her that was crazy, but Astrid and Pepper probably would've offered the same theory. "But . . . why?"

She raised a hand. "I'm not saying he did that. I'm just saying it's possible that someone other than the postal delivery person delivered the envelope. And I probably wouldn't have considered Detective Turner if you hadn't told me that Pepper and Astrid don't trust him."

"I don't know." I opened the door. "I'm not sure why he would be involved in Evangeline's murder, in the first place."

"What do you know about him?" Grandma Anna inquired.

I pictured the spinning symbol that had preceded my

failed Internet search, which I'd repeated twice, with similar results. It was like Lucien Turner didn't exist in cyberspace.

"Nothing, really," I conceded. "But, even if Detective Turner had some kind of motive, why mail *me* evidence that I'd have to return to *him*?"

"To break the chain," Grandma Anna said, sounding like she was familiar with the type of plastic bag Detective Turner had shown me. "To distance himself from the weapon and cast suspicion on you." Then she surprised me by laughing. "But this is just far-fetched speculation. An old lady, playing at being Miss Marple!"

I started to laugh, too, until I looked past my grandmother. My attention had been drawn by a car that was driving up the lane, because it was about time for customers to stop by for fresh eggs. Then I spied a flash of white in the branches of Grandma Anna's hickory tree, where Rembrandt, who *never* ventured out during the day, was sitting and watching me.

Almost like he was on guard.

Chapter 19

As I'd expected, the temperature continued to rise all day, and a bank of dark clouds that rolled in that evening did little to relieve the heat. In fact, the thunderheads, which produced no rain, seemed to compress the warm, damp air, making it heavy, still, and even more oppressive.

Seeking relief, I donned my lightest sundress and joined Luna on the wraparound porch, sprawling out on one of the wicker chaise longues with a whole pitcher of icy mint lemonade by my side and the *Bellamy Book of Spells, Lore & Miscellany* on my lap.

I wasn't sure what I was looking for in the book, and, to be honest, my mind often wandered as I carefully turned the yellowed pages.

Okay, sometimes my eyes wandered, too, to Fletcher Mansion, which was dark and appeared empty, although there were so many rooms that Derek could've easily been in the back of the house, or the secluded backyard, and I never would've known.

Focusing on the book again, I flipped yet another page, discovering a recipe for sweet corn fritters with a spicy dipping sauce, which had been added by my grandmother.

"How did I fail to notice this before?" I mused aloud, dog-earing the page, so I could make the snacks as soon as the heat broke enough to do some frying. And that would surely happen, given the way the clouds were rumbling.

"Is it me, or is this a particularly stormy summer?" I asked Luna, who was curled up on the chaise next to mine. Rembrandt had given me some space since I'd returned home, retreating to the barn, and my very tired pig was passed out in his play shed after his alpaca adventure. I glanced at the clouds again. "I guess Mortimer will be okay, right?"

Luna yawned, which led me to believe she wasn't too concerned, so I resumed reading, intrigued by a spell for protection against poison ivy, until I saw a note that said, *BACKFIRED!* There was also a dried smear of what looked like pink calamine lotion, across a second warning scrawl. *Beware! Outbreak is instantaneous!*

"I won't be using that incantation," I said, nevertheless bending that page, too, because Grandma Anna had scribbled the recipe for the fritter dipping sauce under the lotion.

At least, I tried to create another corner flap, only to realize that the paper was too stiff to fold easily. In fact, it almost felt as though two pages were stuck together— maybe by the old glob of calamine lotion. Yet, when I turned the book sideways, I could barely discern a seam between the fused sheets. Even running my fingernail along the edge did nothing to separate the pages. It was almost as if they were purposely glued together, which made no sense, because whatever had been written would be ruined when someone, like me, tried to pull the sheets apart.

As I continued to pry at the seam, it struck me that one

of my female family members might have sealed the pages not with traditional adhesive, but with a spell, hiding content within the already locked book, like the magical equivalent of locking a safe deposit box within a bigger safe.

"What the . . . ?"

I was totally confused and suddenly very cool when a chilly wind raced across the valley, causing my wind chimes to tinkle chaotically, right before lightning ripped the sky.

Grabbing the book and my pitcher, I hurried inside with Luna on my heels, shutting the door behind us just as rain began to fall in heavy sheets that swept across my lawn. A moment later, Mortimer darted out of his house and ran down the stepping-stone path.

I got the door open just in time for him to scramble inside, all of us gathered in the kitchen, where I sat in the turret, watching the storm and considering my growing list of questions, all of which had arisen since Evangeline's murder.

What is really inside the Bellamy Book?

What went wrong with my first spell, when I tried to see into Evangeline's painting?

Did the symbols I drew—the dog house, the snake, and the fleur-de-lis—mean anything?

And why, really, did Detective Turner warn me to be careful at the gala?

Suddenly frustrated by my failure to find any answers—and, if I was honest, by what felt like cowardice on my part—I decided to take a bold step in what had so far been a rather haphazard investigation. I also needed to take control of my emotions, and I stood up, located my phone, and found Derek's message.

Typing quickly, before I could back out, I sent my reply.

I would love to attend the gala with you—as a friend, if the offer still stands.

Then I called up an old group chat with Pepper and Astrid and texted them, too, using shorthand I knew they'd understand.

 HELP!!

Chapter 20

"Honestly, Willow, why not wear something with a little more color?" my mother suggested, holding up a frothy, pink confection of a dress that reminded me of the calamine-lotion stain I'd recently seen in my family journal.

Pepper and Astrid hadn't been able to go shopping, so Mom had joined me at the Something Borrowed, Something New dress shop, located on the winding road that connected Zephyr Hollow to the nearby town of Sylvan Creek.

I'd hoped my mother could help me find something in the racks of vintage and brand-new dresses that I could wear to the gala, but so far, we hadn't agreed on anything. I was leaning toward a black cocktail dress from the 1960s, while my mother kept gravitating to shiny, colorful, never-before-worn gowns. She continued to shove pink satin and tulle at me while I held up my choice, twisting and turning to catch a glimpse of my reflection in three angled mirrors that flanked a short platform.

"Doesn't this seem festive?" Mom asked, shaking the princess dress at me one more time. "Why must you choose *black*?"

"What's wrong with black?" I inquired, giving up on trying to see myself. "Black is classic."

Mom jammed the fluffy dress back onto a rack, with clear reluctance and no small amount of difficulty, given how huge the skirt was. Then she looked me up and down, whispering. "That dress is kind of *witchy*, don't you think? Do you really want to *add to* your reputation?"

"First of all, I *do* cast the occasional spell, and I usually wear floral prints," I reminded Mom. "And Grandma wears pink boots. So, I don't know how black is 'witchy.' Also, for the record, my reputation is always fine, except for those times Evangeline Fletcher tried to . . ."

I was about to say "ruin it," but the phrase died on my lips when I saw my mother's surprised and disapproving expression.

"Sorry," I said more quietly. I glanced around to see if anyone had overheard, but the shop's young, new owner, who'd introduced himself as Dexter Shipley, was out of earshot and preoccupied, hanging up some discarded dresses and periodically rubbing his temples, like he had a headache. The only other customer—Daphne Templeton, who'd recently booked the painting party for her sister—had been leaving with her basset hound as we'd been arriving. I'd never met Daphne in person, but her name had been painted on her vintage VW van, which advertised her business, Lucky Paws Pet Sitting. Although Mom and I were basically alone, I kept my voice low when I resumed my apology. "I forgot about Evangeline's death for a moment. I feel terrible."

"There's nothing we can do about Evangeline," Mom noted, turning away from me and sliding hangers along the rack, to the degree that was possible. Something Borrowed, Something New was the only bridal shop around, and it was always well stocked with a lot of terrible selections, interspersed with true gems for those willing to search the showroom. Mom paused to check out a poofy, peach-colored dress that I would never wear, and her frown deepened. But I didn't think she disapproved of the gown. "I'm worried about *you*, Willow," she finally said. "Not Evangeline."

I blinked a few times, surprised by that admission. Mayor Celeste Bellamy fretted about her town, her reelection, and her reputation, but she seldom expressed direct concern for me. At least, not since I'd become an adult. "There's no need for you to worry," I assured her. "I've got everything under control."

Mom finally abandoned hunting for a "nonwitchy" gown and turned to me, her skin taking on a rosy glow in the shop's no doubt purposefully forgiving light. "Do you have everything in hand, Willow?" she inquired, and not in the snippy, sarcastic way she sometimes addressed me. She sounded genuinely interested to know if I was coping with the admitted challenges I faced. And before I could respond, she began listing things that did make my life seem a bit out of control. "You're attending the gala with a man who broke your heart, and who is probably leaving town soon—"

"Derek and I are trying to salvage a lifetime of friendship," I interrupted. "We both have realistic expectations going into the party."

I actually felt increasingly good about my decision to attend the gala with my childhood friend and first love. My heart still fluttered when I saw Derek, but I'd grown stronger since he'd left town, and I knew I wouldn't be devastated when he was reassigned. Reestablishing our friendship felt like the right thing to do. Plus, there were a few items we needed to discuss, and the talk might go more smoothly under a moonlit sky with a few glasses of wine behind us.

Mom, understandably, didn't appear convinced that I'd made a good decision, but she didn't press the issue. She continued to list issues of concern for me. "Your love life aside, an *unsolved* murder took place in your backyard, and the weapon, *which you own*, showed up at your house."

"Wait a second!" I interrupted again, speaking too loudly. Mr. Shipley shot us a curious look, and I lowered my voice. "How do you know all that? Have you been talking to Grandma behind my back?"

I honestly didn't think my grandmother would've shared what I'd told her about the curious package without asking me if that was okay. Grandma Anna and I had an unspoken agreement about being circumspect around my mother, who tended to overreact to news, good or bad. But before my mom could respond, I was struck by another thought.

"And do you know more than I do about the shears? Because you seemed to imply that the pair has been positively identified as the murder weapon."

I was trying to speak softly, but Mom shot me a serious "shushing" look. "I don't know anything about positive identification," she whispered. "And I can't even recall how I heard about the mailing." She hesitated, seeming to search her memory, with about as much success as she'd had finding the right dress for me. Then she shrugged, her shoulders lifting a light, white summer cardigan, which she'd paired with black slacks. "Perhaps your grandmother did tell me. Or there was another story in the newspaper."

I studied my mother suspiciously. "Are you in contact with Detective Turner, Mom? Because you are the mayor, and he's probably technically your employee."

Mom lifted her chin and adjusted her purse on her

shoulder. "Detective Turner was hired by Police Chief Dunston Simmons," she informed me. "I am hardly familiar with the young man, and certainly wouldn't meddle in an investigation, even if I had some sort of authority over members of the force. I leave the police work to the chief and those he sees fit to employ. Especially when there would be suspicion of impropriety, like in this case." My mother's usual tone of frustration with me had crept back into her voice. "You *are* a suspect, Willow."

I moved toward the counter to purchase my dress, and Mom followed. "So, you never even saw Detective Turner's résumé?" I asked, suddenly wondering if my own mother might be able to answer questions that the Internet couldn't. "You know *nothing* about him?"

Mom didn't respond, so I kept pressing the issue. "You must've played some role in the hiring process, right?"

"I have no idea where you're going with this, Willow," she finally said, checking her gold wristwatch. "And I've no time to indulge in some cryptic conversation about a man I *do not know*."

"How about his office?" I asked.

Mom looked puzzled. "His . . . what?"

"The palatial space he occupies in the police station. I know you are fully aware of how municipal office space is allocated in every building."

My mother's brow creased. "How do *you* even know where Detective Turner works?"

"I took the shears to him when I received the package. His office was very nice, given that he's brand new to the force, don't you think?"

We'd been getting louder, and Mom glanced nervously at Mr. Shipley, who must've heard at least part of our conversation. He was headed in our direction, his footsteps silent on the thick carpet. Mom checked her watch again. "I *must* return to work, Willow. The Gallery Walk is less than a day away, and there's much to be done. We can talk later, although I'm not sure what there is to say, or what you *want* me to say."

"Fine," I agreed, giving up my attempt to drag information out of my mother and placing the black dress on the counter.

Mr. Shipley slipped behind the cash register, and I smiled at him, then addressed Mom again. "In the meantime, I . . ."

I started to thank my mother for joining me at the shop, even if she hadn't been all that helpful, but when I saw the strange expression on her face, I lost my train of thought, mid-sentence.

"I really am sorry that I can't be of more assistance, Willow," she said. I got the sense that she wasn't talking about gowns. "Truly, truly sorry."

With that, Mom hurried out of the shop, the cheerful tinkling of the bell at odds with her somber demeanor.

I stood there, forgetting my purchase as I tried to figure out why my mother had sounded so uncharacteristically, sincerely apologetic. I also wondered what she was trying to keep from me. Because my mother meddled in every municipal decision, however minor, and she had to know *something* about Detective Turner.

"Keeping secrets is becoming a Bellamy habit," I muttered, still staring at the door, until Dexter Shipley said, "What was that? I didn't quite hear you."

"Nothing important," I promised, facing the shop's owner again and gasping to see what he'd picked up while my attention had been drawn elsewhere.

Chapter 21

"That dress is positively gorgeous," Astrid said, taking a momentary break from whatever the heck she was doing with one of her HappyTime toys crystal balls, which she'd inexplicably set on the Owl & Crescent's farmhouse table. Her laptop was open, too, but she paused in tapping the keys to glance at the 1940s, deep-gray velvet gown I'd hung on a peg near the door, where hopefully it wouldn't get dirty. It was always risky to bring or wear "nice" clothes into my studio, but I'd had to show Astrid and Pepper—who was painting not a canvas, but her toenails—the dress that Dexter Shipley had seemingly conjured from thin air, while I'd been puzzling over my mother's portentous farewell.

Well, the long, strapless sheath hadn't exactly appeared by magic. It had been hanging behind the counter at Something Borrowed, Something New, and, as I'd been staring into space, Mr. Shipley had decided it was perfect for me.

I had to agree. I'd liked the black dress, but I *loved* the simple, yet dramatic gown.

"It's not exactly black, but I'm sure my mother will complain that it's 'witchy,'" I noted, looking up from a watercolor I was painting by the glow of string lights and sandalwood-scented candles. The scene did *not* include any people. I didn't want to run the risk of doing a little conjuring myself, until I could figure out if I'd had anything to do with the arrival of a certain detective in town. "My mother thinks black carries a negative connotation when worn by me, in particular," I added, rinsing my brush in a mason jar full of murky water.

"Black is classic," Pepper said, echoing what I'd told my mother back at the bridal shop. She was lounging on the couch with Luna, who was watching the nail-painting process closely. I was pretty sure my ultra-feminine feline friend would've liked a manicure.

Rembrandt, who probably thought it was strange to paint one's "talons," was also eyeing Pepper from his new favorite spot on Evangeline's easel. I swore he seemed disapproving.

Pepper didn't seem to notice that she was being scrutinized. She blew on her toes, then told me, "I think the gown is magnificent. Derek is going to quit his do-gooder doctor nonsense and decide to stay right here the moment he sees you in that thing."

"Jeez, I hope it doesn't have that kind of power," I said, as Mortimer nudged open the door and let himself into the studio, trotting to the rug, where he snorted a greeting and plopped over sideways.

Abandoning my painting for a moment, I went to close the door. "I don't want Derek to give up a *noble* calling and stay in Zephyr Hollow," I added, mainly addressing Pepper. I wasn't sure if Astrid, who was *running a wire* from the clear globe's battery-powered base to her computer, was even listening. "We just want to be friends, even after he *does* leave for his next assignment."

"Yes, that's why you're attending the gala together,"

Pepper noted slyly, applying more coral polish to her nails. Remi flexed his claws, as if the procedure made him uncomfortable. "You're going on a date because you're 'friends.'"

Ignoring the teasing comment, I returned to my easel, while Astrid continued splicing her laptop to the base of the toy, with a look of intense concentration.

I debated asking her to explain what the heck she was doing, aside from creating some alarming sparks, then spoke again to Pepper.

"Speaking of real romances—and only within the confines of our coven—my grandmother is dating Mr. Van Buskirk. And she seems smitten with him."

My comments didn't draw the positive reaction I'd expected. In fact, Pepper seemed concerned. "I *hope* that's a good thing, Willow. I really do."

Reaching for my paintbrush again, I frowned. "Has he done something new? Seemed confused?"

Pepper bit her lip, like she wasn't sure she should confide in me. Then she said, "I found him outside the pool house, fumbling with his keys. I have no idea why he can't seem to recall that he no longer needs to worry about the cabana. I've told him that I plan to hire a full-service contractor for that job, and he should focus on smaller projects."

I glanced at Rembrandt, who was sitting very still, almost like he was listening. I sometimes swore he understood more than anyone guessed. Then I again looked at Pepper, who was capping the bottle of polish, an action that seemed to disappoint Luna. She jumped down from the couch and trotted to a window, hopping up on the sill.

"Grandma Anna swears that Mr. Van Buskirk is fine," I said. "But please keep me updated, okay? I need to know if my grandmother has any reason to be careful, if he begins to act truly erratically."

Pepper nodded. "Of course. But for now, I'm mainly worried that, once the pool house is under construction, he'll wander in somehow. It could be dangerous."

"Poor Mr. Van Buskirk!" Astrid finally joined the conversation. Whatever she was up to—and it was still a mystery—apparently hadn't prevented her from following along. "I hope he's okay."

"Me, too," Pepper said. "George seems like a very nice man."

"Yes, he is a sweet guy," I agreed. "Let's hope his obsession with the cabana is just some kind of quirky anomaly."

"I have to say, *I'm* pretty curious about the house right next door," Astrid noted, still tapping keys on her laptop, while looking at the crystal ball. "What do you think will happen to Fletcher Mansion if Derek really does leave again, possibly for years? Will the place just sit there, abandoned, and fall apart?"

I'd been applying a sweep of pale blue to my painting's sky, but my hand jerked. "I have no idea," I admitted, not sure why I hadn't thought of that question, myself. "I can't imagine anyone but members of the Fletcher family living there. And yet, I suppose Derek will sell the house *and* restaurant, if he really is the sole heir, as seems likely."

My guess at the estate's future drew no response. I assumed we were all silently calculating how much the Fletchers' properties were probably worth. Given the mansion's size, combined with Evangeline's admittedly good maintenance of the buildings and grounds—and the fact that Zephyr Hollow was a desirable location—I wouldn't have been surprised if a Realtor aimed for well over one million dollars, just for the house. And the restaurant was also prime real estate, probably worth *more* than the mansion.

As I did the math, I could hear Derek's deep voice echoing in my memory.

"*. . . As I've told Aunt Evan, I have no need of a house or fortune—although that money could build more than one hospital in Africa . . .*"

I believed he'd been sincere. Yet I couldn't help thinking that a couple million dollars could also fund a pretty nice life after Derek left his altruistic, but poorly compensated, work abroad, probably at a young age, because the job was dangerous and physically demanding.

And then there was that question I needed to ask him when we attended the gala, if not before . . .

"Got it!"

Astrid's triumphant exclamation broke the silence, and for a second, I thought she'd found the properties' real value online. Or somehow figured out what Derek planned to do with the estate, once he was reassigned. Then I realized Astrid had probably forgotten about her own questions because there was something more interesting, right in front of her.

Something *moving* inside the cheap toy globe.

Chapter 22

"In spite of discounting these things to the point that they were a total loss, I still got stuck with one," Astrid said, crowding close to me and Pepper so we could all gaze into the toy crystal ball.

We weren't seeing the future, but the present that Astrid had tapped into, using an Internet spell that had actually *worked*, was pretty amazing.

Inside the orb, a hologram-like figure—Astrid's cat, Gandalf—prowled around the Astral Emporium. As we watched, Gandalf strolled across the glass counter that held the jewelry and knocked the entire basket full of mood rings—minus the one still stuck on my finger—to the floor. I thought the act looked deliberate, but Astrid didn't seem to care. She grinned with pride over what she'd rigged up. "It's like a paranormal nanny cam!"

"Nicely done." Pepper crossed her arms and tilted her head, the better to watch the feckless feline bat idly at the display of floaty scarves, nearly knocking that down, too. "Your cat's behavior aside, this is quite impressive."

Luna was also clearly captivated by Astrid's feat. She'd joined us on the table and kept tapping at the ball with her white-tipped paw, her head also cocked as she tried to figure out what was happening. Mortimer had woken up and wandered over, too. I doubted he could see anything from his spot on the floor, but he kept lifting his snout and sniffing, like he'd caught a whiff of the excitement.

Only Rembrandt and I seemed to have any misgivings about Astrid's use of good old-fashioned witchcraft, combined with GPS data and a children's novelty item, to peek into others' lives. The owl half of the Owl & Crescent had flown to the rafters right above the table and was peering down at us, ruffling his feathers now and then. I was pretty sure that meant he was agitated.

Tearing my gaze away from Gandalf's mischievous meanderings, I looked up at Remi, silently agreeing that Astrid might've unleashed something a little too powerful inside that plastic orb.

And when I gazed into the ball again, my concerns seemed justified. "Why are we spying on *Mr. Van Buskirk?*" I asked, watching my grandmother's love interest, who moved about his small home.

Although the caretaker's cottage was just across Peddler's Creek, I'd never been inside before. I wasn't surprised to see that the space was tidy and simply decorated.

Mr. Van Buskirk stopped near a window, looking outside at the darkness. Then he bent his head and fidgeted with something he held in his hands. An object or objects too small for me to recognize.

Seeming to give up on whatever puzzle he held, he again stared pensively into the night, his brow knit and his mouth drawn down into an uncharacteristic frown.

"What is he *doing?*" Pepper asked.

Before Astrid or I could venture a guess, the inside of the ball flickered, then turned a milky, murky, pale gray, like fog.

I pulled back, feeling even guiltier, and looked between Pepper and Astrid. "Seriously, why did we just spy on Mr. Van Buskirk? And don't either of you feel the least bit *wrong* about doing it?"

Neither one of my friends, let alone my cat, seemed to have any problem with what we'd just done. Pepper and Astrid exchanged glances, then shrugged to mutually indicate that they weren't concerned about the ethics of the "paranormal nanny cam."

In fact, Astrid started fidgeting with the wires, trying to get the thing to work again. "I tapped into his cottage because I thought we all agreed—in spite of *my* initial reluctance—that we were investigating Evangeline Fletcher's murder," she informed me. "So, I decided to look for a way to check up on the suspects, including Mr. Van Buskirk, who *did* have motive."

"I would think you'd want to look into your grandmother's love interest, Willow," Pepper added, slipping into a seat. She tapped her fingernails, which were also painted coral, on the tabletop, as if she was impatient to see more—or maybe impatient with me. "And not to downplay Astrid's *for once* successful bit of magic . . ."

Astrid paused in her fiddling to shoot Pepper a hurt look. Then she resumed playing with the apparatus she'd created, while Pepper continued justifying Astrid's investigative methods.

". . . We're surrounded by regular cameras, everywhere. In the grocery store, in elevators—on traffic lights, for crying out loud. Most of our moves are monitored by someone, and we don't think twice about it."

"But—" I tried to form an objection, but Pepper overrode my attempt to argue.

"Plus, real investigators conduct surveillance," she

reminded me, leaning back and crossing her arms again. "They just don't do it *intelligently*, like us, from the comfort of a lovely art studio. They sit in cars for hours, cameras at the ready to snap secret pictures of people doing bad things. It's an entire industry."

"Maybe so, but Mr. Van Buskirk has an alibi—"

I was trying to explain when Astrid cried out. "Look! It's working again!"

I knew I wouldn't be able to resist looking, but I quickly told my friends, "You have to *promise* me that you won't let the snooping get out of hand. We're trying to solve a murder, not invade people's privacy."

"Fine, fine," Pepper agreed halfheartedly, pointing at the toy. "Now, look!"

I peered into the globe, which had cleared of its mist to reveal Penelope Dandridge, who stood before a glass case inside the large, indoor part of her flea market, which was nearly as dark as the night outside.

I couldn't see much, beyond some knickknacks, household goods, and furniture, including a tall grandfather clock. And Penny's back was hunched, her face hidden and her shoulders shaking.

Bending closer again—and cursing my curiosity—I tried to see what she was doing, only to jump when the ball faded back to gray.

I looked to Astrid. "What happened now?"

She seemed unsure. "I . . . I plugged a bunch of addresses into the computer before casting the spell. Maybe it's working like a slideshow, advancing on its own?"

That seemed to be the case. As we all bent closer—I'd given up resisting, at least temporarily—Myrna Crickle suddenly appeared in the orb. I recognized the upper floor of her gallery, where I'd seen the painting from the Silver

Spoon, the Duvalier, which she was taking from its hiding
place. . . .

There was no chance to see more. The gray mist descended again, and I, at least, held my breath to see who it
would reveal next. Yet the interior remained obscured for
a long time, actually growing even darker, until I realized
that there *was* motion in the center.

My friends must've seen it, too, because we all leaned
in until our noses were practically against the plastic.

"Benedict Blodgett!" Pepper was the first to recognize
the filmmaker. She swiveled her head to look at Astrid.
"Where *is* he? What address did you plug in?"

"I used the address for Take 666 Studio," she said.
"We're only snooping in people's homes when there's no
other choice, like with Mr. Van Buskirk, who lives where
he works."

Her explanation was questionable, but I found myself
squinting, trying to see the studio's interior. However, all
I could make out was Benedict's pale face—then a glint
of silver, near his hands.

"What was . . . ?" I thought Pepper was again about to
ask the same question that was on my mind.

What was that?

But before Pepper could finish her thought, the haze
again obscured the view, only to lift moments later, rising
like a curtain to reveal the interior of Fletcher Mansion.

I shot Astrid a sharp look. "I thought we were only
snooping in people's homes as a last resort!"

She waved off my concerns. "This is Derek. The rules
of privacy don't apply to former boyfriends."

I wasn't sure that was the case, but I also knew by then
that the image would only last a few moments, and I looked

down to see Derek sitting in the study, bent over, rubbing his eyes, like he was exhausted. A coffee table near his knees held a tall stack of papers.

Maybe Evangeline's will?

His transfer orders?

Something else?

It was impossible to tell, and, as I'd anticipated, the picture quickly dissolved away to gray.

"That's it," Astrid announced, stepping back from the table. "That's all the people I used the spell to find."

Pepper sat back, and I straightened, too, suddenly feeling a little sick. "Astrid, you said you were only checking up on suspects. Yet, you included Derek."

My friend's plump cheeks grew pink. "I don't *really* suspect him. But you did mention that he was likely to inherit the whole Fletcher estate upon Evangeline's death."

Pepper crossed her arms on the table. "That is true, Willow. And, while I don't believe he's a killer, either, Derek probably did have motive, and he was the first to note that Evangeline was missing. What if there was an argument, and some kind of accident, and now he's afraid to come forward? Even truly good people might panic if they get mixed up in someone's death." Her gaze cut to the ball for a second. "And he looked almost *anguished*, a few moments ago."

That was also true. And there was that niggling doubt in my mind, too, related to something Pepper and Astrid didn't even know about. That strange suspicion *I* harbored. Yet I refused to believe that Derek Fletcher could harm a flea, nor that he'd be a coward if, as Pepper had noted, he'd been involved in some sort of accident that had resulted in his aunt's death.

"Derek is innocent." I spoke firmly, with conviction. "Whatever was weighing him down, it wasn't a guilty conscience."

Pepper and Astrid exchanged looks that told me they hoped I was right. "Well, it doesn't hurt to keep an eye on Derek, if only to help him," Pepper said. "Because he's likely still on someone else's radar. Someone I, for one, definitely don't trust."

We all knew who she meant, and Astrid raised an eyebrow, silently asking for permission that I didn't plan to give. Not surprisingly, Pepper grinned and nodded. "Go ahead, Astrid. Let's see what your twenty-first-century crystal ball reveals about Detective Turner."

I opened my mouth to protest that we'd spied on enough people for one night, and that Lucien Turner probably wasn't at his office so late, but Astrid was already typing away. A moment later, the mist in the sphere began to swirl wildly enough that we humans drew back.

Luna and Mortimer, meanwhile, crept closer again. Luna's eyes were huge with interest, while Mortimer danced on nervous hooves. And Rembrandt flapped his wings, taking off and flying a protective circle around the barn.

"Should we . . ." I was about to suggest that perhaps Astrid should try to cancel the spell, if that was possible, when the swirling clouds finally parted to reveal the office on the top floor of the police station. And, standing behind his desk, his arms braced on either side of the old-fashioned blotter, in the intimidating pose he'd struck when inspecting the envelope and shears, was Detective Lucien Turner.

Marinette was there, too, lying on the carpet. And someone sat in one of the chairs for guests. The room was shadowed, and the person's back was to me, so I couldn't make out who'd come to see the detective at such a late hour.

And I wouldn't get a chance to identify the individual, because all at once, Detective Turner straightened and seemed to stare right at us—directly at *me*—right before the crystal ball's interior *didn't* fade to gray, as before, but snapped to an inky, almost viscous, swirling black.

Or maybe that never really happened, because at nearly that exact moment, an owl with normally perfect manners and perfectly honed claws swooped down from the sky and knocked the toy to the floor, with such force that the plastic exploded into a thousand little ice pick–sharp shards.

Chapter 23

"What was that all about?" I asked Rembrandt, who was pretending to doze in the rafters. It was the morning after he'd smashed the crystal ball, and I was sweeping the Owl & Crescent's floor by the light of day, making sure I hadn't missed any sharp pieces of plastic when I'd cleaned up more hastily the night before.

The day was sunny and hot—thankfully clear for the night's Gallery Walk—and I caught my hair up into a high ponytail, using an elastic I'd slipped onto my wrist when I'd donned my white capris and T-shirt. Then I looked up at my avian tenant, who was my sole animal companion that day. Luna was sunning herself on top of the potting shed, and Mortimer was keeping cool in his playhouse, where I'd placed a fan that morning.

"I know you're listening," I told Remi. "So why in the world did you destroy the ball? And don't pretend it was an accident, because you can pluck a running field mouse from high grass on a moonless night. There's no way you just bumped into a big toy."

The owl who finally did open his eyes didn't respond.

And I'd misspoken when I called the orb a "toy." Astrid had transformed the ball into something quite serious.

I couldn't stop thinking about things we'd seen inside the globe, including the image of Detective Turner, who had emerged from a turbulent mist, and who had seemed to stare straight at me, as if he'd known he was being observed—right before the ball had been plunged into blackness. The kind of profound darkness that I recalled swallowing *me* up, the night I'd cast the spell to look into Evangeline's painting. A blackness I'd seen again, during a flash of lightning, when Detective Turner had stood close to me . . .

Shuddering in spite of the heat, I once more looked up at Rembrandt, whose eyes were closed again.

Was there a chance he'd been protecting us—or me— by destroying the ball before we somehow "summoned" Lucien Turner again? Or angered him?

I had no idea if I was making any sense, and I shook off my concerns, wondering if I was starting to get paranoid.

"I should probably focus on something more practical, like my business," I noted softly, moving to the counter where I kept my appointment book. Resting my broom against the wall, I opened the ledger, noting that I would soon host the party scheduled by bridesmaid Daphne Templeton, for her sister, Piper. And a scrawl I'd left in the margin—*basset hound and poodle??*—reminded me that there was a chance we'd have canine guests, too.

The note also gave me an idea for a project the group could complete at the event.

However, I didn't have the necessary materials. But I knew where there was a good chance I could find what I needed, even if the objects were quirky and random: Penelope Dandridge's Penny For Your Stuff flea market, which I'd last visited in an unconventional way. And where I was almost certain I'd seen Penny alone in the dark, either laughing or crying.

Penny Dandridge's indoor-outdoor flea market was located on the outskirts of Zephyr Hollow, in a shaded grove that had once been a fairground. I had many happy memories of attending carnivals, county fairs, and even a few small, itinerant circuses, which would imbue the spot with an aura of mystery and magic for a day or two.

The market still retained a bit of enchantment for me. I swore, whenever I needed something, however obscure, I'd find the object somewhere among the antiques, crafts, and junk waiting to be rescued and repurposed.

Picking my way through a maze of wooden tables and white tents, which were packed with everything from vintage toasters to old wire egg baskets and Depression glass, I scanned the vendors' displays—some haphazard and some quaintly curated—for basset hound and poodle figurines, preferably close to the same size.

Since the dogs were part of the bridal party, I thought it might be fun to have the bridesmaids paint a scene with two similar pups, perhaps situated in front of a wedding cake, top hat, or other wedding-related object.

As always happened at Penny For Your Stuff, I quickly lost track of time. However, I supposed that at least a half hour passed before I started to fear that, for the first time I could recall, the market's magic might have failed.

"There has to be at least one dog figurine here some-where," I said, under my breath. Not that anyone could hear me. The market was surprisingly quiet, in spite of the nice weather. In fact, I thought I was alone until I noticed someone standing in the doorway to a building that used to house displays of homemade pies, jams, and cakes entered for judging during the county fair.

I hardly ever ventured into the indoor part of the market, where Penny sold her own collection of pricier antiques, but I found myself waving my arm and opening my mouth to call to her, just as Penelope Dandridge seemed to vanish into thin air.

Chapter 24

"Penny?" I called, stepping through the open door into the quiet space, where some lazily spinning ceiling fans created a nice breeze. Pausing at the threshold, I surveyed the selection of ever-changing, unique goods, which included small things in glass display cases and larger pieces, such as the grandfather clock I'd seen in Astrid's "paranormal nanny cam."

Moving closer to the clock, I flipped a paper tag and read the price. *$21,500.* Forgetting that Penny was likely nearby, I whistled and whispered under my breath, "It's a *pretty* penny for the stuff in here."

Then I wandered over to one of the display cases, thinking I might find my hoped-for canine figurines, if at a higher price than I wanted to pay.

However, I didn't see anything that interested me except a bracelet that stood out among the other knickknacks.

The silver cuff appeared to be vintage, and, to my untrained eye, the "topaz" stone that was central to an engraved pattern of geometric shapes looked real. Much more authentic than the plastic gem that was glowing a neutral green on my finger.

Interested in the unique item, in part because my birthstone was topaz, I again looked around for Penny, who was still absent, or, more likely, concealed in the warren of armoires and stacked chairs and end tables. Confident that she'd trust me, as a longtime customer, I stepped around the case and reached inside, pulling out the bracelet.

The piece was surprisingly hefty, and I wondered if Penny had made a mistake and was displaying something of real value alongside some cut-crystal salt-and-pepper shakers and tarnished silverware with gold trim on the handles—a pattern that looked familiar to me.

I glanced at the clock again, thinking I'd also seen that somewhere, aside from inside the crystal ball.

Then I turned over the cuff to discover that it was engraved.

The words were difficult to read on the dark underside of the curved metal, and I squinted until I could make out the phrase, "Believe in the beauty and strength of woman's devotion."

The quote was unexpected and poetic, and I again checked out the jewel and pattern, which reminded me of a symbol I might find in my *Book of Miscellany*, inked as part of some long-forgotten attempt at a spell. The circular topaz was set within an engraved square, which was within a triangle, all within a larger circle.

"I wonder if I could trace the former owner using my art and soul spell," I said quietly even as I realized I'd never waste precious energy to satisfy a vague, temporary curiosity.

But the bracelet *was* like a piece of art, and there might be a way to tweak the spell, which I'd only used on paintings.

"I should probably put you back, before I get any crazy ideas," I added, bending to place the bracelet in the case, just as Penelope Dandridge finally emerged from the tangled maze of furniture, crying, "Stop right there, thief!"

"I'm so sorry, Willow," Penny said, fiddling anxiously with a dreamcatcher pendant that dangled from a leather thong around her neck. She also wore a faded tie-dyed T-shirt and rumpled khaki shorts, and her long, frizzy, gray-streaked brown hair was disheveled. Between her outfit and her eyes—which were tired and watery—I wondered if she'd been sneaking in a nap. "I couldn't see your face when you were bent down," she added, gesturing half-heartedly around her shop. "You're always welcome to check out anything you want." Her eyes—a light shade of caramel brown—brightened, just slightly. "Were you interested in something in the case?"

I was still standing next to the display, and I reached in again to retrieve the bracelet, which I'd dropped when Penny startled me. "I was looking at this," I said, holding up the cuff. "I don't buy a lot of jewelry, but this is so unusual. And the gem—my birthstone—looks like the real thing. At least, to my untrained eye."

I added that last part because I still feared that Penny, who had far more experience appraising objects than I did, might nevertheless have mistaken the bracelet for the type of costume jewelry she probably usually ran across at local auctions and estate sales.

In fact, I was about to ask, point blank, if the cuff should be evaluated by a jeweler.

However, Penny got a pinched, almost pained, expression on her face. "I'm not sure I'm even really selling that sorry thing," she informed me, nevertheless holding out her hand to take the bracelet from me. "I honestly don't know what to do with it, so I just stuck it in the case until I could decide its fate."

I thought "fate" was an odd word to use, related to jewelry, and I gave Penny a funny look. "What makes you say it's 'sorry'? Because I think it's very interesting."

"The sorry part is the sentimental hogwash," Penny said, scowling at the inscription. "It's embarrassingly personal, not to mention meaningless, and ruins the piece."

"I thought it was poetic," I disagreed, thinking her obvious foul mood was coloring her opinion. "Do you remember where the cuff came from? Or know anything about its story?"

Penny's eyes were again trained on the bracelet, which she was rubbing with her fingers, as if to remove tarnish that didn't exist.

"I can't tell you anything, Willow," she said glumly. I swore I also heard a tinge of bitterness in her voice. "There's really no story, at all. Which is probably the saddest thing about this homeless, unwanted relic of the past."

I kind of wanted the relic, and I debated whether to make an offer.

And as I tried to decide how much I'd be willing to pay, I realized that Penny was standing right where she'd been the night before, when Astrid's crystal ball had shown her in the same physical position, too. Hunched over, with the distinctive clock right behind her.

She looked like her shoulders might be about to start shaking again, too. And not with laughter.

"Penny?" I asked. "Are you okay? You seem kind of . . . weary."

"I am exhausted, Willow," she admitted, setting the bracelet on the case. "I'm leaving for a vacation—visiting my family's lake house, in the Midwest—a few weeks from now. It's the first time I've been home in quite a while, and I need the break."

"Oh, good for you," I said, although she didn't seem thrilled about her upcoming trip. Still, I added, "I'm sure you'll appreciate the time off. I know what it's like, being an entrepreneur. Everyone thinks you make your own hours, but, in truth, it can be hard to get away."

It struck me then that I hadn't taken a vacation in over a year. Fortunately, my home felt like a retreat. Even so, I thought I should probably close up the Owl & Crescent at some point and get out of town. I didn't want to reach the point of exhaustion, like Penny who, I suddenly recalled, had recently been to my place of business, which meant that I owed her something.

"Oh, gosh, Penny," I said. "I can't believe I forgot to bring your painting, from the night . . ." I started to say ". . . that Evangeline Fletcher was killed," but that didn't seem like a good way to describe the party, so I quickly changed course. "The night of the Small Business Alliance gathering."

Not that I'd really needed to clarify when Penny had been at the Owl & Crescent. I doubted anyone who'd attended that gathering had forgotten about it.

Penny certainly hadn't. "Please don't worry about my painting, Willow," she assured me, her voice tight. I wasn't sure what to make of her unusual mood. She was normally easygoing, with a ready smile. "I'm not much of an artist," she said. "And I don't . . . I don't need a reminder of . . . of . . ."

Penny's lip quivered, and for a second, I thought she might break down completely, perhaps over Evangeline's death. Neither one of us had spoken directly about the murder, but I couldn't think of another reason Penny might be so upset about the party.

And yet, I was also almost certain that Penny had been talking about Evangeline when she'd made that comment about "destroying" someone, back at my studio.

So why would she be so obviously shaken by the homicide?

Given that Penny and I weren't the closest friends, and our conversations usually centered on old objects, I didn't know if I should ask what was troubling her. We both got quiet, studying each other while the ceiling fans whirred softly overhead. And as I stared into Penny's brown eyes, I began to wonder if she was emotional about Evangeline's death because she felt *guilty*.

If I'd murdered someone, perhaps in an impulsive fit of rage, I wouldn't want a reminder of the incident—like a painting I'd created the night of the killing.

And carrying guilt could be exhausting, too.

I might also want to get out of town, if I'd committed homicide. Maybe even leave—or flee—the state.

As pieces fell into place, and the silence stretched on, I watched Penny even more closely and warily, although it was difficult for me to believe that the owner of one of my favorite spots on earth could have killed someone in cold blood.

Then again, Detective Turner said people were always surprised to learn that their friends and neighbors were capable of homicide.

Penny was also observing me, and it struck me that similar thoughts might be going through her head. She might very well be considering whether an herb-growing artist with a rescue pig might be pushed to commit murder, too. Especially if Penny knew about Evangeline's attempt to take away my animals and property—a crusade that hadn't exactly been a secret.

I probably should've backed away and pedaled home, but I heard myself asking, "Did you know Evangeline well, Penny? Is that why you don't want your painting, because it would make you think of her loss?"

I was careful not to say "murder," in case Penny had committed the crime. I didn't want her to think I had any suspicions, however weak and unfounded they might be. I wanted her to think I believed she might be upset about the passing of a friend—which may have been the case, in spite of Penny's harsh comment during the party.

"Were you and Evangeline friends?" I asked, when Penny didn't answer right away.

"Everyone knew Evangeline Fletcher," she finally said, sounding less glum and more guarded. A bit *stronger*. "Zephyr Hollow is a small town. A place where it's very difficult to keep secrets."

I had no idea why she'd added that last part, which seemed directed at me.

But I didn't have any secrets. Discounting those that might be hidden in the pages of my family's double-sealed spell book.

However, I seriously doubted that Penny Dandridge knew about the old journal. I didn't go to pains to keep it hidden, but I didn't brag about it, either, because there wasn't much reason to boast about a bunch of recipes and a spell that could likely *worsen* a case of poison ivy.

"I . . ."

I started to speak, although I had no idea what I planned to say. And Penny cut me off, anyway, steering the conversation back to the bracelet, which I'd completely forgotten about.

"I want you to have the cuff, Willow," she said, speaking more firmly. Her eyes had lost their watery, exhausted sadness, too. In fact, she seemed more like the woman who usually helped me when I visited the flea market. She even forced a smile. "I don't know why I got so upset before. Take the bracelet as my apology for acting so strangely. I know I seem out of sorts."

"No, I'd have to pay you," I insisted. "I really think it might be valuable."

"Nonsense." Penny practically forced the cuff into my hand. "You can pay me by telling everyone where you got it. Drum up some business, because things have been slow this summer."

I accepted her gift, thinking I would have it appraised and either return it, or come back with cash, if it proved to be valuable. "Thanks, Penny. It's a lovely present."

She waved off my gratitude. "It's nothing. Now, tell me what really brought you to Penny For Your Stuff. Is there something I can help you find?"

I'd almost forgotten my quest, too, and I shook off the last remnants of the weird, suspicious moments we'd just shared. "Oh, yes," I told her. "I did come here for something special."

"What might that be?"

It was hard for me to believe I'd just suspected Penny of murder as she nodded thoughtfully, listening to me describe the objects I sought for the bridesmaids' painting party.

Penny didn't seem to think my quest was crazy, but I nevertheless expected her to tell me I was out of luck. However, the magic of the flea market must've been working again, because gradually, some of the light came back to Penny's eyes, and she beckoned me to follow her, telling me, "I think I have the perfect thing for you and your party!"

Chapter 25

"Can you believe Penny was able to find miniature versions of the two dog breeds I needed, in the same booth?" I asked Luna, who sat on my bed, clearly more interested in the dresses I was rummaging through than the canine couple, silky gloves, and top hat that sat on my dresser, with the bracelet Penny had given me. Still, as I pulled yet another outfit from my closet, I added, "What were the odds she'd find a basset hound and a poodle for the wedding party to paint?"

Luna flattened her ears, and for a second, I thought she disapproved of my planned scene. Then I realized she was making a truly catty comment about the green dress I was holding up to myself.

"I agree," I said, tossing the shift onto my bed, next to the disapproving feline.

Then I pushed aside the hanger with the *perfect* gown I'd wear the next night and spied a maxi-dress with a black sleeveless bodice and black-and-white floral pattern on the long skirt.

Smiling, I grabbed the hanger and spun around, showing Luna the dress. "What do you think of this for the Gallery Walk?"

Luna's tail twitched with approval, and I quickly changed. Then I slipped on some sandals, tickled Luna under the chin, and headed out into the night, which was warm and humid, but thankfully not rainy. In fact, the sky was filled with stars, a nearly full moon, and a barn owl, who was turning lazy, sweeping circles overhead, as if patrolling the perimeter of my property.

"Don't worry so much, Remi," I told him, climbing into my Subaru. "This evening is supposed to be fun!"

I was talking to myself, of course. And I didn't really think Rembrandt was concerned about me. He was probably just hoping to spy a mouse sneaking around in the garden.

However, I couldn't help feeling uneasy when Remi disappeared into the woods, flying low, right down the path where Derek and I had found Evangeline's body.

And when I joined the walk, stopping first at the Well-Dressed Wall, I discovered that gallery owner Myrna Crickle was waiting for me. And she had some interesting news to share.

A bit of information that initially seemed great, but which I quickly realized might be cause for concern.

"I can't believe three of my paintings sold already," I told Myrna, who stood with me before bare spots where my watercolors had been hanging. If the rumors Evangeline Fletcher had tried to spread about Myrna's sale of inauthentic paintings had dissuaded customers for a while, that no longer seemed to be the case in the wake of my neighbor's death. The gallery was packed with locals and tourists, and I was lucky to snag Myrna's attention for even a few minutes. "Thanks so much for letting me display my art here, for such a ridiculously small commission."

"Nonsense." Myrna waved off my gratitude with a be-jeweled hand. "It's my pleasure to display your wonderful works, which quite obviously make people happy. And that's good for business, overall."

"Sometimes I wish the Owl & Crescent was more centrally located, so I could be part of the walk," I noted, gesturing at the crowd of people who were sipping champagne and snacking on crab salad croustades as light jazz played in the background. "But this is definitely the next best thing."

"Oh, your property is perfect for you, Willow." Myrna patted my arm. "You wouldn't be happy in town. I imagine you're more likely to move *farther* into the country, like your grandmother."

I glanced out one of the gallery's large windows, and, as if on cue, my Grandma Anna strolled by, hand-in-hand with George Van Buskirk.

That shouldn't have surprised me, but I hesitated, watching until they were out of sight.

I was thinking about Mr. Van Buskirk's health and feeling guilty for spying on him, via crystal ball.

Yet I couldn't help wondering what he'd been holding, as he'd gazed pensively out the window.

And where had Myrna been taking the Duvalier, when I'd seen *her*?

I was debating whether I should quietly inquire about the painting's fate when Myrna, obviously noting the funny expression on my face, asked, "Are you feeling all right, dear? You don't look very happy for someone who just made a substantial amount of money."

"It's not that much," I reminded her again. "A very modest profit for both of us."

"Oh, goodness . . ." Myrna rested her hand on her chest. "I should've told you. There was a small *bidding war* for one of your works."

I wasn't sure I'd heard correctly. "But this isn't an auction house. The prices are firm."

Myrna's eyes twinkled, and she took a step backward, probably because she needed to mingle with other guests.

Or maybe she was yielding the floor to the person who stepped up next to me, telling me with a gleam in *his* dark eyes, "I know the prices are set. But I couldn't let someone else own a painting of *my dog and me*—which I first saw, much to my surprise, at the Owl & Crescent."

My mouth kept opening and closing as I tried to figure out how to respond to Detective Lucien Turner's admission that he *had* seen the watercolor I still feared had somehow brought him into my life. Not to mention the fact that he now owned the painting.

But before I could say anything, he tossed me another curveball, asking, "Are you here with anyone?"

I expected him to give me another warning. And I *really* didn't know how to answer when he offered, "Because, if you're on your own, you're welcome to join me for the evening."

Chapter 26

The summer weather might have been unpredictable that year, but the balmy first night of the Gallery Walk was perfect for strolling along Zephyr Hollow's historic Main Street, which was lit by flickering paper bag luminaries and thousands of fairy lights that were strung in the branches of the many trees that arched overhead. Most of the merchants—even those who didn't usually sell art—displayed pieces in their windows, and some independent artists were featuring their works on tables in the roped-off street.

The village looked perfectly charming, and I couldn't help thinking that my companion for the evening was awfully attractive, too. As we moved down the crowded lane, sharing an order of deep-fried pecan hand pies from Baguettes & Beignets, I noticed quite a few women casting surreptitious glances at Detective Lucien Turner and his dog, Marinette, who had been waiting for him outside the Well-Dressed Wall.

The pensive pup, who stuck closely by Detective Turner's side, was technically leashed, as per a local ordinance my mother ensured was strictly enforced. However, Marinette carried her own lead in her mouth, leaving Detective Turner free to enjoy his share of a Southern treat, updated to be handheld, but still gooey and sugary-sweet.

I was savoring my snack, and the festive atmosphere, too. But I also kept sneaking glances at Detective Turner.

Apparently, he'd noticed the guarded way I repeatedly looked up at him. "Would you rather walk alone?" he finally asked, after a fairly long, but not necessarily uncomfortable, silence. He smiled at me, his expression very different from the imposing on-duty stare I'd endured at his office. "You don't need to feel obligated to stay with me."

I took my time answering, trying to decide if *he* wanted to ditch *me*. If maybe I hadn't turned out to be such great company, after all. Then, licking the last few crumbs from my fingers, I said, "No. I'm just trying to figure out why you asked me to walk with you. I'm a little concerned that you plan to question me some more."

He shook his head. "No, Willow. I'm off duty tonight. I don't plan to interrogate you."

"Then why ask me . . . ?"

"I just thought I'd get to know the artist who painted my portrait—unbeknown to me," he said. He'd finished his pie, too, and he wiped his fingers with a napkin he then tossed into a curbside bin. "Did you happen to snap a picture of me and Marinette, one rainy night? Was I some random stranger, walking through town, who happened to pass by the lens of your camera or phone, only to end up investigating you for murder?"

We'd reached the corner near Astrid's Astral Emporium, where the door was propped open, so I could see that quite a few people were inside, checking out the glow-in-the-dark paintings of unicorns and fairies, rendered on black velvet, that Astrid displayed every year. Not only was she the only merchant who would agree to host the artist, an eccentric young man who went by the single name "StarGazer," but she claimed to like his works, which definitely suited her unique aesthetic.

What *wouldn't* Astrid like?

The sight of me walking with Detective Turner, and I hoped she wouldn't see me stop him by resting a hand on his arm, so I could blurt out a bunch of questions I couldn't keep bottled up one more second. Not even long enough to step out of Astrid's potential sight line.

"Can I finally call you by your first name?" I asked, leading with the least urgent inquiry. Glancing down, I noticed that Marinette was on guard, as if she didn't like me touching her person, and I withdrew my hand. I lowered my voice, too, although passersby were engaged in their own conversations. "And am I still a murder suspect? Were the shears the weapon? And, last but not least, is there a tiny chance I summoned you to Zephyr Hollow— or to *life*—when I painted you?"

Detective Turner didn't jump to invite me to use his first name. Nor did he back away, like he thought that last question was crazy. Instead, he took my elbow in his cool, strong hand and said, "I think we should talk. In private."

Bistro Ruelle—translation, "back alley bistro"—was named literally, and, even though Zephyr Hollow was busy during the Gallery Walk, the somewhat secret little café was, as always, quiet. Owner Maurice Ledoc mainly operated the restaurant as a hobby, and a way to bring the taste and feel of his native city of Paris to his adopted nation. A glimpse of lights strung across narrow, cobbled Blackberry Alley, hidden away from the town's main thoroughfare, provided the only hint to tourists that the place even existed, and few ventured down the tight, twisting lane, which was hemmed in on either side by rows of attached, historic homes, the doors of which were lit with flickering gas lamps.

The few seats inside the bistro were occupied, so Detective Turner pulled out a chair at one of the outdoor tables.

I accepted the seat. "Thanks, Detective—"

"Please, call me Lucien," he interrupted, taking the chair opposite mine, while Marinette lay down at our feet. "I thought we'd already done away with the formality."

"Actually, no."

I started to remind Detective Turner . . . er, Lucien . . . that he'd never given me the go ahead to use his first name when someone who was apparently quite familiar with him came bursting through the door, rubbing his hands together, then clapping Lucien on the back in a hearty greeting.

"*Bonjour, mon ami,*" Maurice Ledoc said, grinning and completely overlooking me. "*C'est bon de te voir!*" The short, stocky chef had a bottle of wine tucked in the crook of one arm, and he used his free hand to pull something from the deep pockets of his white apron. Bending, he offered Marinette a real bone. The normally standoffish canine stood up, accepted the treat, and walked a few feet away, where she stretched out on the cobblestones in a pool of moonlight to chew her prize. Straightening, Maurice smiled at Lucien again. "*Tu as amené un ami ce soir!*"

Lucien laughed, sounding more relaxed than I could recall since meeting him, perhaps because the bistro was reminiscent of both Paris and New Orleans. He shrugged, still grinning. "*Ami, tueur . . . qui pourrait être certain?*"

"Ahem." I cleared my throat, reminding them both that one of us only spoke high school French, and not very well. And yet, I was pretty sure I'd translated most of their short, simple conversation.

"My apologies!" Maurice's brown eyes glimmered with merriment. "I always leap at the chance to speak French with my detective friend. I did not mean to be rude, Willow."

"You two know each other?" Lucien asked, slipping back into English, and his distinctive British-Cajun accent. He'd sounded like a native Parisian, himself, when he'd spoken French. "No introductions are necessary, I take it?"

"No, no, of course not!" Maurice placed the bottle and two tumblers he pulled from his capacious pockets onto the table. He winked at me and began to back away, his cheeks ruddy, like maybe he'd had a few sips of wine, himself, that evening. "You are looking quite lovely tonight, *Mademoiselle* Bellamy."

"Merci," I said, trying to add my own two *centimes* in French, and immediately wishing I hadn't. "I mean, thanks."

The men exchanged amused glances, then Maurice clapped Lucien on the shoulder again before hurrying back inside, without taking our orders because Chef Ledoc only cooked one dish a night, based on his whims and whatever was in season locally. He dictated the drinks, too. Bubbling water or something from his selection of imported, European wine.

Grabbing the bottle, Lucien checked the label, nodding like he approved. Then he lifted the vessel, silently asking if I wanted a glass.

I nodded my reply, and he poured—nearly spilling some of the Burgundy when I leaned forward and said, "Why did you just tell Maurice Ledoc that I might be a *killer*?"

Chapter 27

"I was just joking," Lucien said, resting back in his chair and stretching out his long legs. A sultry, bluesy Billie Holiday song played in the background, on the bistro's old turntable, and I could hear couples laughing inside. The air smelled of whatever mouthwateringly garlicky fare Maurice was whipping up in the kitchen, and I had a feeling that, although we hadn't ordered food, we were getting some, anyway. "I wouldn't have risked using the word *tueur* . . . killer . . . if I really believed you were still a suspect," Lucien added. "However, please don't share that news widely. I really just made an impromptu call, on the spot, to eliminate you from my current list."

Hunching my shoulders, I ran a finger around the rim of my tumbler. "Based on?"

Lucien smiled in a lopsided way and dragged one hand through his thick hair. "Gut instinct? The fact that, the more I ask around, the more enemies *I* make, just by insinuating that you might've committed homicide. You're quite loved in this town." He shrugged. "And you've got that rescue pig. Try as I might, I just can't reconcile you as a killer."

I sat back, my mood ring glowing a happy light blue. "It's nice to know my community is defending me."

I was pleased, but Lucien grew more serious, leaning forward, so I could better see his eyes. "I hope I'm right, Willow. I'm taking a leap of faith, ruling you out when the weapon *does* belong to you. And it reappeared rather suspiciously. Not to mention the fact that your alibi is as thin as they come."

He'd just said something important, maybe let a fact slip, and I sucked in a sharp breath, which was a bad idea, because I'd been sipping my wine.

Choking, I set down my glass and thumped my chest, coughing while Lucien waited for me to compose myself. When I could breathe again, I asked, "So, you've positively identified my old pruners as the weapon?"

He nodded. "Yes."

I was the one who'd harbored a murder weapon, but I studied Lucien with renewed suspicion. "Did you tell my mother about the shears' definite connection to Evangeline's death? She seemed to have that information yesterday."

Lucien averted his gaze, sipping his wine, too. Then he said, "I file frequent updates on my investigation. All of which are available to your mother."

He hadn't answered me directly, but I decided not to press the issue. "So, were there any fingerprints—aside from mine—on the pruners?"

"I can't tell you that, Willow. Just suffice it to say that your prints, at least, were wiped clean."

A shadow passed over our table, and I looked up to see a familiar owl gliding down the alley. Lucien didn't act like he noticed Rembrandt's arrival, but Marinette stopped gnawing her bone long enough to glance skyward.

Not sure why Remi had joined us, I returned my attention to the conversation. "So, you mentioned a 'current list' of suspects. Since I'm no longer on that roster, might I ask who *is*?"

Lucien's white teeth flashed when he laughed. "No. You may not."

I smiled, too. "I didn't think so, but I had to take a shot."

Lucien cocked his head. "Why? Why would you need to know? Because I feel like you asked out of more than just curiosity."

My grin faded. "I'm worried about Derek. Worried that you're targeting him—"

"I don't 'target' anyone," Lucien interrupted. "I look at the facts."

"What if the facts are misleading?"

"Then they weren't really facts, were they?"

We locked eyes for a minute, while I tried to decide whether I believed that was true. I honestly wasn't sure. I didn't see the world in black and white, and I suspected that Lucien didn't really do that, either. However, he might have a point about certain facts leading to the truth.

For example, whoever had sent me the murder weapon had obviously possessed it, at some point, after it had been taken from the Owl & Crescent. That was irrefutable, and potentially damning.

"Do you have something to tell me, Willow?" Lucien asked, breaking an increasingly tense silence. "Maybe something about your friend, Derek, who showed up in town the night of the murder and who might inherit a fortune in the wake of his aunt's death?"

"No," I whispered, my throat tightening. "I don't have anything to say."

Lucien continued to watch me, and I couldn't break his gaze, even when Rembrandt swooped over us again. "Maybe you've had time to think about the envelope," he noted, "and you've decided you *do* have some insights, after all?"

"I . . . no . . . I . . ."

It was like he'd read my mind, and I started to stammer a denial—just as, thank goodness, Maurice emerged from the bistro, humming cheerfully while he set two bundles of silverware and a single plate, holding the strange combination of a crepe and some pommes frites, between Lucien and me. Apparently, we were sharing.

"Thanks," I mumbled, simultaneous to Lucien's, *"Merci."*

"De rien! You are welcome!" Maurice grinned broadly and backed away, his head bobbing. "Enjoy!"

"I'm sure we will," Lucien promised, right before Maurice disappeared inside the bistro. Then Lucien reached for his napkin, unrolling it to expose a silver fork and knife.

I did the same, and for a split second, I flashed back to the flea market, where I'd seen the silverware with gold details, which had seemed familiar to me.

I must've stared for a moment too long.

"Something wrong?"

I looked up to discover Lucien watching me again, but some of the warmth and humor had returned to his eyes. "Is the silverware dirty? Or maybe you don't like mushrooms?"

For a moment, I didn't know why he'd asked about my preferences, regarding fungi. Then he cut into the crepe, and I realized it was savory, and stuffed with mushrooms and melty cheese. Probably Gruyere, if I knew Maurice.

"No, the utensils are fine, and this looks delicious." I reached for my fork as Lucien pushed part of the crepe toward my half of the plate. However, tempting as the meal looked, I didn't dig in right away, like Lucien did. My stomach was still twisting from the recent tension between us. And something else was bothering me, too. "Lucien?"

He looked up. "Yes?"

"What if I was told something, in confidence, but which might be pertinent to your investigation?"

He set down his fork, giving me his full attention. Light from the candle was reflected in his eyes. "I can't give you guidance, regarding ethics. But I do think there's a moral imperative to bring killers to justice, especially if there's a chance they might kill again."

If the person I was thinking about had killed Evangeline Fletcher, I didn't think she'd kill anyone else. And I seriously doubted she was guilty. Yet our conversation continued to weigh on my mind, and I ventured, tentatively, "Did anyone ever mention having a fight with Evangeline, the night before her death? One that ended in a shoving match?"

I was relieved when Lucien nodded. "Yes. You're talking about Myrna Crickle. She finally—belatedly—unburdened herself of the whole story, in a fit of guilt and gratitude."

I didn't understand. "Why *gratitude*?"

"I helped her locate experts who authenticated the Duvalier that was the source of contention between the two women," Lucien explained. "A battle that, I am certain, *didn't* end with Ms. Crickle committing homicide. Her extensive personal security system clearly shows her at home when the killing took place."

I was glad Myrna had been exonerated but struck by something else Lucien had said. "*You* found an authority to authenticate the painting?" I asked, surprised. I finally picked up my fork and dug into the crepe. "How—and who?"

The corners of Lucien's mouth quirked with amusement. "The 'who' was my father, and some of his associates. And Doctor Turner was rather easy to find. He's in my contacts."

I dropped the fork again. "Your father?"

"Is a professor with Tulane's art department, and a very respected scholar." Lucien reached for one of the thin, crispy French fries. "Contemporary French painting isn't his area of expertise. But it was easy for him to track down several people qualified to authenticate the Duvalier. Which is worth a cool quarter million and which, I suppose, will likely be inherited by Derek Fletcher."

I ignored his comment about Derek. "What, exactly, is your father's area of expertise?" I asked, picturing the book I'd seen in Lucien's office. The one by D. W. Turner. "What does he study?"

"Art and the paranormal," Lucien said, clearly watching me for a reaction. "He's the author of a definitive book on the subject—"

"*The Conjured Canvas: Intersections of Art & Magic*," I interrupted, nodding. "I saw it on your bookshelves."

Neither one of us spoke for a moment. The couples in the bistro were quieter, too, and a soft, scratchy recording of Sarah Vaughan seemed to roll like mist through the alley. Having finished her bone, Marinette slunk back under the table and took her place at Lucien's feet. I was also keenly aware of an owl who sat on a plantation-style wooden shutter a few yards down the street.

"You're not here by accident or coincidence, are you?" I finally asked, pushing the nearly empty plate closer to Lucien. My stomach felt too fluttery to eat any more. "You . . . We . . . really do have some sort of connection."

Lucien didn't answer me. Without breaking our gaze, he pushed the plate back to center, almost like it was a game piece, or object up for negotiation. The candle continued to reflect in his eyes, which suddenly seemed darker. Peering into them, I sought a glimpse of whatever

I'd seen a few nights before, when we'd stood on my porch and the lightning had pierced the darkness.

Or maybe I *didn't* want to see that again.

Yet I found myself leaning even closer, also searching for the truth, or reassurance, which I feared might be two different things.

"Pepper once joked that I should summon you to life from my painting," I finally whispered, thinking the possibility sounded crazier the second time I'd voiced it. But Lucien didn't so much as blink. "Did something like that actually happen?" I asked. "Because I never saw you or Marinette before I painted you both." I recalled my dream, too, but decided not to mention it. "And, suddenly, here you are, talking about Voodoo, and familiars, and art and the paranormal, which are both related to me. It seems awfully strange. Especially since the Internet seems to break when I type your name into a search engine."

His eyebrows shot up. "You *Googled* me?"

I rolled my eyes. "You've asked every resident of Zephyr Hollow about me." He opened his mouth to reply, but I cut him off. "So. What's going on?"

Lucien sat back, sighed, and rubbed his jaw. "You *didn't* breathe me to life," he told me, in a low, deep voice. "But, yes, we do have a connection. There's a chance that you somehow anticipated my arrival. You are obviously intuitive, and I saw your spell book. You dabble in dreams and travel between planes."

"Why would I anticipate . . . ?"

I was asking a question that I thought was important, but Lucien was pulling money from his pocket, placing the bills on the table, and rising to leave.

"Wait," I said, too loudly. The sudden noise caused

Rembrandt to flap his wings, and Marinette jolted and rose, too. "Where are you going?"

"I really can't tell you more, right now." Lucien tucked the cash under the plate. "And I need to go."

I also pushed back my chair and stood up, grabbing Lucien's arm. Marinette tensed, visibly, and Lucien cast a surprised glance at the spot where my hand met his wrist.

I again quickly released him. "Just tell me if you saw anything the other night." That was awfully vague, but I didn't know how to ask if he'd seen me watching him in a crystal ball. "I swore, you looked right at me. Maybe saw me in my studio, but from a distance . . . ?"

I still wasn't being clear, but I thought he understood what I was talking about.

"Did we communicate in some different way?" I asked. "Through a strange medium?"

Lucien gave me a dead level stare, reminiscent of the way he'd looked at me in his office—probably because we'd circled back to a conversation we'd had there.

"I'll answer your questions truthfully, Willow," he finally said, "when you're honest with me about the handwriting on the envelope that held the murder weapon."

And without another word, Detective Lucien Turner turned and walked into the darkness, followed by his dog, who looked back once at me, and an owl that I was starting to fear might be not an ally, but a *traitor*.

Chapter 28

With its soft lighting and Old World charm, Blackberry Alley had seemed like a cozy enclave while I'd sat at the bistro with Lucien. At least, the narrow lane had felt welcoming until he'd called me on the fib my grandmother had warned me about telling. But as I walked toward Main Street, away from the restaurant's music and laughter, the buildings seemed to close in a bit, and I found myself hurrying, my footsteps echoing on the uneven cobblestones.

My ears, pricked for the slightest sound, picked up another faint noise, too. One that I couldn't place.

It wasn't the sound of someone following me, although I kept looking over my shoulder, the farther I got from the bistro.

It was a faint whirring and clacking, coming from in front of me, in a dark passage between two buildings.

I knew that I had no real reason to be afraid, and I was only on edge because of the recent murder, but I picked up my pace even more, thinking that once I was past the strange noise, I would be just a half-block from the busy Gallery Walk. I could see people strolling in the distance.

In fact, lots of people would hear me if I needed to

scream, although no one came running when I let out a high-pitched yelp, because a shadowy figure suddenly darted out from the passage, blinding me with a bright light, so I stumbled on the uneven cobblestones and tumbled to the ground.

"Benedict, what are you doing, lurking in the dark with a video camera?" I asked Benedict Blodgett, who hadn't come to my aid, either. In fact, he'd continued filming for a moment too long while I'd struggled to pick myself up off the ground.

My use of the word "lurking" was probably rude, but Benedict seemed more offended by my characterization of his equipment.

"Oh, dear, dear, no!" he cried softly. My eyes were still readjusting to the darkness after he'd blinded me with the light on his camera, but I was able to see him rest the object against his narrow chest. A protective gesture. "This isn't just some 'video camera,' Willow," he corrected me. "It's a 1944 Paillard Bolex sixteen-millimeter *movie* camera. A piece of equipment as classic as the films made in its heyday!"

I dusted off my rear end, which was going to be bruised. "Well, what are you doing with it in a dark alley, aside from scaring the heck out of me and causing me to fall?"

"Did I scare you? I thought perhaps you just tripped."

My eyes were functioning normally again, and I saw his lips curve into a self-satisfied smile that made me want to resume walking quickly toward Main Street. However, he was blocking my path.

"The footing here is always tricky at night," he added, taking a step closer. "Even I've taken a few spills."

"You . . . you hang out here a lot, after dark?" I asked, sidestepping to get around him, only to have him match my movement, so he was still in front of me. My skin prickled, and I glanced at the dark buildings that hemmed in the alley, hoping there was a logical explanation for his frequent presence in such a secluded spot. "Do you live in one of these houses?"

Benedict shook his head. "No. I just like to shoot here. It's very atmospheric."

That was true. The gas lamps cast eerie shadows on a street that looked trapped in the eighteenth century. But what the heck was Benedict filming? There were no actors—not so much as a stray cat—to capture.

Unless he was lying in wait . . .

"I really need to get going," I said more firmly, stepping around him again. My bare shoulder brushed his arm, and I twitched, half afraid he'd grab me. Fortunately, he let me pass. "Take care, Benedict."

"Willow?"

I didn't want to turn back, but I did. "Yes?"

He stood in the center of the alley, the camera still cradled against his chest and the flames reflecting off the lenses of his small eyeglasses. "I film lots of things after dark, you know? Sometimes I capture the patrons at the bistro. So many interesting people and animals show up. Often, individuals and pets you wouldn't expect to see together!"

My blood was running cold. I was pretty sure he was trying to say that he'd filmed me with Lucien. But I didn't know what he was insinuating.

Maybe that, as a murder suspect, I shouldn't have been splitting a crepe with the investigating detective?

"What are you trying to say?" I asked point blank.

He shrugged. "Nothing. I just thought that, as an artist, you might be interested in my process. Filming after dark, with a traditional camera, is something of an art, itself." He stepped closer again. "And I practice all the time. Not just in this alley. But all over the place. You might be interested in some of the things I've captured near your property, late at night."

My blood was *frozen*. "Near my property . . . ?"

He nodded. "Yes. There are things you might want to see. Things I could show you. And not just at your place."

I backed away. "I don't think so. Thanks, though." Why did I add *that*? "Good night, Benedict."

He made a move to follow me. "Willow . . . my painting."

"Your what?"

"My painting. Of the rabbit. From the night of Evangeline's death."

I was still backing away, being careful on the cobblestones. I did *not* want to fall again. "What about it?"

"Would you mind dropping that off at my studio? You *did* mention that you would deliver the works, once they dried."

Had I made that promise? Because I usually had customers pick up their canvases. I was only delivering the batch from the recent party because no one was claiming them.

All at once, I was struck by a worrisome thought. Was there a chance Benedict had seen me load the box of paintings into my car?

How often did he creep around my neighborhood at any time of day?

Regardless, I didn't want to invite him to stop by my studio. It seemed like he "visited" enough.

"Sure, I can deliver the canvas," I said, gesturing behind

me. "In fact, I have the paintings in my car. You could walk with me and get yours."

I didn't want to extend that invitation, either, but it seemed like the least objectionable of several bad options. If I gave him the painting that night, on a busy, public street, Benedict wouldn't have a legitimate reason to visit the Owl & Crescent. And once rid of his painting, I wouldn't have to go to Take 666.

Unfortunately, Benedict had other plans. "No, I'm afraid I need to stay here. I'm not quite done with my work this evening, and the moonlight . . . and darkness . . . are just right for a project I'd like to finish while I still have my space under the Silver Spoon."

I was ready to flee, but I needed him to explain that last comment. "What do you mean, while you still have your space? Are you moving out? Or is the building being sold or something?"

"What?" He jolted. It was clear he felt like he'd said too much.

"What's happening with your studio? Because I haven't heard about any plans for the Silver Spoon."

"I . . . I just *think* the building might be sold, now that Evangeline is dead. And perhaps the new owner will have different plans for the cellar."

He was lying, while I was quickly connecting dots. Or, more accurately, notes I'd seen in Evangeline's planner.

Place Whisper ad—New TNT!

Evangeline hadn't been planning a classified ad to buy or sell dynamite in Zephyr Hollow's weekly newspaper. She'd been seeking a new *tenant*.

"*Evangeline* was evicting you, wasn't she?" I asked. "You were worried about your studio space before she was killed, weren't you?"

Benedict's silence spoke volumes, and I felt a prickle of excitement, to have pieced together a possible clue to my neighbor's murder. That was quickly followed by a new, stronger creeping sensation of fear. Yet I dared to ask another question. "What happened? Did you fall behind on your rent?"

The alley was dim, but I could tell Benedict's face was paler than usual. However, there were two spots of red on his cheeks, too. "I might've been a month or two behind. But she wanted me gone because she hated my work," he said. "Called it 'disgusting' and, worse yet, 'derivative'!"

As an artist, myself, I also flinched at that latter insult, which was worse than "disgusting." "Sorry," I told him.

He jutted his chin. "My work pays homage to classic horror films. But it is original!"

I wasn't really concerned about the stylistic elements of his movies. I wanted to know more about his possible eviction.

"You were fighting to keep the space, weren't you?" I ventured, keeping my tone neutral. I didn't want to agitate him further, but I wanted him to share more. "You didn't mention anything about moving when you invited me to one of your classes. You thought you'd be able to stay, didn't you?"

"I . . . I wasn't sure." He squeezed the camera to himself. "I'd come up with the rent money, but when I delivered the check, in person, Evangeline refused to take it. Said my studio reflected badly on her fancy restaurant, and that I should start packing my things. I told her that I had rights, as a tenant. I'd signed a lease, and I was willing to fight her in court, if necessary!"

I continued to act almost disinterested. "I imagine that didn't go over well with Evangeline, huh?"

Benedict shook his head, his voice deepening to a low growl. "No, that mean old miser threatened . . ."

My skin was crawling, because I could imagine Benedict lurking around my property after the party, waiting for Evangeline in the woods with the shears he'd rendered as weapon-like in his painting.

"No!" Benedict's sudden cry echoed down the alley. He must've known was I was thinking, and he caught himself, mid-sentence, before he incriminated himself further. He took another step toward me. "It's not what you think!" He sounded like a hurt child. A *desperate*, hurt child. "We did argue, but I didn't kill her! Just because I make horror films doesn't make *me* a monster!"

Hanging his head, he hugged his camera tighter, and I could also picture him in a basement studio, working alone on films that hardly anyone saw. A part of me felt sorry for him. However, I wasn't sure I believed he was innocent, and I resumed backing away.

"Willow, I didn't kill anyone," he insisted, raising his eyes to meet mine again, although I still couldn't see past his glasses. "I can prove it. The next time you're near the studio, please stop by. I *really* need to show you some things that I believe you'll find of interest." He cleared his throat. "Perhaps of *benefit*. Honestly, Willow!"

I caught another subtle change in his voice. A nervous, almost pleading hitch.

I took my time responding. Then I nodded. "Okay. I'll stop by sometime."

I turned to walk away, and he called after me again, softly but insistently. "Soon, Willow. I think it would be best if you visited soon!"

I didn't answer.

And I didn't fully understand why I intended to heed

that summons, which lingered in my mind as I drove home, where I brought Mortimer inside with me and Luna. Then I locked my doors and first-floor windows, turning in early, because, in spite of my initial reluctance, I'd decided to attend a funeral that was scheduled for the following morning.

Chapter 29

"Given how I felt about the deceased, I feel like a hypocrite," Pepper whispered, nudging me in the ribs, by accident. Like Astrid, who stood on my other side, she was trying to silence her cell phone before Evangeline Fletcher's memorial service began in a very crowded, hilly Wildwood Cemetery, on the outskirts of Zephyr Hollow. The ground around the Fletcher family's imposing mausoleum, located in a grove of tall oaks, was filled with genuine mourners, as well as individuals who probably felt compelled to pay their respects to a community leader, and, I suspected, some folks who were merely gawkers, trying to play a peripheral role in the town's first murder in decades.

Craning my neck, I searched for familiar faces and quickly located Myrna Crickle and Linh Tran, who both likely fell into category two.

Myrna, who wore a buglike pair of oversized black sunglasses, must've sensed that someone was watching her. She caught my eye and nodded a greeting.

Linh, more subdued in a linen suit, did the same, her expression solemn.

I dipped my head in reply, then searched the crowd again, spotting Penelope Dandridge, who hung back at the very edge of the throng, her hair disheveled and a handkerchief pressed to her mouth. She didn't appear to be crying, but she was clearly on the verge.

"Why do you think Penny Dandridge is so shaken up about Evangeline?" I whispered, turning back around. "I swear, she was furious with her at the painting party."

"Maybe she feels guilty for being angry with Evangeline, right before her death," Astrid said quietly. She'd made the mistake of wearing all black, and she fluttered her dolman sleeves in a futile attempt to create a breeze. "Maybe their last words were cross."

"Or maybe Penny feels guilty because her last words to Evangeline were, 'Sorry, dear, but I'm about to stab you,'" Pepper suggested, dropping her phone into her purse.

"Pepper!" My blurted rebuke caused a few heads to swivel in our direction.

"I don't think she would've announced it like that," Astrid said, missing the point. "The stabbing was probably more spur of the moment."

As I was deciding whether to reply, the purr of an engine drew everyone's attention to the twisting lane. A respectful silence fell over the crowd as two black Cadillacs and one hearse pulled to the side of the road.

A moment later, Derek and some other men I didn't know—perhaps distant relatives or representatives of the funeral home—emerged from the vehicles.

Derek took a second to survey the crowd, like I'd just done. The sunlight gleamed on his blond hair, and, forgetting the solemn circumstances for a moment, my heart hitched a little.

"He makes a quite handsome mourner," Pepper whispered, nudging me again, this time on purpose.

I didn't respond to that, either, except to shoot her a look that suggested she be more respectful.

Pepper merely grinned. She felt very strongly in an afterlife, and she didn't take death quite as seriously as most people. Still, I shook my head, reminding her to mind her manners.

By the time I looked at the vehicles again, Derek and the other men were pulling the casket from the hearse.

The crowd parted so the pallbearers, with Derek at the front, right-hand side, could carry Evangeline's body toward a white tent, where a minister waited. Derek's mouth was set in a grim line, but I didn't think he was straining under the weight of the coffin. I was pretty sure he was grieving the loss of an entire generation of Fletchers. Although he and his aunt hadn't gotten along, she *was* the last member of his immediate family. And he was probably again upset with himself for missing his parents' burials, although he wasn't to blame.

A lump formed in my throat for all the deceased and Derek. And someone else was touched by the sad spectacle, too. A sob cut through the silence, and I shifted to see Penelope's shoulders shaking.

Should I go to her . . . ?

"Willow, look!"

Astrid's quiet cry, accompanied by a tap on my arm, drew my attention back to my friends.

"What?" I whispered, leaning closer to her—right before I spied what she had also seen: Benedict Blodgett, who stood half hidden behind a tree, in the shadows, a small, modern video camera in his hand.

"Is he *videotaping* the funeral?" Pepper spoke softly, but she sounded horrified. I'd told her and Astrid about my encounter with Benedict, and she muttered, "What is *wrong* with him?"

A horrible thought crossed my mind, and I feared that something might be desperately amiss.

What if Benedict was capturing footage for the end of a *real-life* horror film, involving a murder by the director, because no one would think that was "derivative"?

I kept staring at Benedict until the minister stepped forward, near the casket that had been placed on a draped stand. A moment later, the service was underway, and I did my best to concentrate on the prayers and sermon about the brevity of life.

However, my thoughts kept straying, and my eyes wandered, too.

I wasn't the only one who was distracted. Pepper suddenly drew a sharp breath, and I saw her head turn, right before she stiffened at my side.

Following her gaze, I spotted Lucien Turner standing under one of the majestic oaks, not far from where Benjamin had just been skulking.

Lucien, who listened attentively, his hands clasped, was probably also trying to be inconspicuous in a dark, sober suit. But the perfectly fitted jacket and crisp, white shirt only made him command even more attention than usual.

Whether it was because Pepper distrusted Lucien or found him attractive—or likely both—she couldn't seem to take her eyes off him, just like a certain owl, who sat in the branches above the detective, peering down.

Astrid had seen Lucien, too, and she clutched my arm. "Oh, my goodness!" she whispered, fanning herself with her free hand. "He's even . . . *more*, in real life!"

I understood what she meant, and, as I shushed her with one finger to my lips, I mentally supplied some of the adjectives that had failed my friend.

Handsome. Compelling. Contradictory. Enigmatic.

Okay, Astrid was probably just thinking "handsome," and possibly "compelling."

Like Myrna, Lucien must've sensed that he was under scrutiny, because he met my gaze and tilted his chin, just slightly, in acknowledgment.

Embarrassed to have been caught staring, I replied in kind and faced forward again, in time to hear the minister call the first eulogist, telling us all, "Mayor Celeste Bellamy would like to say a few words about her *dearest childhood friend.*"

I looked between Pepper and Astrid, and we all spoke too loudly, asking the same, single-word question.

"What?"

Chapter 30

"It feels kind of strange, going from a funeral in the morning to a party at night," I told my grandmother, who'd volunteered to help me with a hairstyle for the gala at the Crooked Chimneys. I could *not* work magic with hair. Not even with a spell book. Checking my reflection in my bedroom mirror, I lightly touched the tendrils that were purposely loose from the artfully chaotic updo Grandma Anna had created for me, thinking the look was perfect.

Luna, who sat on my vanity, seemed to agree. Her yellow eyes were alight, like she sensed that the evening promised to be special, although I'd reminded her several times that I wasn't going on a real date.

Mortimer, meanwhile, couldn't have cared less about updos or dances. He was happily munching on a bowl of pitted apricots Grandma had brought him from her farm.

I met Anna's eyes, reflected in the glass. "Should I feel guilty about going out tonight? Or should *Derek*?"

Grandma rested her hands on my shoulders, which were covered by my flannel robe. "By the time you're my age, you'll be grateful for every moment *you* have to live, and you'll understand that life goes on." Releasing me, she stepped back from her handiwork, nodding with approval, even as she continued to address my concerns. "Would it be more proper if the party was tomorrow? Or three days later?" She shrugged and turned away, giving me some privacy so I could get dressed. "Besides, I didn't even attend the service, so if anyone should feel badly, it's me. But I had no dealings with Evangeline, lately, and we certainly weren't friendly."

"Grandma . . ." I rose from my seat at my vanity, tossed off my robe and shimmied into my body-conscious velvet dress. "Were *Mom* and Evangeline great pals at some point? Because the minister described them as 'dearest' friends, before Mom gave her eulogy."

My grandmother had moved to the turret, where she was looking out the windows at the setting sun, and I thought her back stiffened for just a second. But she was smiling when she faced me again. "Celeste and Evangeline were the same age and lived next door to one another growing up. Of course, they played together at times. But I think the minister exaggerated, perhaps for dramatic effect."

That made sense, and my mother's remarks hadn't been overly sentimental. Yet I felt my grandmother was keeping something from me. And my mother had acted oddly, too, the last time I'd seen her. Plus, I'd found what appeared to be a locked page in the spell book.

"Grandma, what's going on?" I asked, turning and gesturing for her to help me with my zipper. She obliged, and I turned back around. "There's something you're not telling me. And I feel like Mom's keeping secrets, too." I could tell that I'd struck a nerve, and I hurried to add, "There's something hidden in *Book of Miscellany*, too. Pages that someone fused together."

Grandma Anna averted her gaze. Then she sighed

deeply and met my eyes again. "Willow, I've been trying to piece together some things, myself. But perhaps it is time we talk. You and I—and your mother, too."

My grandmother and I shared a lot of confidences, but we seldom . . . no, never . . . included my mom.

"What's happening?" I asked again, with a flutter of concern. The sun had nearly set, and it was difficult to read my grandmother's expression. "Should I be worried? About you? Or Mom?" I recalled Detective Turner's warning to me about the gala, and my mother's cryptic comment about wishing she could help me more. "About *myself*?"

Grandma Anna smiled and rubbed my bare arm with her warm, rough hand. "Oh, goodness, Willow! Nothing's so grave that you need to ruin a perfectly lovely evening, fretting. Perhaps nothing's wrong at all."

That didn't sound very reassuring, and I wanted to ask more questions. But my grandmother was leaving. She shouldered her tote and kissed my cheek. "Have a wonderful time, dear. We will chat soon."

With that, she disappeared from my room. I heard the front door open and close, then her truck rumbling away.

"Mysterious detectives, cagey family members, and homicide," I said, as the very last rays of the setting sun caused something on my vanity to twinkle. The gemstone in the bracelet Penny had given me.

I reached for the cuff, thinking the topaz stone would be a good complement to the deep gray gown.

Slipping the bracelet onto my wrist, I twisted my arm, noting that the mood ring, which I'd grown rather fond of, was glowing red, meaning I was nervous. And not just related to my grandmother's admission that we needed to talk. I was getting butterflies for a different reason as the dance grew closer.

"I'm being ridiculous," I chided myself, addressing Luna, who was pacing the mattress. "There's no reason to be nervous around Derek. We've known each other since childhood!"

I told myself that, but my heart still jumped when the doorbell rang, causing Luna and Mortimer to jolt, too.

Both pig and cat followed me down the stairs and to the door, which I opened to greet Derek, who had a strange look on his face. And he sounded odd, too, when, instead of hello, he said, "Oh, Willow . . ."

Chapter 31

"I'm sorry I started babbling when I saw you," Derek said, grinning sheepishly. He laced his fingers with mine, and we joined other couples who were turning slow, rhythmic circles on the flagstone patio behind the Crooked Chimneys, to the soft sounds of a trio of musicians.

As always, Pepper, whom I hadn't seen yet, had outdone herself with the gala, which was in full swing on a clear, moonlit night. Hundreds of tiny lanterns hung from the trees around the pool, where more candles floated like stars in the dark water. The cabana was strung with twinkle lights, and the windows of the inn, which was crowded with mingling people, glowed softly.

The atmosphere was over-the-top romantic, and I kept reminding myself not to fall under its spell, or be too charmed by my dance partner, who was complimenting me again. "You took my breath away when you opened the door in that dress."

"You look pretty handsome, yourself," I told Derek, placing my free hand on his shoulder and letting him draw me closer.

Looking around, I checked to see if Astrid, my mother,

or my grandmother were watching, because I knew they'd all have opinions about the wisdom of me dancing with the guy who'd broken my heart. But I didn't see any of them, either, and I took a deep breath, allowing myself to sway to the music.

Derek and I had been quiet on the ride to the party, both of us probably trying to sort out our feelings, to be on a date after years apart, and we stopped talking entirely as we fell into the rhythm of the song.

It felt strange to be in his arms again. Both familiar and . . . different.

Was this how I'd felt back at our high school prom, when we'd first danced like this?

Or the night of our first kiss?

How did it compare to the last time Derek had embraced me at the airport, when we'd said goodbye?

He drew me even closer, and I could feel his warm breath tickling my neck.

Was I about to get my heart broken again, in a gentler, bittersweet way?

"Willow?" Derek's voice was soft in my ear, and I pulled back to see his blue eyes, which I'd gazed into so many times as we'd moved from childhood friends to teenage sweethearts to adults in a romance foiled by our conflicting visions for the future. "Willow, I've missed you."

I'd spent what felt like countless nights dreaming of the moment Derek Fletcher would return to Zephyr Hollow and say those words to me. Nights I'd also wished I didn't selfishly want to pull him away from lifesaving work on a continent that needed doctors.

And now that my dream was coming true, if only for an evening. . . .

"Derek." I shifted my hand on his shoulder, putting a

little space between us. When I moved my arm, the gem in my cuff glittered in the moonlight while my mood ring was glowing red again.

But I didn't feel the same type of butterflies, now that I was in his arms. I felt nervous about a conversation Derek and I needed to have, before he voiced what I sensed he was thinking. Because if he expressed what I was seeing in his eyes, I didn't know how I'd respond.

I needed the truth first, and I squeezed his shoulder, asking him, point blank, "Derek . . . You have to tell me. Did you put a *murder weapon* in my mailbox?"

"Willow, I'm so sorry." Derek's voice was muffled, because he was bent over, his fingers dug into his thick hair.

We'd retreated to a cement bench in a secluded glade at the very edge of Pepper's property, a place where we could talk privately, and I rested my hand on his back, gently urging him to sit up and face me.

Straightening at my touch, he smoothed his hair back into place and sighed deeply, finally meeting my gaze again. He looked miserable. "You recognized my handwriting, didn't you? Even though I tried to conceal it."

"Yes. I thought one of the letters looked familiar. But I wasn't sure."

"Yet another thing I botched." He offered me a crooked, rueful smile. "I can't seem to do anything right, anymore. I'm constantly fixing mistakes—with new mistakes. And so things continue to spin out of control, getting worse and worse."

I had this terrible feeling that the guy who'd once done everything right—the high school sports hero turned humanitarian—might have made the *ultimate* mistake, taking a human life. Yet I wasn't afraid to be alone with him.

In fact, our whole evening had been remarkable for the lack of emotion I'd felt once the date had gotten underway.

That was the bittersweet heartbreak. I felt like a part of my youth had officially come to a close. But I would mourn that loss another time.

"Derek, you need to be honest with me," I said. "Did something happen between you and Evangeline? Maybe an argument that got out of hand?"

He shook his head so vigorously that I stopped trying to lay out a possible scenario.

"No, Willow! It's not like that," he promised. "It's . . . I don't know what happened. It'll sound crazy, but . . ."

"Derek, I'm a witch who casts spells from a recipe book," I reminded him. "Whatever you have to say, it's probably not crazier than that."

Derek didn't laugh. He nodded solemnly. "Okay. Maybe you will believe me when I tell you that the shears—which were covered in blood—were on my kitchen counter when I woke up the morning after Aunt Evan's murder. And when I saw them . . . saw the blood . . ."

He covered his face with his hands, as if to shut out the memory, while I grew even more confused. He was a doctor, who sometimes operated in the field. Wasn't blood a pretty big part of the job?

I rested one hand lightly on his arm, trying to connect with and steady him, because he seemed close to breaking down. "What's going on, Derek? What's the bigger story?"

He ground his palms into his eyes, then pulled his hands away, so he could meet my gaze again. To my surprise, he looked almost relieved, probably because he was about to unburden himself of some secrets he'd been keeping for quite a while.

"I've been having panic attacks, Willow. From the stress of working in constant danger. And the things I've seen . . ." He shook his head. "I'm not being reassigned, Willow. I had to quit, to save myself and my patients. I wasn't functioning anymore in the field. I was a danger to my teammates and those in my care."

"Why didn't you tell me?"

"I was ashamed. You thought I was some kind of hero when I left here. But I couldn't hack it."

I shook his arm, wanting him to believe me. "Derek, you're still a hero. Most people *never* do what you did. They don't have the courage or commitment. You made a real difference, for years. And you're certainly not the first person to suffer PTSD from serving in a conflict zone. You have *nothing* to be ashamed of."

He smiled wanly. "No? Not even the fact that I started shaking and hyperventilating when I saw the shears? Not just because of the blood, but because I knew I was being framed, and had motives that would make me look doubly guilty." He looked away, unable to meet my eyes. "I . . . I washed them and stuck them in the envelope, giving them back to you."

I felt too sorry for him to be angry. "Why me?"

"I was in a panic, not thinking straight. I just had to get rid of what I *knew* was the murder weapon. And I couldn't imagine that you'd ever be seriously accused of homicide," he explained. "I also thought maybe you, Pepper, and Astrid would find a way to make the shears disappear. If not with some sort of hocus pocus, with your combined cleverness."

I pulled my hand away. "Derek, you know I couldn't do that."

He rubbed his eyes again, seeming weary. "It seemed possible at the time. I'm telling you, when I lose control, I don't think straight. I go into survival mode."

Derek's admission that he "lost control" gave me pause, and he must've understood what I was thinking. He pulled back. "I don't black out, though. And I don't get violent. I've seen enough violence to last me a lifetime. I swear, I was reading, I fell asleep, and I came to get you when I realized Aunt Evan had never come home."

"I believe you," I promised him. "But you have to tell Detective Turner. And you have to get help. You need counseling."

"I know." He hunched over again, his hands hanging between his knees. He seemed exhausted, and his tone was flat, defeated. "It's just difficult for me to admit. And other things are such a mess, too."

I recalled the image I'd seen of Derek in the crystal ball. He'd sat before a pile of papers, looking overwhelmed then, too.

"What else is happening?"

He turned to me, his face bathed in moonlight. "I've been going through the estate since Evangeline died. It's a disaster, Willow. We're nearly broke. I'm almost certain that's why she was leaving bad reviews everywhere and using cheap ingredients. And some items are missing from the house, too. Pawned, for all I know."

I snapped my fingers. "The grandfather clock!"

Derek gave me a funny look. "How did you know about that? Because a clock that was in our formal parlor for as long as I can remember is gone."

"I saw a familiar clock and some distinctive silverware that I'm pretty sure is yours, too, at Penny For Your Stuff.

It just never occurred to me that Evangeline would be pawning items, so I didn't make the connection."

"Well, I'm not going to bother trying to get anything back," Derek said sadly. "I doubt I have the resources!"

The Fletchers *always* had resources. "How can that be?" I asked. "What happened?"

"As it turns out, Aunt Evangeline was a terrible investor, and even worse entrepreneur," he said. "It seems like my mother had all the business sense, and once she was gone, Evangeline basically ran the Silver Spoon, and our portfolio, into the ground."

"I'm so sorry, Derek." Yet I thought there might be a small silver lining to his financial problems. "But maybe this gives you less motive. If there wasn't much to inherit, why would you kill your aunt?"

Derek rose from the bench. "I wish that was the case. But I didn't know we were nearly broke until after her death. And, even if I had known earlier, her recklessness and incompetence seem like issues we would've argued about."

He was right, and I didn't know what to say. I stood up, too, and reached for his hand. "Come on. Let's go enjoy the rest of the evening. Everything else can sort itself out later."

"I don't think so, Willow." He pulled away from me.

My hand hung in the warm air, then I dropped it to my side. "Why not?"

"You don't feel the same about me anymore. I could tell when we were dancing that things really have changed between us. Even more than I thought."

I swallowed thickly, knowing he was right, and hoping he wasn't hurt. "Have they changed for you, too?"

"I'm not sure. There's so much going on that it's hard for me to sort out my feelings."

"I understand."

Derek took a step away from me, gesturing toward the inn. "Would you mind if I leave? I'd like to just head home, if you won't be stranded."

My heart was aching again, because that part of my life I'd been letting go of, all evening, had officially come to an end. But I forced a smile. "Yes. Of course. I'm sure my grandmother, Pepper, or someone else can give me a ride home."

Derek hesitated, then leaned in to kiss my cheek. "Good night, Willow."

"Good night."

I watched him walk off into the darkness, toward the lights and laughter that lay a few yards beyond the secluded glade. Then I sank back down onto the bench, trying to process everything that had just happened—and reconcile the man who'd come back to Zephyr Hollow with the boy who'd left for medical school and then Africa.

I also wondered who in the world would want to frame Derek, and have access to his house in the middle of the night.

George Van Buskirk, obviously, much as I hated to admit it.

And perhaps Penelope Dandridge, who probably had a collection of skeleton keys at her flea market that would fit an old mansion's simple, vintage locks.

Or maybe Benedict Blodgett, who'd confessed to creeping around in the wee hours?

Was there even a tiny chance that Derek wasn't being completely truthful with me?

I sat there for a long time, lost in thought, until a flash of white, overhead, brought me back to reality.

"Rembrandt!" I greeted the owl who settled onto a branch above my seat. "What are you doing . . . ?"

I didn't get to finish that question before someone else joined me, stepping into the clearing and asking, in a deep and strangely accented voice, "I don't suppose you'd care to dance, would you, Willow?"

I rose as Lucien extended his hand, and, in the distance, a woodpecker began to rap against a tree, just like in my dream.

Chapter 32

The gala had grown even more crowded while I'd been off alone, and the area near the pool was filled with dancing couples by the time Lucien and I made our way down the narrow path that led back to the party.

We paused at the edge of the patio, under a magnolia tree, where Rembrandt alit on a high branch, and I first looked up at the owl.

I wasn't sure if Remi was there for me or if his allegiance had switched to the tall detective who was surveying the scene, probably searching for a spot we could claim, since I'd agreed somewhat hesitantly to his request for a dance.

Then I shifted to see Lucien, who was by far the most handsome man at the gathering. He wore another dark suit, like the one he'd donned for the funeral, and I swore, this one was cut even better to fit his broad shoulders. His hair was glossy black in the light from the lanterns that hung above us, and when he looked down at me, his dark, dark eyes . . .

"Maybe we should just get a drink," I suggested, nodding to a bar that was set up near the pool house.

"If that's what you prefer."

I didn't know what I preferred. My heart was hammering like the woodpecker's beak, and I tried to read Lucien's thoughts, which he soon made clear, adding, "But if it's all the same, I'd like to dance with you."

I was at a busy party, yet I felt more imperiled than I had when I'd been alone in the alley with Benedict Blodgett.

I didn't feel like Lucien was going to physically harm me. Yet I definitely felt at risk, in some way.

To make matters more confusing, I kind of liked the feeling.

That couldn't be good, right?

"Willow?" Lucien prompted. "Dance? Drink? Both— or neither?"

I stared into his eyes, where I'd once seen a flash of darkness so profound that it continued to haunt me. Yet, in spite of Pepper and Astrid's concerns, I didn't think he was truly dangerous. Okay, maybe a little dangerous. But my gut told me that whatever had surfaced during the lightning strike was related to some pain or loss he'd suffered, not some evil lurking inside him.

Or maybe I was fooling myself because I just plain wanted to dance with the mysterious man who'd appeared on my easel and in my dreams, and who was smiling down at me with what I believed was genuine warmth.

I knew Pepper, especially, would disapprove if she saw me with Lucien, but I nevertheless told him, "I would like to dance, thanks. If we can find room."

"I don't think that will be a problem," he said, resting one hand on the small of my back. His touch was cool, even through the fabric of my dress, and I shivered a little. That didn't feel bad, either—not at all—and I forced myself to remember Pepper's warnings, and the fleur-de-lis I'd drawn while under the influence of a spell, as Lucien guided me through a crowd that seemed to part for us.

Reaching a spot close to the still, dark pool, where the candles floated, he turned to me, arched his eyebrows and offered a hand. "Shall we?"

It was too late to back out, so I nodded and slipped my hand into his. I was struck again by that restless energy that I always sensed in him, and which seemed to course through his palm. Then he wrapped his other arm around my waist, leaving a bit of distance between us. But that small space was charged with electricity, at least for me. The spark that had been missing when I'd danced with Derek.

"Be careful, Willow."

I heard Lucien, himself, warning me in memory to be cautious at the party—which he hadn't mentioned planning to attend.

And I felt as if a whole bunch of other people were whispering in my ear, too.

Looking around, I saw Pepper standing just outside the Crooked Chimneys' French doors, and I knew she was watching me and willing me to walk away from Lucien.

I spotted my grandmother, too, talking with Mr. Van Buskirk near the cabana. They were deep in conversation and seemed oblivious to me. But I was certain that Grandma Anna was keeping one protective eye on me, even as she took Mr. Van Buskirk's hand, biting her lower lip and shaking her head.

Was my grandmother asking about his confusion, related to the pool house? Because they looked very serious.

And was there a chance I'd seen *keys* in Mr. Van

Buskirk's hand, the night Astrid had rigged up the crystal ball . . . ?

Lucien turned us slightly, and that was when I saw my mother—and my mother saw me from across the patio.

Her eyes got *huge*, and she fumbled with a cocktail she balanced in one hand. The drink was still in jeopardy, the moment frozen in time, when Lucien and I shifted again.

Ignoring the waves of disapproval and concern I could feel radiating from my friend and at least one relative, I let Lucien draw me a tiny bit closer. Inhaling, I smelled the bergamot and sandalwood in his cologne—made with essential oils used to ward off evil.

Was I in peril or protected?

"You look especially beautiful tonight." Lucien's compliment interrupted my thoughts. His voice was even lower and softer than usual, and there was something new in his eyes, too. Something I hadn't seen in a man's eyes in a long time.

Could he see what I was feeling?

"Be careful, Willow."

I could've returned his compliment—gushed for an hour about how great he looked—but I squeezed Lucien's shoulder, making the slightest effort to break the spell he was casting over me.

That word—spell—echoed in my increasingly foggy brain, and I pictured the way Lucien had met my gaze through the crystal ball, right before it had snapped to black.

Pepper was right about one thing. Detective Lucien Turner had some kind of special power, whether it came from a spell book, or just existed inside of him. Either way, there was something different, compelling about him, and I let him move my hand to his shoulder, so he could rest both his hands near my hips. He was drawing me closer, his dark eyes hypnotic, the flecks of gold I saw there echoing the candles in the dark pool, which mimicked the stars in the inky sky. Black, like my mood ring, which seemed to be overworked by my shifting, intense emotions.

I struggled not to completely lose my head when Lucien smiled down at me, just the slightest curve of his lips.

Was there a chance he was casting a *real* spell over me?

Maybe some New Orleans Voodoo, or a different kind of magic?

I stepped back. Reluctantly. "Lucien . . . You need to be honest with me."

"And you with me," he said quietly. "About the envelope."

I licked my lips, buying myself a moment. Then I said, "Derek is going to tell you everything. I'll let him explain."

A mix of interest and frustration flickered in Lucien's eyes, and he released me. We were no longer dancing. Just standing at the edge of the pool, the moment between us over, for better or worse. Probably for the better.

"So, Fletcher did have the shears at some point?" Lucien asked quietly. "And you recognized his handwriting when he dumped them on you?"

I didn't like the word "dumped," but if I'd been in Lucien's shoes, not knowing everything Derek was going through, I might've used the same term.

Heck, I knew all about Derek's travails, and it was still difficult for me not to feel a bit betrayed.

"Yes, he had the pruners," I said. "But it's not as simple as that. He'll explain."

"I hope so." Lucien's gaze flicked to the inn. "I should go see him now."

I rested one hand on his arm. "Derek went home, and

he's not going anywhere beyond the mansion tonight. He's had a difficult evening. Just leave him be until morning, okay?"

Lucien didn't look convinced, but he nodded. "Fine. But if Fletcher disappears, it's on you. To be honest, I'm not sure why I'm trusting you, after you covered for him about his handwriting."

"I only recognized one letter, and I wasn't sure," I said. "I wanted to give him a chance to explain before I cast more suspicion on him."

There was warning in Lucien's voice. "Willow—"

"I've shared something with you," I interrupted, before he could tell me how much trouble I was probably in. "Or, at the very least, I convinced Derek to tell you how he ended up with the pruners. Now you need to share something with me. Because you saw me, Astrid, and Pepper . . ." I glanced at the French doors, but Pepper was gone. Astrid was probably around somewhere, but I hadn't seen her yet. I looked up at Lucien again. "You saw us when we used the crystal ball."

Lucien drew back, a glimmer of welcome amusement in his eyes. "That's what you used to watch me?"

I lightly smacked his shoulder. "So, you *did* see us!"

"Not exactly." He lowered his voice again. Not that anyone was listening to us. The couples around us were focused on each other, casting their own spells in the magical atmosphere Pepper had created. Not far from me, Grandma Anna and Mr. Van Buskirk were turning slow circles, like teenagers at a prom.

I *couldn't* suspect my grandmother's date of doing any harm, and I smiled at them before returning my attention to Lucien, who rested a hand on the small of my back again. He nodded toward the cabana, beside which Pepper had set up a few tables. However, because the little cottage wasn't in use that year, few people were venturing there. The spot would be good for a private chat, and I allowed Lucien to again guide me, this time around the edge of the pool.

Reaching the tables, I took a seat while he went to retrieve two of Pepper's signature Midsummer Night's Dream cocktails.

Setting the potent drinks next to a lit candle, he claimed the chair opposite mine while Rembrandt moved to the highest point on the cabana's peaked roof. The stealthy owl was so silent that I doubted anyone even noticed him, except for Lucien, who glanced upward.

I drew his attention back to me. "What happened, the night I saw you in your office?"

"Ah, yes, the night you spied." Lucien sat back, grinning, while my ears got warm. "I was working late when Marinette started growling at the ceiling. And when I looked up, there was a mist forming. I had a strong sense that I was being observed, somehow. And I could feel your presence, at least, in the room. But when I tried to look more closely, the blackness sort of *shattered*."

So, Marinette had tipped him off about our surveillance. And why didn't he seem more surprised by a mysterious fog?

My thoughts must've been written all over my face. "I told you," he said, "Voodoo, hoodoo, and witchcraft are nothing new to me. Art—and arts of the magical, mystical sort—were common topics at my dinner table, growing up. Of interest to both my father *and* mother. Strange things happened around us, all the time."

I saw the faintest hint of that darkness I'd seen flicker in his eyes, and I wondered if the pain had to do with his mother's passing. But I didn't think it was the right time to inquire. Besides, I had another question for him, related to the crystal ball, before Astrid and Pepper inevitably hunted us down and dragged me away from Lucien. "Who was with you that night? Because I saw someone sitting in one of the chairs."

"Do you think I'm going to tell you that?" The shadows in his eyes had already vanished, and he was close to laughing. "Shouldn't you explain why you were spying on me?"

I sipped my drink, hoping the icy potion would cool the heat I could still feel in my cheeks. "That was Astrid's idea," I explained. "I had no clue what she was even doing, until images started appearing in the ball. Pictures, like holograms, of you and other people."

"Let me guess." Lucien absently swiped at the condensation on his glass. "Your coven was investigating. On behalf of Fletcher."

I nodded. "He was—is—important to us. Especially to me."

Lucien grew quiet, and I was aware of the music in the air and the chatter of conversation drifting across the water at our feet. Then he inquired, gravely, "How important?"

I wasn't sure if he asked because Derek was in big trouble, and he wanted to prepare me for the worst, or if he wanted to know whether Derek and I were still an item. "Is that question personal or professional?" I finally ventured.

"Personal," he admitted. "And I'm sorry. It was out of line."

"It's okay," I whispered, searching his face. He'd just apologized, but he didn't look very sorry. "But why . . . ?"

"Willow, you must know that you and I are . . ." Leaning forward, he reached to clasp my wrist—only to be distracted when his hand met the cuff on my arm. He glanced down at the bracelet, and I noticed that the symbol engraved into the metal was practically glowing under his fingers. Not unlike my mood ring, which was pulsing a traitorous purple at his touch. Lucien met my eyes again, with a questioning look. "Where did you get this?"

"At Penny Dandridge's flea market. Why?"

"Take it off."

I withdrew my arm, and he softened his tone. "Sorry. I was just surprised by the design. Let me try that again, in a more civilized manner. Would you please let me see it more closely?"

"Since you said please." I wiggled the cuff from my wrist and handed it over. "What's wrong?"

Lucien studied the bracelet. "Do you know what the symbol means?"

"No clue," I admitted. "Do you?"

Lucien nodded, still not looking at me. "Yes. It's the alchemical symbol for the philosopher's stone."

I searched my memory. "A mythical element, right? That can supposedly turn base metals into gold?"

"Correct." Lucien ran his finger over the design, bringing it to life again. He *definitely* had powers. "It's also the symbol for one of the most powerful and selective covens in the world. A group so underground that they are nameless, but often referred to as the 'rich witches.' A nickname that's seldom used fondly." He raised his eyes to mine again. "So where did you get this?"

"It was a gift—"

"From Pepper?" he interrupted, his voice sharp with interest. "Because I've wondered . . ."

I shook my head. "No. Pepper's rich, and a witch. And every now and then, you can replace the 'w' with a 'b.' But she didn't give me the bracelet. I got it from Penelope Dandridge. She didn't like the piece, or its inscription, which she considered sappy and too personal. She thought it devalued the cuff."

Lucien was already turning over the bracelet and pulling out his cell phone. Hitting the flashlight app, he shined it on the inside of the metal arc, illuminating the part of the engraving I hadn't been able to see at Penny For Your Stuff, and which I'd subsequently forgotten about.

"Why do I also forget about that app?" I mused aloud.

Lucien wasn't paying attention. He was reading. "Believe in the beauty and strength of woman's devotion. Yours forever, P."

I sucked in a sharp breath.

Lucien's gaze snapped to me. "What?"

"Nothing. Maybe," I said.

"You do play it close to the vest," Lucien muttered, resting back and handing me the cuff. "I hope you're not again hampering my investigation."

I slipped the bracelet back onto my wrist. "I'm not trying to hamper anything. I'm just—"

"Protecting a friend?"

"Sorting things out."

"Yes, I'll be 'sorting,' too," he said, gesturing to my wrist. "And I hope this *possible* clue doesn't also lead to Fletcher. Or your friend with the initial 'p.'"

I didn't think it would lead to either of those people. Especially not to Pepper, whose taste ran to pearls, and who never set foot in a flea market because she was a shameless snob and certainly didn't need to pawn things.

I could see why Lucien might wonder if Pepper belonged to a group of wealthy witches.

What I *didn't* understand was why he knew about the coven at all.

"So, what's your connection to the 'rich witches'?" I asked. "A group I've never heard of, even though I'm a witch, myself—"

"Willow!" My mother's sharp rebuke startled me and caused Rembrandt to flap his wings. Taking off, he wheeled around the cabana in crazy circles before flying off into a sky that seemed darker, somehow.

I shifted to look up at Mom, and although I couldn't see her face very well, her tone was as ominous as the night that seemed to be engulfing us. "Willow and Detective Turner. What is going . . . ?"

She didn't get a chance to finish her thought, either, because fat, icy raindrops suddenly fell in sheets from the sky, the tempest ending the gala and sending us all hurrying for cover.

Chapter 33

"I can't believe you ruined your own party by conjuring a storm," I told Pepper, who had driven me home from the rained-out gala, with Astrid in tow. Both of them had been inside the Crooked Chimneys when the skies had opened up, so I was the only one wearing a towel turban as I served them tea—chamomile, no spells attached—in my snug, eclectically furnished parlor, which overflowed with antiques, books, and plants. Bending, I offered Pepper, who was reclining on my favorite old fainting couch, a steaming drink, to dispel the chill of the rain that continued to patter softly against the tin roof. "That was a little drastic, don't you think?"

"I can't believe the spell worked," Pepper said, grinning and plucking a delicate, china cup from the tray I held. She still looked lovely in an elegant, cream-colored gown, while I'd ditched my dress and jewelry in favor of baggy sweats. "I was as surprised as anyone when the sky cut loose!"

"I can't believe I missed the whole party," Astrid said glumly from her favorite spot on a tufted ottoman, near the fireplace.

Stepping over Mortimer, who was sprawled on my worn

Persian rug, I offered Astrid a cup, too. "Where were you all night?"

Luna also seemed curious about Astrid's absence from the gala. She jumped onto the ottoman and peered at my friend. The little feline was also keenly interested in the gold tassels that were part of Astrid's unique, deep-blue ensemble, which looked like it had been assembled from a display cloth and various objects left over in the Astral Emporium stockroom.

Astrid, meanwhile, averted her gaze, staring into the dark fireplace. "I was busy, and time got away from me."

"Busy doing what?" Pepper inquired, no longer smiling. She sounded disapproving, as if, like me, she'd already guessed what had kept Astrid preoccupied. "Spill, Astrid!"

"I . . ."

"You rigged up another crystal ball, didn't you?" I asked, setting the tray on my coffee table and curling up on my couch. "You were spying, weren't you?"

Astrid's voice was small. "I found one more crystal ball in the stock room."

I groaned, because she shouldn't have been using the spell again, and I was pretty sure she really had cobbled together her strange outfit. "Astrid!"

She grew defensive. "It's just for fun!"

"Who were you watching?" Pepper spoke sharply.

I turned to her. "I thought you didn't care about the ethics of the paranormal nanny cam."

"I *didn't* care when we were investigating. But I don't think using the spell should become a habit." She stared hard at Astrid. "Who were you watching?"

"Just random people," Astrid said, petting Luna with her free hand. The cat purred loudly, while Astrid winced, admitting, sheepishly, "Like, maybe, StarGazer."

Pepper, who was always too busy planning the gala to attend the Gallery Walk, blinked with confusion. "What is a stargazer?"

"He's a painter," I explained. "He creates unicorns and things like that on velvet." I smiled at Astrid. "And *somebody* has a crush on him, right?"

Astrid's chin jutted. "I just find him interesting."

Pepper balanced her teacup on the arm of the fainting chair. "Well, he's not going to be interested in return if he learns that you've been spying on him. I think I can speak for Willow when I say that our coven rules should henceforth include a prohibition on crystal ball surveillance under most circumstances."

"Yes," I agreed. "In fact, I would say *all* circumstances. As we suspected, Detective Turner did know that we were watching him. The mist we saw in the ball was visible in his office and caught his dog's attention. We're probably lucky no one else noticed it."

"Fine," Astrid grumbled. "I promise I'll destroy the ball tonight."

Pepper gave me the side eye, and I knew we were about to return to a topic she, Astrid, and I had already covered on the ride to my house.

"Speaking of promises, Willow," Pepper said. "You have to promise Astrid and me that you will stop being *seduced* by Detective Turner."

"I told you before. I was not 'seduced'!"

"Honestly, Willow?" Pepper rolled her eyes. "I had to literally hose you two down, and destroy the gala, to pull you both apart."

"You know, you could've just come over, greeted Lucien—"

Pepper nearly spilled her tea. "He's Lucien now? Not Detective Turner?"

"Oh, that's *such* a dreamy name, to match a dreamy guy," Astrid sighed.

Luna purred again in agreement before hopping onto the mantel, where she settled in, her ears pricked, as if she hoped to hear more about the handsome visitor who'd captured *her* fancy.

Pepper, on the other hand, was giving Astrid a withering look, and Astrid quickly added, "But you need to look past all that dreaminess, Willow. We still know nothing about Detective Turner!"

"I do know a little," I admitted. "But I don't think anything I've learned will reassure you."

Pepper narrowed her blue eyes. "Tell us anyway, please."

I searched my brain for key bits of information. "His father is an expert on the intersection of art and the paranormal. He knows a little about alchemy. His mother is deceased." I wasn't sure why I added that, or why I omitted my fears that Lucien had been casting a real spell on me while we'd danced. Instead, I concluded, "And Rembrandt seems to be following him."

My friends took a moment to digest all that.

"I think Pepper did the right thing, conjuring the storm and pulling you away from Detective Turner tonight," Astrid finally said. "If she hadn't ruined the whole party, you two probably would've kept dancing and talking and . . . Who knows what might've happened!"

I'd wondered that, myself, and the possibilities walked a fine line between exciting and terrifying. I probably should've been grateful for Pepper's intervention—and the bracelet's interference, too.

What had Lucien been about to say when he'd grabbed my wrist, telling me, "Willow, you must know . . ."

Who I am?

What I am?

Why we seem to have a strange connection?

"Willow!" Pepper snapped me back to reality. "You're daydreaming about him now, aren't you?"

"Not the way you think," I told my friends. "There might've been a moment or two, while we danced, when I got a little swept away, but for the most part, we were discussing the murder."

Pepper didn't seem as happy about that as I'd hoped. "What about it? And, now that I think of it, what the heck happened to Derek? How did you end up with a different date, anyhow?"

"That's all intertwined," I said, glancing at Luna, who, I swore, was hanging on every word, while Mortimer snored away. Then I looked between my human friends. "Promise me you won't think less of Derek, if I share some of what he told me tonight."

Pepper nodded, and Astrid crisscrossed her chest with her index finger, disturbing her tassels.

"He's having a very difficult time, personally and financially," I said. "He's left Physicians for Peace, and I think he might be suffering from PTSD."

Astrid gasped. "Oh, poor Derek!"

"On top of that, Evangeline squandered most of the family fortune, and . . ."

"He's still in love with you—while you've fallen for a dashing, *duplicitous* detective."

I ignored Pepper's comment, because I wasn't sure she was right about Derek, and I wasn't certain of my own feelings, either.

"This is the really confusing part." I lowered my voice, although obviously we were alone. "You know the shears that were used to kill Evangeline?" I didn't wait for a response. "Someone planted them in Fletcher Mansion."

"Then how did you end up with them?" Pepper asked, swinging her legs off the couch. She was either getting more involved in the story or preparing to go. Maybe both. She probably did need to get back to the Crooked Chimneys to oversee the staff cleaning up after the party. "I don't want to believe that Derek tried to frame you, but—"

"He panicked," I interrupted. "He was terrified, knowing he was already under suspicion. He kind of lost control and gave the shears to me, hoping I might use a bit of magic, or our combined wits, to make them disappear."

"I understand," Astrid said sadly.

Pepper wasn't as forgiving. "It seems to me like there's another snake in the grass. One I never suspected."

She rose to leave, and Astrid and I stood up, too. "Pepper," I said, following her to the front door. "I asked you to please have a little sympathy."

The most vocal leader of our coven turned back to me. "And I asked you to please look out for yourself. What Derek did was *wrong*. I honestly don't know who I'm more worried about, right now. The mysterious detective or the untrustworthy ex!"

I felt like the whole situation was more complicated than Pepper was making it out to be, but she had a point, too, and her words bothered me long after she and Astrid had left. The storm seemed to follow its mistress, and soon the air was still and warm again.

As I prepared for bed, I opened the windows in the turret. Then, while Luna and my increasingly indoor pig found spots to sleep, I sat on my reading chair, looking out at my garden, the barn, and the dark path that Evangeline had followed one final time, on an even stormier night.

> *"This is the forest primeval. The murmuring pines*
>   *and the hemlocks,*
> *Bearded with moss, and in garments green,*
>   *indistinct in the twilight . . ."*

I spoke those words softly, like an incantation, but I had no idea where I'd ever heard or read them. They certainly weren't from my spell book and seemed to rise unbidden from some distant memory.

I absently rubbed my wrist, where I'd worn the cuff, trying to think—only to be interrupted by a swift and stealthy hunter, who winged in through the open window and perched on my bookshelf, high up near the ceiling.

"Rembrandt." I greeted him with a smile. "Unlike certain pigs, you almost never come inside the cottage."

Remi blinked down at me, and I stood up, the better to see him. His eyes always fascinated me, especially at night, when they were pure black in his snowy white face.

Climbing onto a step stool, I drew even closer to him. "What is *your* fascination with Lucien Turner?" I asked, half expecting him to answer. "Are you keeping tabs on him for me—or joining forces?"

Of course, Rembrandt didn't really respond. Yet I felt that he was communicating with me when he swiveled his head, so my attention was drawn to a dusty old volume by Henry Wadsworth Longfellow.

I hadn't read the book since childhood, but I had nevertheless quoted it, moments before, maybe because earlier that night, my brain had been jogged by a phrase I'd *worn*, from that same long poem: *Evangeline.*

Chapter 34

The Penny For Your Stuff flea market was again quiet the next day at dawn, the white, canvas tents sealed up and the tables unmanned. The deserted scene reminded me of a spectral Civil War encampment, and I had the eerie sense that I was being watched as I threaded my way through the mazelike grounds, headed for the building where I'd last seen Penelope Dandridge.

I was fairly certain she would already be there, since vendors and shoppers would start arriving soon, yet I still jumped when the door to the indoor market swung open, and Penny stepped out into the slanted sunlight, greeting me with obvious confusion.

"Willow . . . ?"

She was staring at the cuff on my arm, while my attention had been drawn to the vintage suitcases dangling from her hands.

I wanted to ask if her plans had changed, and she was heading to her family's lake house a few weeks early. But first I needed to know something equally or more important, and I asked, point blank, "Were you and Evangeline *lovers*?"

* * *

"Our relationship started out the way it ended—which was terribly," Penny told me sadly, toying with the bracelet I'd insisted she take back.

She obviously still cared about Evangeline, and I thought someday she might recall their time together more fondly and want the memento, engraved with the line from the Longfellow poem.

But for now, she set the cuff on the linoleum table in the trailer she occupied near the market. I'd never even noticed the mobile home, tucked behind some trees, until Penny had pointed it out, suggesting we go inside to talk.

"Evangeline first approached me to sell off some of her antiques, and we always bickered about price." Penny smiled wanly and shrugged. "But the spats took a turn at some point. Became less petty and more passionate."

It was difficult for me to imagine my former neighbor being anything but mean in a fight. Then again, if anyone was going to find heated arguments romantic, it probably would've been Evangeline.

"How did you figure it out?" Penny asked, drawing my attention back to the conversation. I'd been distracted for a moment, looking around at the cramped but cozy little house, which reflected Penny's passion for collecting. Little objects cluttered every surface, but the place felt clean and organized in its own way. "Evangeline took great pains to keep our relationship secret—which is what eventually ruined it. She was ashamed of me. The way I dress in thrift store clothes, instead of expensive outfits. And the way I live, in a trailer, instead of a mansion."

"Upcycling is all the rage right now, and I think your home is quite charming," I said honestly. "As for figuring things out . . . It took me quite a while, because I'd never known Evangeline to date anyone. It never occurred to me that she might have a romantic partner. And I might not have figured it out without the help of . . ."

I started to say "a crystal ball," but that would sound crazy, and force me to confess that I'd spied on Penny. Instead, I said something equally odd.

"An owl. I had some assistance from an owl named Rembrandt, who flew into my window and perched right next to a copy of *Evangeline*. Having read the poem several times, I finally realized why the engraving was familiar— and who likely owned the bracelet, at one point."

Penny gave no indication that she thought I was off my rocker for consulting with an avian advisor. "You saw my initial, and recalled my bitter comments about the cuff, right?"

I nodded. "Yes. It was clear you were heartbroken, the day you gave me the bracelet. And I'd seen Evangeline's planner at the Silver Spoon, too. She'd crossed off a planned trip to a state with the abbreviation 'MN.' Which I mistakenly believed was probably Montana. Until I thought back to what you'd said about planning a trip to a Midwestern lake house."

"In Minnesota," Penny interrupted, brushing some frizzy hair off her forehead and pushing back from the table. "You're quite the sleuth."

I wasn't sure if that was a compliment, and, although I'd felt safe joining Penny in her trailer, because the nearby flea market was coming to life, I suddenly felt a bit hemmed in and uneasy.

"I'm not accusing you of anything," I clarified, pushing my seat back, too. "Just because you two broke up . . ."

"Which would seem to give me motive." Penny finished

my thought in a completely different way than I'd intended. "Plus, I was at the Owl & Crescent the night she died."

I couldn't help glancing at the suitcases, which Penny had claimed from one of her vendors, who owed back rent on his tent. The bags, hastily obtained, sat near the door to her bedroom, ready to be packed.

Penny clearly understood what I was thinking. "And my decision to leave town soon looks suspicious, too, doesn't it?"

I really did think that was the case. And Penny didn't even know that I'd overheard her talking about "destroying" Evangeline.

Next to Derek, Penny honestly seemed like the most likely suspect. Especially since she'd hidden her real connection to Evangeline, even after the murder.

But as I looked into the red-rimmed, tired eyes of a woman who was still devastated by Evangeline's loss— who was perhaps the *only* person truly grieving—I didn't see a killer.

I dared to reach across the table and squeeze her arm. "Penny, you were the only one who cried—really wept— at Evangeline's funeral. I *don't* think you killed her."

Penny's lower lip quivered, and tears formed in her eyes again. "I couldn't have done it," she said, her voice shaking, too. She reached for the bracelet. "I loved her too much. And I always hoped someday she'd set aside her pride and realize that money and status and clothes aren't important."

I rose to leave. "Penny . . . You need to tell all this to Detective Turner, if you haven't already. And you need to do it before you leave town."

Standing up, too, she shook her head. "No. I can't do that."

"He's already seen the bracelet with your initial," I told her. "And he's sharp." I pictured Lucien's bookshelves. "Not to mention well read." *And maybe supernatural.* "He's probably already figured everything out, too."

Swiping her fingers under her eyes, Penelope pulled herself together, throwing back her shoulders. "Well, let him come question me, then. But he'd better do it quickly. Because I *am* leaving soon." She glanced at the suitcases. "I'll be gone before you can call him and get him here, if that's your plan." Then she gestured around the trailer, and I thought she was including the flea market when she said, "Gone from all this stuff that weighs me down! Possessions that are just pointless when we're dead and buried!"

I suddenly had the sense that Penny Dandridge wasn't going on vacation. She was leaving Zephyr Hollow for good. Leaving behind a messy murder and memories of an intense, if doomed, love affair, not to mention objects that probably did start to feel like overwhelming burdens, over time.

"Well, Willow?" she prompted me. "Are you going to call the detective?"

"I don't know," I admitted, moving to the door. "I was being honest when I said I believe you didn't kill Evangeline. And I don't think Detective Turner appreciates my help with his investigation." I immediately remembered that he'd also told me not to be a hindrance if I had information about the bracelet, in particular. "But I probably have to share what I know."

Before Penny could respond, I opened the door and stepped into the fresh morning air. I hadn't really felt like

I was in danger, but I was still relieved to be outside the confines of the isolated trailer.

Then I turned back to Penny, who was about to shut the door, no doubt so she could grab a few things and hurry off.

"Penny, wait!"

To my surprise, she kept the door open, just a crack. "What?"

"The symbol on the bracelet? Did you design that? Or choose it for a reason? Or was it a consignment piece you had engraved?"

Penny opened the door a tiny bit wider. Just enough for me to see the regret, mingled with anger, in her brown eyes.

"I commissioned the design specifically for Evange-line," she told me, her voice throaty and low. "It seemed like a good idea, at first. But her obsession with that symbol . . . an obsession that kept growing . . . was driving *me* from *her*, even before she broke my heart!"

Chapter 35

I had a feeling that, no matter how quickly I contacted Lucien, Penny would make good on her promise—or threat—to skip town before he could get to Penny For Your Stuff, if he even rushed right over there. Penny had indicated that she planned to travel lightly, which meant she didn't have much packing to do. And for all I knew, Lucien had figured out that Penny and Evangeline had been lovers before I did.

After all, he'd known all about Myrna Crickle and the semi-stolen painting long before I'd spilled the beans. Long enough to have the Duvalier authenticated and confirm Myrna's alibi.

Still, I kept debating whether to pull over and text him while I drove down Zephyr Hollow's Main Street, heading for my cottage, where I definitely planned to call my grandmother and mother.

"I wonder what *they* know about alchemy, and what they're hiding, related to Evangeline and Lucien Turner," I muttered, stopping at a traffic light. I drummed my fingers on the steering wheel, pondering Penny's stunning admission about Evangeline's interest in one of the oldest, most elusive spells around, and a symbol that was related to a powerful coven, according to Lucien. I also kept picturing the way the engraving had glowed under Lucien's touch, and recalling how my grandmother had jolted when I'd mentioned Mom's past relationship with Evangeline. Someone needed to explain the sealed pages within the *Book of Miscellany*, too.

Everyone was keeping secrets, and at least some of them had to be intertwined.

Resolving to get some answers, at least from my own family members, I pressed on the gas pedal, growing increasingly eager to get home.

And yet, at the last second, I spied a big white sign with red letters, taped to a lamppost, and I spun the wheel, heeding an invitation and following a gory-looking, dripping arrow that pointed to the parking lot behind the Silver Spoon.

"Benedict?" I called, struggling to get through the subterranean door to Take 666 Studio with his creepy canvas clutched in my hands. Although he was supposedly hosting a free screening of an original horror film—an unsanctioned addition to the Gallery Walk weekend—the dark basement seemed empty.

I wasn't surprised. The sign Benedict had tacked up wasn't exactly welcoming, and the cement steps leading down to the studio were dark and forbidding, too. Even though Benedict had invited me to Take 666, and I was on a mission to drop off his painting, which had still been stashed in my car, I had stalled at the top of the steps. I could imagine that other people had done the same.

"Yoo hoo, Benedict," I called again, propping the painting against a wall, right inside the door.

No one answered. But listening more closely, I heard a faint noise, like a muted conversation, coming from a room deep in the basement, which was like a warren—and a complete mess. It looked like a whirlwind had passed through, and I thought Benedict should've cleaned up before inviting the public.

"I left your painting, like I promised," I said more loudly. "I'll see you later, okay?"

Hopefully not lurking near the Owl & Crescent or in a dark alley.

"Help!"

I was turning to leave, but the cry stopped me in my tracks.

And as I was deciding whether to run to the person in distress, or run away to get help, I heard a blood-curdling scream that made the choice for me.

"I'm coming!" I called, stumbling through the dim cellar, toward the sound and a soft, glowing light. I tried to move quickly, but the place really was a disaster, filled with boxes and scattered camera equipment and what I assumed were props. Mannequins and masks and *weapons* that I told myself were probably fake. Then my feet slipped and slid on something that felt like crumpled plastic, right before I burst into a small room where I immediately felt like an idiot.

"It's his movie," I whispered, fighting to calm my thudding heart. "Just a movie!"

Fortunately for me—and unfortunately for Benedict—no one was sitting in the empty folding chairs that were scattered around a TV-DVD combo.

The room was also a shambles, one of the chairs knocked

over, and I again thought Benedict should put as much effort into his business as he obviously did his art. Because I had to admit that I'd already been drawn into the obviously low-budget film, about someone who had apparently wandered into some dangerous woods. Alone.

The shaky footage was from the victim's point of view, the camera repeatedly swinging around, as if the person was looking over his shoulder, his fear apparent by his panting breath.

At least, I assumed I was watching Benedict in action, both playing a role and operating the camera. He'd been alone when I'd met him in the alley, and he hadn't mentioned bringing any actors when he sneaked around on my property, which looked a lot like the woods captured on the film.

Specifically, the place where Evangeline had been murdered.

Had she run like that . . . ?

I took a step backward, pressing one hand against my stomach, because I suddenly felt queasy, and the room seemed to grow darker. But it was a darkness that came from inside me.

I hadn't cast a spell, or touched Evangeline's painting again, yet I felt myself slipping into that state. The one in which I might be able to see something . . .

I closed my eyes, trying to push aside the memories I'd so desperately wanted to see when I'd first tried the spell, because I wasn't in the right place and felt vulnerable. Scared, even.

Yet another part of me thought I should try to recall whatever I'd witnessed, before I'd woken up to discover Lucien testing my pulse . . .

"No!"

I was so confused that I wasn't sure if I spoke, or if the voice had come from the television, but my eyes snapped open, and I saw that the camera was moving crazily through the trees, like the person in peril was running away at a reckless pace.

I needed to get away, too. Find a place to breathe and compose myself, because I was shaking, and I hurried out of the room, stumbling toward the exit—only to get my feet tangled in the crinkly stuff I'd just waded through.

I fought to keep my footing, but the floor beneath me was slick, and I fell facedown.

Forcing myself to calm down, I moved to stand up, finally realizing that I was surrounded by *unspooled film*, and crouched next to a realistic and horrific prop.

A mannequin that looked *incredibly* like Benedict Blodgett, only lifeless, its eyes wide open and staring at nothing.

I stared back for a long time, then tentatively reached out a hand—barely stifling a scream of my own when my fingers rested against Benedict's icy cold cheek.

Chapter 36

"How are you doing, dear?" my grandmother asked, tucking a throw around my feet before taking a seat on my sofa.

My mother was pacing around my living room, while I had been assigned the fainting couch, although I was nowhere close to fainting. Just a little shaken after discovering Benedict Blodgett's body, surrounded by yards and yards of unspooled film, earlier that day.

Although I kept insisting I was fine, all the animals who lived in and around my cottage seemed concerned about me, too. Luna was crouched on the back of my chair, peering over my shoulder, and Mortimer was pacing in my mother's wake—a situation that seemed to unsettle her.

Even Rembrandt had come inside. He was perched on the mantel, a sight that was also throwing Mom for a loop. I could tell by the way she kept looking over her shoulder at the pig and casting wary glances at the owl.

She was also fretting over me in an uncharacteristic way, like she'd done at the bridal shop.

"I can't stop thinking about what might've happened if you'd arrived earlier," she said, finally taking a seat on the tufted ottoman, where Astrid usually sat. Mortimer plopped down at her feet, and I thought he might've taken an inexplicable shine to Mom, who didn't usually connect well with animals, and who certainly hadn't done anything to encourage the little porker's affection. She completely ignored him, addressing me. "What in the world possessed you to attend a *literal* underground screening of a no-budget horror film?"

I kicked off the blanket, because the evening was hot and sticky. "I wasn't there to see the movie, which, in retrospect, was a lot like the *Blair Witch Project*," I said, immediately regretting my critique, which echoed Evangeline's hurtful assessment of Benedict's films as "derivative." I'd forgotten for a moment that the director had just been murdered.

At least, that's what I assumed, given Lucien Turner's arrival on the scene, before I'd been dismissed by the uniformed officers who'd responded first to my 911 call. I'd been told I would likely be questioned the next day, if the death was officially ruled a homicide.

"So, why were you at the studio?" Grandma Anna prompted, because I hadn't yet explained myself.

"I was dropping off Benedict's painting, from the Small Business Alliance party," I said, stroking Luna, who'd jumped onto my lap. "And Benedict had invited me to stop by to talk, too. Practically begged me, actually. He said he had something to show me, and that I needed to see it soon."

My mother and grandmother exchanged concerned, confused glances.

"I'm sure he was killed because he'd witnessed something," I continued, my grave pronouncement at odds with Luna's contented purrs. "Maybe the night of Evangeline's murder."

Grandma Anna moved to the edge of her seat. "What do you mean, Willow?"

I tried to explain better. "I ran into Benedict the night of the Gallery Walk." I decided to leave out the part about having dinner with Lucien. "He confessed that he sometimes shot footage near the Owl & Crescent, and a bunch of other places, late at night. He hinted that he might've seen something while spooking around."

Mom rubbed her throat, like it was tight. "Like . . . the murder, itself?"

I nodded. "Maybe. And maybe he wasn't quite as stealthy as he thought. Maybe the killer saw Benedict spying and decided to silence him."

"If he saw the crime, why didn't he go to the police?" Grandma Anna's question was logical.

"I don't know," I admitted. "Maybe he was scared of the killer? Or afraid *he'd* be accused? Because creeping around alone, filming things, isn't much of an alibi. On the contrary, it sounds like a habit a homicidal person might enjoy."

"So, why tell *you*?" Mom mused.

"That's an excellent question, too." I glanced at Rembrandt, who was observing everything with his intelligent eyes. I wished there was a way to know what *he'd* seen the night of Evangeline's death. "I guess I'll never know, because I didn't visit him soon enough."

That was the first time I suffered a pang of guilt over Benedict's death, and my grandmother must've understood what I was feeling.

"You did not cause Benedict Blodgett's demise," she said. "He shouldn't have been sneaking around other people's property without permission, and if he saw something, he should've gone to the police."

"Yes, Willow," my mother agreed, standing up to pace again. Mortimer followed suit. His little snout was raised in the air, and he trotted with an air of importance, like he hoped to be helpful. "If Benedict feared he was in danger, he also shouldn't have tried to involve you!"

I watched my mother, who was twisting a strand of pearls and gnawing her lower lip while she walked around. "Mom?" I asked suspiciously. "Why aren't you freaking out about your town's reputation? Why are you more worried about me?"

My mother stopped pacing, and Mortimer bumped into the back of her Ann Taylor Loft pants. She shot the pig an exasperated look, then turned to me. "Because I honestly think you might be in danger. When Evangeline was murdered, I told myself it was related to her abrasive personality, because she rubbed everyone the wrong way. I also quietly wondered if money was the motive, and Derek was hoping to claim the Fletcher fortune."

I didn't argue with Mom for suspecting my former boyfriend or tell her that the Fletcher family's finances were in ruin. I let her keep talking.

"But now that a second person is dead . . . someone who might've seen the killing or *other* things, late at night . . . I'm starting to wonder if there really isn't something more nefarious going on here. I didn't want to believe it, but it might be the case."

As Mom finished speaking, she and Grandma Anna again shared a strange look. A *knowing* look.

Setting aside Luna, I moved to the edge of my seat. "What is going on with you two?" I asked, staring hard at Mom. "What's your real connection to Evangeline?" Before she could answer, I questioned my grandmother. "And why is part of our family spell book sealed? Because

I don't think the pages are stuck together with calamine lotion!"

Mom and Grandma Anna didn't answer right away. They were too busy communicating silently again, with only their eyes. Then they must've reached some sort of agreement, because Mom nodded, giving my grandmother the go-ahead to speak first.

"The *Book of Miscellany* is doubly sealed because it contains a very powerful spell," Grandma Anna said, rising to turn on a lamp. The sun had set, and the room had grown rather dark. By the dim light, I saw that her expression was very grave. She paused before Rembrandt, admiring his talons, which were curved around the mantel's edge. Then my grandmother returned her attention to me. "The pages you finally discovered have been under lock and key for many years, for your safety, and the safety of other witches and nonpractitioners, too."

I almost wanted to laugh. "But the book is mainly full of Jell-O recipes!" I looked to Mom, expecting her to roll her eyes, because she thought witchcraft was nonsense. However, to my surprise, she also appeared somber. I didn't know what to make of that. "Mom . . . ?"

"Your grandmother is right," she said, sinking down onto the ottoman again. Mortimer snorted, like he wished she would pick a spot and stick with it, before resuming his place at her feet. "I've always tried to act like the book is full of nonsense, and discourage you from dabbling in the craft, because I know how dangerous it can be." She shot Grandma Anna a dark look. "I still think the book should've been destroyed!"

"You know that we would've run the risk of unleashing the magic," my grandmother said evenly. "We weren't skilled enough to guarantee that, if the book went up in a puff of smoke, some other, more adept witch might not literally pull the information from the air." I couldn't believe they'd had this discussion before, but it was obvious that was the case. "It was safer to seal up the book, locking out everyone—including Evangeline, even though I didn't think she ever truly believed what she saw. I was pretty sure she thought everything you were doing was make believe."

I tensed, my fingers curling around the edge of my seat. "What in the world are you two talking about?"

Grandma Anna closed her eyes and took a deep breath. Exhaling, she said, "During her childhood, your mother was fascinated by the *Book of Miscellany*—and quite a skilled witch." While I struggled to digest that information, my grandmother beamed at Mom, whose expression remained neutral, like she wasn't proud of her past. Then Grandma Anna grew serious again, too. "Sometimes Evangeline would wander over from next door, observing while Celeste dabbled in the craft. And she was there when, working from an old spell—"

"I discovered the philosopher's stone," Mom interrupted, speaking quite coolly, like that was no big deal. "Not a stone, per se," she clarified. "But a spell that could turn nearly any object into gold. Not *quite* the Holy Grail of alchemists. But very close."

That revelation was shocking, and someday I would need to hear more about my mother's aptitude for, then abandonment of, witchcraft. But right then, I was fixated on a very bizarre coincidence. "I don't know if Evangeline thought it was all a game," I said. "She was obsessed with the old symbol for the philosopher's stone. That's kind of weird, isn't it?"

"How do you know that?" Grandma Anna spoke sharply.

"Penny Dandridge, who was Evangeline's lover—"

"What?"

I'd surprised my mother, and probably my grandmother, too. "It's true," I told them. "Evangeline and Penny were a couple for a while. And Penny gave Evangeline a bracelet engraved with the old alchemical symbol, because Evangeline was intrigued by it. But her obsession became so strong that it drove Penny away."

I didn't think any of us really knew what to make of all that, and we all took time to think. Even the animals seemed to feel the tension in the air. Luna and Mortimer remained still, and Remi looked like a statue.

Grandma Anna was the first to break the silence. "George also thought Evangeline was involved in something strange, right before her death. He's mentioned, several times, that she'd been away from home a lot, and acting erratically, in the months leading up to the murder."

"Maybe Evangeline was with Penny," I suggested. "They *did* keep the relationship secret. And she might've been acting strangely because she was nearly broke."

Mom's eyes snapped wide open. "You're kidding!"

"That's also regrettably true," I confirmed. "Derek has been going over the family finances, and he says their assets are pretty much wiped out. In fact, that's how Evangeline and Penny got close. Evangeline was pawning family heirlooms." I was struck by a thought. "That's probably why she was extra furious about the Duvalier, when she believed Myrna had sold her a fake. The painting was probably the next item to go, and she wouldn't get top dollar for a forgery."

As I put those pieces in place, I also figured out why Evangeline probably hadn't reported Myrna's "theft" of the artwork. She had likely been considering whether she could submit an insurance claim for the "stolen" painting. She wouldn't have needed to tell the police she knew who'd taken the canvas, because Myrna certainly wouldn't have bragged about the embarrassing and *illegal* incident.

With everything kept quiet, Evangeline could've filed for an insurance payout before Myrna had the Duvalier appraised and returned it. If Lucien hadn't used his connections, it might've taken quite a while to find an expert or experts who could authenticate the work—or declare it worthless. At which point, the painting might've just disappeared. Or been quietly sold on the black market, passed off as the real thing by *Evangeline*, who could've doubled her profit.

"Willow, what are you talking about?" Mom asked. "What is a 'Duvalier'?"

I had forgotten that Mom and Grandma Anna probably didn't know anything about the painting, which wasn't important, anymore. The piece had been evaluated, and Myrna had been removed from the list of murder suspects.

"It's nothing," I said. "I'm more interested in Mr. Van Buskirk's observations. Because maybe Evangeline was hiding more than just a romance."

"I believe so," Grandma Anna said. "Although, he wouldn't tell me more. In fact, he wanted to talk to you first, Willow."

"Why?"

"I'm not sure."

I knew my grandmother very well, and she was thinking the same thing as me.

The last person who wanted to share cryptic information with me, for unknown reasons, was dead.

"Keep a good eye on Mr. Van Buskirk, okay, Grandma?" I urged.

She nodded, outwardly calm, as always. But I saw anxiety in her green eyes. "Yes. I'll do that."

Mom was more visibly fretful. "Something bigger really is going on here," she said, worrying her pearls again. "I *truly* believe it now."

That was the second time she'd mentioned believing that some bigger force than we perhaps suspected was behind Evangeline's death. It was almost like someone had clued her in. Or *warned* her.

"What kind of 'bigger' thing?" I asked. "And why would the spell to turn matter into gold be so dangerous, anyhow?"

Grandma Anna answered my second question. "Can you imagine how many witches would want to use the spell, if it ever leaked out? And the power struggles that would ensue, as some sought to gain sole control over it?"

"There's a chance two lives have already been lost, somehow related to alchemy," Mom added. "I hate to think what might happen if even a handful of witches knew the secret!"

A handful. Or a coven. A very powerful coven.

"Mom, you make it sound like someone told you there was a conspiracy unfolding. Did someone from a coven of 'rich witches' approach you?"

I could tell my mother was still holding back information, while Grandma Anna looked baffled.

Fortunately, someone was able to answer my question.

Lucien, whom I hadn't even heard enter the house with Marinette, and who stepped from the shadowed foyer into the room, telling me, "*I* was the one who warned your mother. Right before she reluctantly agreed to let me quietly watch over you, in hopes of saving your life."

Chapter 37

"Your grandmother—and your mother, who knows and should trust me—weren't happy about being dismissed," Lucien noted, speaking to me from the living room.

I was in the foyer, closing the door after practically shoving Mom and Grandma Anna out onto the porch.

They'd wanted to stay, but I felt like Lucien and I needed to speak privately, finishing a bunch of conversations that had never yielded all the answers I planned to get that evening.

I wasn't afraid. And not only because Lucien had just said he wanted to protect me. I was trusting my instincts, which told me I wasn't about to come to any harm. I also had faith in Luna and Mortimer's judgment. My cat and pig companions weren't the least bit nervous around Lucien or Marinette. And Rembrandt wasn't acting protective of me, either, although he didn't fly off to hunt.

In fact, when I returned to the living room, I discovered that Remi had found a new perch.

One that made me gasp with surprise.

* * *

"I've never seen Rembrandt get so close to a human," I said, reclaiming my seat on the fainting couch. I kept watching Remi, whose talons were wrapped lightly around Lucien's wrist. My owl companion looked quite comfortable on our visitor's arm, like a falcon awaiting instruction from a falconer. Not that Remi took orders. "Except for me," I added, suffering another pang of doubt about Rembrandt's loyalty. "And I *never* touch him."

"It took me quite a bit of time to gain his confidence," Lucien said, lifting his arm, so Rembrandt could take his spot on the mantel again, above the dark fireplace, where Marinette lay watchful by the hearth.

Luna was curled on the ottoman, and Mortimer scrambled awkwardly up to join her. Apparently, he was now an indoor pig who sat on furniture, too. I probably should've told him to get down, but it was incredibly cute when he snuggled in next to his feline friend.

I also ignored Mortimer's behavior because I was distracted by the tall, handsome detective who was shaking out his wrist, which had to have been scratched, before taking a seat, uninvited, at the end of my chair.

I edged back, giving him some space and hoping I hadn't made a mistake by shooing the other humans away. I still didn't believe Lucien planned to harm me, but I once again felt vulnerable in his presence, in a different way, and my tell-tale, traitorous mood ring was glowing purple, for attraction.

"That's the first time I've ever invited Rembrandt to come that close," Lucien added, shifting so I could see his dark eyes by the single lamp that lit the crowded parlor. A space that felt even smaller than usual, thanks to the addition of an imposing investigator who wore a black T-shirt and jeans that emphasized his lean, but muscular, frame. "I was surprised he accepted the offer—which might've been a way to remind me that he could inflict serious damage, if his trust in me proved to be groundless." Lucien turned over his wrist, which was, indeed, laced with red marks. "I wouldn't want him for an enemy."

"When did you become friends?" I asked, with a glance at the mantel. Remi was watching us with his inscrutable stare. Marinette was doing the same. "When, exactly, did this trust-building happen?"

"Your familiar has been keeping an eye on me since the first day I came to town and met with your mother," Lucien said. I didn't normally use that word, familiar, to describe Remi, but I supposed it was accurate. "I think he sensed my connection to you before we even met." Lucien's gaze cut to Remi, too. "We've spent quite a bit of time together."

"Lucien . . ." I had so many questions that I didn't know what to ask first. I decided to start at the beginning. "Why did you contact my mother? Who are you, and why are you really here?"

Lucien paused, then said, "This is going to sound strange to you. Perhaps unbelievable."

"Why do people keep thinking I'll find things unbelievable?" I asked. "I'm a *witch*. One who can connect with other souls across the astral plane, via art."

"You make a good point," Lucien conceded. "Perhaps you *won't* find it odd when I tell you that I am part of an alliance. A well-organized group of individuals who work to protect vulnerable practitioners of various forms of witchcraft and magic from those who dabble in dark arts."

Most of that just confused me more, because I had

never heard of any sort of body that governed witches, warlocks, and the like. "Who does this 'alliance' report to?"

"We operate on our own authority," Lucien said.

That admission made me uneasy. "Like . . . paranormal vigilantes?"

Lucien must've sensed that I was concerned. "Something like that," he explained. "But within our small ranks, we follow strict codes of conduct, to protect our identities, safeguard those we watch over and ensure that *we* do as little harm as possible." A shadow darkened his eyes. "Trust me. The rules I follow are uncompromising, and I would break them at my peril."

I'd believed that Lucien's clothing—the jeans, dress shirt, and slightly askew tie that he usually wore—had signaled some sort of rebellion against the local police force. But apparently he operated far outside the bounds of that agency.

"We are not some rogue group, acting impulsively," he added. "We serve thoughtfully to fill a vacuum in a community that operates with great power, and no governing authority—a situation that sometimes costs lives."

I curled my legs up under myself, because the night was getting chilly and rainy. Droplets spattered against the windows. I also wanted to put a little more space between myself and Lucien, whose story raised more questions than it answered—and who nevertheless drew me in a way that I wanted, but was unable, to deny. Finally, I was probably curling into a defensive position because I was suddenly very concerned about external threats to my well-being.

"Why are you here for me?" I asked softly. "I don't have any connections to 'dark arts.'"

Or did alchemy count?

"At least, no intentional connections," I clarified. "And

I certainly don't consort with any practitioners. My little coven is pretty isolated and, let's face it, innocent. We don't even allow crystal ball spying anymore!"

"Your friends might be innocent, but I was starting to hear rumblings about your spell book," he told me. "My sources in the dark underground were telling me that the coven I spoke to you about—the world's most wealthy and powerful witches—had it on good authority that someone in your family had come very close to unlocking the secrets to alchemy. A secret now sealed in your innocuous-looking *Book of Miscellany*."

"Hey!" I rose to the defense of my family spell book, only to realize that "innocuous" was probably putting it kindly. Marinette, who'd jerked to alertness when I'd raised my voice, settled back down, while I made a rolling motion with my hand. "Sorry. Go on."

Lucien rose and began to pace the small room. He wasn't fretful, like my mother. Just thinking, his hands clasped behind his back. "Of course, I'd traced the source of the rumors to Evangeline Fletcher."

"Who saw my mother use the spell, years ago, and who did believe it was more than a game, or trick, like my grandmother believed."

"Yes. Exactly. And now, I think the members of the coven are determined to get your book and find a way to unlock it, probably by bending their rules and embracing you, in spite of your humble lifestyle."

I considered protesting again, but I hadn't really been insulted. I was content with my chosen circumstances. "And if I don't want to be 'embraced'?" I asked, rubbing my throat, because I feared I knew the answer.

Lucien stopped right in front of me, so I could see that

his expression was deadly serious. "They would have no qualms about eliminating you."

I'd thought Luna and Mortimer were asleep, but the little cat mewed, as if she'd understood, and Mortimer snuffled, too. His upturned mouth didn't look quite so much like a smile. Rembrandt was stock-still again, but I saw his talons flex, the motion tiny but telling.

Only Marinette remained impassive, as if she'd been in similar situations—had similar discussions—before.

I took a moment to observe the dog with the blessing-like spot on her forehead. "Marinette is . . ."

"Special." Lucien finished my thought, offering the perceptive canine an appreciative look. "Not a pet, but a partner." He turned back to me. "I can't tell you more than that. Except to say that, like Rembrandt, you wouldn't want to cross her. And you are fortunate that she's on your side."

"And you?" I asked warily. "Are you . . . special? Or in possession of any special powers? Because Pepper, especially, suspects . . ."

Lucien kept his eyes locked on mine, but he raised one hand, palm open, to the fireplace. Some logs left over from the past spring burst into flame. Mortimer and Luna jumped, while Remi and Marinette, closest to the hearth, didn't so much as flinch.

"Not bad," I said softly, as the fire crackled in the grate, dispelling the chill that had settled over the room. "Not bad at all."

Lucien dropped his hand to his side. "My mother taught me a thing or two."

I wanted to know more, but first I had to learn if I was about to be *killed*. I looked up at Lucien, fighting to keep my voice even and my concerns in check. "Getting back to the possible 'elimination,' as you call it."

"It isn't *likely* imminent," he quickly reassured me, resuming his restless pacing. "As I said, from what I understand, the plan is to court you. Gain your trust and win you over to a lifestyle that's already pretty lavish, even without alchemy."

"That's why you thought Pepper might be a member of the coven."

Lucien nodded. "I've still got my eye on her. Although, her wealth, by the standards of this group, is negligible."

Pepper was like a sister to me, and I would always trust her. But, thinking objectively, I could understand Lucien's doubts. "Was *Evangeline* part of the coven?" I asked. "Was her 'horror' of witchcraft just a sham?"

"She might've been afraid of the craft at some point, but she was trying hard to join the sisterhood—which was an absurd goal, unless she could deliver up the alchemy spell," Lucien said. "She had no other skills, nothing to offer. Not even money." So, he knew about the squandered fortune. "But then, of course, something went wrong. Or so it seems."

"Do you still think there's any chance Evangeline was murdered for some other reason?"

"I honestly did suspect Derek or Van Buskirk until I saw the cuff. Then I became almost certain that Evangeline's death was related to the quest for the alchemy spell. And now I fear that the entire plan has been compromised, and the timeline to get to you altered."

I drew back. "Meaning . . . ?"

Lucien didn't answer right away. He sat down near me again, so close that I could see the faint stubble on his jaw and the flecks of gold in his eyes, and smell bergamot and sandalwood. "My concern," he finally said, "is that someone has botched the effort to access the spell and is now running scared. Getting sloppy and doing rash things to avoid getting caught."

"Like killing Benedict Blodgett, too. Because he likely saw something."

Lucien nodded. "Yes. That was the act of someone desperate. And desperate people—and witches—tend to stray from the best laid plans."

I understood what he was saying. That I might be in more immediate danger than he'd initially believed when he'd come to Zephyr Hollow. "I thought you said . . ."

"I still don't think you're immediately imperiled," he said. "But I am more alert than I was just a few days ago."

I scooched up straighter on the fainting couch, struck by an idea—and suddenly very concerned for two women I loved. My mood ring turned a nervous orange. "Lucien, why target me, and not my grandmother or mother, who created the spell? And why did *you* approach my mom?"

"To be honest, I was afraid you might have already been working with the coven," he said. "And if you weren't, you might panic if I told you the truth. I went to your mother because I knew she didn't practice anymore. I thought she was my best potential source of objective information. I'd also studied her for a while, and I knew she wouldn't risk her reputation by telling anyone she believed a crazy story about a paranormal protector coming to town."

His instincts were dead on.

"Finally," he added, "she could offer me a job that would give me a valid reason to snoop around town, asking questions. It's honestly the best cover I've ever had, coming into a community."

"Mom was with you when Astrid cast the crystal ball spell, wasn't she?" I asked. "She's been meeting with you, getting updates. That's how she knew about the murder weapon. And why she acted so strangely at the bridal shop, when she said she wished she could do more to help me. She wasn't talking about finding me a party dress. She was worried about my safety."

Lucien probably had no idea what half of that meant, but he got the part about the crystal ball. "Yes. She was with me the night you saw me in my office. I know you two are very different, in some ways, but she's deeply concerned for you."

"I still don't understand," I said. "My mother doesn't practice, but she created the spell. Why is this coven focused on me?"

"From what I've gathered, the leaders believe that, if your mother and grandmother had the willpower to lock the key to alchemy away, they would never give up the secret. You're considered more . . . *malleable*."

"In other words, they think I'm weak and can be coerced, or tricked."

Lucien nodded, but reluctantly.

I stared him straight in the eyes, challenging him. "Do you believe that?"

"I did," he admitted. "Based on the colorful flowers, the wind chimes, the kids' parties, and the rescue pig who's allowed to jump on the furniture."

We both looked at Mortimer, whose snout was raised in the air, so he looked a bit smug, curled up next to Luna. "Maybe I could have a few more rules," I conceded.

Lucien grinned. "Perhaps one or two." His smile faded away. "But as I've come to know you, I've changed my mind. You nearly killed *yourself* with a spell to find a murderer, seeking justice for someone you didn't even like. And you've fought hard to defend your friends. I've actually kept you in the dark about certain things, because you seem too willing to take matters into your own hands. I started to fear that you would do even more investigating on your own, and possibly wind up in grave danger. In short, I think the coven has underestimated you."

"Actually, they've *over*estimated me," I reminded him. "I really don't know how to unlock the spell."

"But it's your family spell book," he pointed out. "You know its quirks, not to mention passwords or meaningful phrases."

"*Periculosum opibus.*" I inadvertently muttered the phrase that opened the spell book.

"A dangerous resource."

I pulled back. "What?"

"You just said something like 'dangerous resource' in Latin." He studied me closely. "Is that the password to open the book?"

I nodded, wishing I'd kept my mouth shut, although I increasingly trusted Lucien.

"See," he said. "You might possess more knowledge and insights than you even realize. And sometimes spells and spell books are particular to bloodlines. The spell might not work for anyone but a Bellamy. That's why they haven't just taken the book already."

"Maybe they have."

Lucien arched one eyebrow. "What do you mean?"

"I thought the *Book of Miscellany* had been moved the other day. I assumed Luna had just managed to bump it, while climbing on the shelves. Although, that seemed unlikely, even at the time."

"I suspect the cat wasn't to blame," Lucien said quietly. "Someone might be borrowing the book—"

"Taking it where?" I interrupted, making a mental note to apologize to Luna, who was mewing a soft rebuke.

"I have a few theories," Lucien noted. I waited, but he didn't tell me more, except to say, "Obviously, the borrower hasn't unlocked the spell, which is why you are no doubt still considered potentially valuable."

"And what if I later prove worthless?" I asked, dreading the answer.

"I'm pretty sure they're prepared for that eventuality." Lucien's eyes grew nearly as black as the night outside. Blacker than my mood ring, which had gone on overload again. "If worse came to worst, and you proved uncooperative, or really couldn't unlock the spell, I suspect that they would use you as a pawn. Hold you hostage to force your relatives to unseal the pages." He hesitated, then admitted, "To be honest, that was . . . is . . . probably the most likely scenario."

I should've been getting scared, but I was growing increasingly angry. "I don't like being manipulated," I said evenly. Rembrandt—the hunter, never the hunted—ruffled his feathers, like he agreed. "Tell me what I should be doing to fight back."

Lucien rose again and looked around the room, like he was assessing the entry points. "For now, there's not much you can do, beyond remaining watchful." He met my eyes again. "And I think Marinette and I should stay here, because this place isn't exactly a fortress."

"No," I told him firmly. I stood up, too, along with Marinette, who moved to Lucien's side. "You don't need to do that."

"I think I do."

"For how long?" I challenged him, trying to be realistic. "One night? Two? A month? A *year*?"

He knew that I was making sense. And I got the feeling

we were both uncertain about the wisdom of Lucien Turner staying overnight with me for reasons we weren't discussing.

We remained in a standoff, everyone, even the animals on edge. I studied Lucien's face by the changeable firelight, looking deeply into his eyes, where I saw something unexpected. The tiniest flicker of fear.

Not for himself. For me.

"Lucien," I whispered. "How did you end up in this alliance? What happened to your mother?"

I asked that second question on a hunch, and I knew I'd hit a mark when the concern he felt for me became pain that he fought hard to hide.

"My mother was deeply involved in Voodoo, and had a power greater than alchemy," he said, his voice low but steady with controlled emotion. "An artistic power, quite close to your gift."

"What could she do?"

"Raise the dead," he said matter-of-factly. "Paint them to life. You *thought* you might've done that with me. But my mother figured out how to use her two talents to reanimate corpses. Only, she quickly realized that people don't come back quite the same. They're damaged and dangerous. Which didn't stop some of the world's most powerful practitioners of dark arts from demanding that she use her skills toward their ends. Requests that my mother refused."

"And . . ."

"I tried to protect her, as did my father. But at the time, we were just three people, fighting alone. And we lost."

"I'm so sorry."

Lucien shrugged, but he wasn't downplaying his mother's death. He was still mastering his feelings. "My father buried himself in his studies, while I found some people who'd suffered in similar ways, and we formed the alliance."

I didn't know what else to say except, "I appreciate that you're here for me. But I will be fine tonight. I promise."

Lucien looked like he was about to protest again. Then he nodded to Marinette. "Will you let her stay? She can prove very helpful in an emergency."

To be honest, I still wasn't sure if Marinette was purely canine, and I was a tiny bit afraid of her. But I could sense her quiet power. "Sure," I agreed. "That sounds like a compromise."

"Thank you," Lucien said, while Marinette returned to her spot near the fire, as if she'd understood. "And let's check all the windows and doors," Lucien added. "I want to at least make sure they're locked before I leave."

He was being reasonable. "Fine."

"Upstairs and down."

He knew me better than I thought. I probably wouldn't have bothered to lock up the second floor. "Just give me a minute," I said, heading for the staircase.

Lucien was already moving around the living room, testing windows and locking those that opened.

I went upstairs and did the same, hurrying, because there was one more thing I needed to ask Lucien before he left.

But when I got downstairs, the fire was blazing, the animals were still settled in their spots, yet the cottage felt strangely cold and empty, and I didn't even bother to call for my protector, who had quietly vanished into the night, locking the front door behind himself.

Chapter 38

I lay awake listening to the rain, while Luna and Mortimer dozed by the fire I'd lit in my room, too, to ward off the chill and add some cheer to the sealed-up cottage. Marinette and Rembrandt had also joined us upstairs, but they were as wakeful as me. And poor Remi had to be hungry, but he wasn't leaving my side, in spite of Lucien's assurance that I was probably relatively safe, in the short term.

"I wish I had a snack that would appeal to you," I told Rembrandt, kicking off my covers and getting out of bed. I'd already fed the other animals. "But I am fresh out of live mice." I went to a window and, ignoring Lucien's directive for a moment, opened it, gesturing for Remi to fly out, in case he was feeling trapped. "Go have dinner. I'll be fine."

As I said that, I looked at Marinette, whose eyes flickered with the reflected fire, and I again hoped the real threat wasn't inside my home. Then I assured myself that Lucien wouldn't have left me alone with an honest-to-goodness dangerous loa. She was probably just a very skilled guard dog.

I locked eyes with Marinette.

Yeah, right.

Breaking our gaze, I swept my hand toward the window again. "Go on, Rembrandt. Go hunt!"

The owl who'd perched on my bookcase didn't budge, so I closed the window, which was letting in rain and chilly air. Joining him in the turret, I sat down on my reading chair and reached for my sketchbook, which sat on the table.

Opening the pad, I studied the drawings I'd created while under the influence of the weaker memory spell.

A snake on a jagged stick.

A doghouse.

And a spade or fleur-de-lis

I considered all those sketches, while my mind wandered back over the last few days, replaying snippets of conversations and trying to piece things together.

". . . another snake in the grass . . ."

*A caretaker's cottage, a piggy playhouse—and
    another small structure.*

*"George also thought Evangeline was involved in
    something strange . . ."*

". . . he's saying things that don't make sense . . ."

*"Things I could show you. And not just at your
    place . . ."*

The symbol of New Orleans. . .

Pulling the sketchbook right up under my nose, I looked more closely at the fleur-de-lis and swallowed hard.

Then I tossed the pad onto the table, stood up and went to the window again, looking out over the Owl & Crescent, which was dark and quiet.

I weighed my options for a long moment, then I pulled my robe over my pajamas and crept downstairs to the kitchen, where I assembled a bunch of herbs and oils. Once everything was packed into a basket, I dragged some oversized galoshes onto my feet and led Marinette, Rembrandt, and a very confused, groggy pig and cat duo splashing out into the wet night.

If my hunch was correct, Lucien was right. I wasn't in any imminent danger. Yet I still felt uneasy until I'd locked the studio's door behind me and my mismatched crew of animals.

For the first time ever, I also took the precaution of locking the windows.

Once everything was secured, I took a deep, calming breath and realized I felt safer in the sturdy, cozy space than I had in my cottage.

Rembrandt flew up to his usual spot in the rafters, while Luna hopped onto the table. Mortimer nosed around, snorting loudly, like he wanted to go back to bed. And Marinette sat watch by the door.

"Thank you," I told her, pulling Evangeline's easel into the middle of the room and quickly surrounding it with candles.

My hands shook when I tried to light them. I wasn't afraid anymore. Just heartsick, angry, and hopeful that I was wrong.

Unfortunately, I wouldn't know for sure until I cast the art and souls spell again, and returned to the realm within Evangeline's canvas, where this time, if I was right, I would see and remember what had happened in her final moments.

Pulling the spell book, the silver bowl, and Rembrandt's feather from my bookshelves, I assembled everything on the table. Opening the book with the Latin phrase Lucien had recognized, I began to add the camphor, carnation oil, bladderwrack, honeysuckle, and agrimony to the bowl.

I'd taken time to perfect the measurements for the potion, but at the last moment, I added an extra drop of camphor, to boost my psychic power—and another pinch of agrimony, to help ensure my safe return.

"I hope that wasn't a mistake," I said under my breath.

My comment seemed to worry the animals. Remi swooped down to sit on the easel, like he needed to be closer to me, and Luna was rubbing against my arm.

Forcing a smile, I tickled her under the chin, where she had the crescent-shaped mark. "I will be fine," I promised her and Mortimer, who was bumping against my legs. I bent to give him a reassuring pat, too, and locked eyes with Marinette, who lay against the door, like a canine doorstop. Her expression seemed to have softened, which, paradoxically, made her presence more reassuring.

"Now, to get this over with," I said, reaching for the feather as lightning flickered outside.

Willing my hand to be steady, I dipped the plume into the mixture, stirred clockwise seven times, then spread the infused oil onto my right palm.

As I'd done before, I stepped into the circle of candles and closed my eyes, first picturing my neighbor as I'd last seen her. Then I lightly rested my hand against Evangeline Fletcher's canvas.

"Art and soul, uniquely combined," I whispered, feeling a too-familiar surge of energy spark from my fingertips. Energy I would probably never regain. But I had to know the truth, and I completed the spell. *"From brush to canvas, a story unwinds. Hidden dreams within each work. Show me where the TRUE soul lurks."*

Before the words died on my lips, I felt myself being whisked away into a profound and thunderous darkness.

Chapter 39

The water is still.

It's supposed to be moving. But this isn't Peddler's Creek at my feet. And the trees are different, too. Not what I expected.

I stand in the darkness, waiting impatiently for someone to unlock the door. It's still raining and chilly, and I want to get inside. Or, better yet, go home.

"There's nothing we can accomplish tonight," I complain. "Why are we here?"

Still fumbling with the door to the pool house, she turns and smiles.

An evil smile that makes me uneasy, and I ask, weakly . . .

"Pepper?"

My own voice, and a flash of intense fear, drew me back from the darkness, and my eyes fluttered open, struggling to focus and adjust to the candlelight and bursts of bright lightning in the otherwise dark barn.

Then I scrambled backward, my hands scraping against the rough boards.

"Pepper?" I repeated with alarm. "What are you doing here?"

"I can't believe you committed murder—and schemed to betray me," I told Pepper, who had trapped me in the barn, while a tempest raged outside. Still weak and drained from traversing astral planes, I sat on the couch where, not too long ago, my *former* best friend had painted her toenails. Now Pepper was pacing around, tapping a large chef's knife against her palm. I dared to glance at the *Book of Miscellany*, which was still open on the table. "I had to do the spell again, and go back to the scene of the crime, to believe it was true. I *couldn't* have believed it, otherwise. Never."

"Sorry, Willow." Pepper didn't sound the least bit apologetic. She stood before me, her tanned arms crossed, so the big blade jutted upward near her shoulder. "Try not to take it personally. It's business."

My eyes nearly popped out of my head. "Your 'business' is homicide? And treachery?"

Luna, who was pacing on the table, hissed in agreement, and Mortimer squealed. I thought it was brave of him to speak up, although he was hiding under the protective piece of furniture. Not that I blamed him. What pig wouldn't fear a knife?

Marinette, meanwhile, had disappeared, and if Remi was there, he was making himself scarce. I wasn't sure if I hoped he was concealed somewhere, biding his time. I didn't want him to get hurt, but he was also a very skilled predator. If any of the animals who might've stuck around were going to be helpful, it would be my familiar.

Luna's assistance was less practical, but I appreciated

the support when she hissed again. At least *some* friends were loyal.

Pepper glared at the cat, and I made a shooing motion, urging Luna to run away.

Thankfully, Pepper quickly returned her attention to me. "My business—like that of all of the Armbrusters before me—is to *make money*," she informed me. "And when Evangeline approached me, confiding that she honestly believed your mother had created a spell to turn almost any object into gold—"

I was exhausted, but I was also furious, and I snapped at her. "When did she seek you out? And why *you*?"

Pepper grinned, her teeth gleaming like the blade she continued to clutch. "Dear old Evan came to the Crooked Chimneys a few months ago, hat in hand, telling me a sob story about being broke in spite of undermining every restaurant in town, and overhyping her place all over the Internet."

"So, you knew for a fact that she really was leaving bad reviews."

Pepper scowled. "Yes, and I made her knock it off, for my inn, before I agreed to team up."

"I'm still confused."

Pepper stepped closer, addressing me like I was an idiot, although, to be honest, I'd pieced together most of the story. I just needed her to keep talking while I gained enough strength to either leap for the knife or fight back, when the right time came.

"Evangeline remembered your mother doing what she thought was a magic trick, years ago, when this place"— uncrossing her arms, Pepper gazed around the Owl & Crescent—"was a rundown hideout, where she and Celeste played sometimes. Evangeline didn't believe in magic or witchcraft, then. But, having *spied on* you Bellamy women for years, she came to realize that there might be something to the old book." She gestured to my family journal with the tip of the knife. "Something hidden in there, that could make us a lot of money."

"I still don't understand. Why contact *you*?"

Pepper's eyes gleamed with pride. "Evangeline knew that I was part of our little coven. And she was smart enough to realize that I was the most powerful witch. She'd done her research and knew my heritage."

Outside, lightning flashed, and I hoped more firmly that Rembrandt was inside, not to help me, but for his own safety. I didn't think even skilled flyers should be out in the storm, which Pepper had to have conjured. When not busy running an inn, plotting against me and killing people, she'd obviously been honing her skills.

"You're the reason the weather's so awful this summer, aren't you?" I asked.

Pepper looked up to the ceiling. "Yes. It's almost like the weather is starting to respond to my moods. The night you first cast the spell, to see the murder, and I tried to block it—"

"You did what?"

Pepper's eyes gleamed with triumph. "I knew what you were doing when you texted me. I hurried over and cast a spell to block your memories. I was quite concerned, and the storm reflected that." Her expression hardened. "I have to say, you were surprisingly strong. I was half afraid I hadn't succeeded, until you assured me otherwise, at Astrid's *ridiculous* emporium."

I drew back at the harsh assessment of Astrid's shop, wondering how long Pepper had despised us both.

And why had we placed that stupid prohibition on

crystal ball gazing? Because maybe the *nicer* member of our coven would've checked on me that night, while she was checking out StarGazer, if we hadn't stopped her from spying.

I knew Astrid would follow the rules, though. If anyone was going to save me, it would be me—or a missing spirit dog, or an absent owl.

Given that I was still completely drained, like I had the flu, my odds didn't seem good.

"You messed more directly with the sketchbook, didn't you?" I asked, sounding as weary as I felt. "You drew the fleur-de-lis."

Pepper looked almost pleased with me. "How did you know?"

"You have great taste," I admitted. "But you're not an artist, and you don't sketch like one. Especially not an artist under the influence of a spell. When I looked more closely at the symbol, I saw that it was outlined and colored in."

"I tried to block your second spell, too," Pepper said. "But I didn't interfere in time."

I had this creepy image of her standing over my bed while I was completely vulnerable.

I shook it off, forcing myself to listen while she explained, "I wanted to add a drawing that would cause you to be even more suspicious of the mysterious Detective Turner, and less suspect of your friends. Because you'd already drawn a snake in the grass."

"Which symbolized you, not Derek. Who you framed, leaving the shears in his house."

Pepper didn't seem offended to be characterized as a slithering reptile. "Correct. It was easy enough to break into the mansion with a simple unlocking spell." She laughed. "I knew Derek was damaged, but I had no idea he'd ditch the pruners with *you*, muddying the waters more. It was such a nice turn of events."

My fists balled up, but I swallowed my rage, not wanting to act rashly. "I drew your cabana, too."

"Yes. I knew the truth. But I certainly didn't discourage you from interpreting it as a dog house."

"That's where you've been taking my spell book, right?" I asked. "To work with it." Pepper didn't contradict me, so I kept adding to my theory. "You and Evangeline would borrow the book, because my foolishly trusting self rarely locked the Owl & Crescent, and I probably let you overhear the phrase that unlocks the cover, too." Pepper's smug smile told me I was correct. "And you would work in the pool house, trying to unlock the alchemy spell—which became like an obsession for Evangeline."

Pepper rolled her eyes. "It was kind of pathetic."

I remembered Pepper's strong reaction the second time Astrid used the crystal ball to spy without us. "You got upset, and forbade Astrid from using her 'paranormal nanny cam' because you were afraid she'd catch you doing something evil and underhanded, right?"

Pepper didn't respond, but I knew I'd guessed correctly.

"And Mr. Van Buskirk suspected something was up," I continued. "That's why you sealed up the cabana and told me that I should ignore him, if he started saying crazy things."

"I didn't think he knew anything about witchcraft, until I learned he was *dating your grandmother*." Pepper was growing agitated, and she began to pace. Thunder roared overhead, and I again feared that, even if by some miracle Marinette had run for help, or Remi was winging his way to Lucien, the ferocious storm would impede their progress or, worse yet, harm them. "By then, George had already been inside the cabana," Pepper added. "Had keys, even!"

I pictured Mr. Van Buskirk, as we'd seen him in the crystal ball. He'd been puzzling over a small object. I'd thought it was a set of keys, but hadn't been sure. Now I understood why he'd looked so pensive, and why he might've wanted to speak to me.

"He saw the spell book in the cabana, didn't he?"

"Yes," Pepper said. "Who would've thought an old fool like George Van Buskirk would think anything of a tattered book? But one night he came back to check on a leak I'd hired him to repair, and he walked in on Evangeline and me poring over the old Jell-O recipes and mumbo jumbo. He asked why in the world we had your family's book, and 'what in the dickens' we were doing with it. In spite of the old-timey, innocent phrasing, I knew he was suspicious after that. Not about alchemy, but of me and Evangeline, who stammered out a weak explanation before I could even talk."

Luna and Mortimer had grown very quiet, and my mood ring was a sickly green. "Mr. Van Buskirk is lucky . . ."

"He's alive, yes." Pepper finished my thought, absently tapping the blade against her palm. "I *knew* I had to eliminate Benedict Blodgett, whom I suspected had actually seen me kill Evangeline, and I couldn't have bodies piling up *too* fast."

I was probably as green as my ring. "The footage Benedict wanted to show me . . . that wasn't taken near Peddler's Creek. Because I saw the cabana when I cast the spell tonight. Evangeline's last moments took place at the Crooked Chimneys. You brought her body back to plant it on the property line, casting even more suspicion on me and Derek."

Pepper's eyes glittered strangely, almost like she'd relished her morbid adventure. "You've almost pieced it together," she said. "The night I killed Evangeline, I first helped greedy little Astrid—"

"Hey!"

Pepper spoke over my defense of Astrid, who wasn't so much greedy as perpetually hungry.

"I helped her load up my car with leftover food. Then I drove her home and returned to the Owl & Crescent, where I quietly grabbed the book and the shears before meeting Evangeline."

"Why the shears . . . ?" I knew the answer before the question was fully out of my mouth.

"I had decided that I *had* to do away with her that night," Pepper said, confirming my suspicion. "The opportunity was too good. She was surrounded by people who hated her—potential suspects—even before her rival for the admittedly decimated Fletcher estate came bursting in, as if on cue."

"But *why* kill her?"

Pepper drew herself up taller, and I sat up straighter, too. I could finally feel some energy returning to my body. I hoped it wasn't coming back too late, because Pepper had to be close to finished with bragging about her penchant for homicide—and her new friends.

"The coven I'm joining no longer found Evangeline useful, once she'd delivered your spell book and its secrets," Pepper said, her chest puffing with pride, like she'd infiltrated the "cool kids'" table at a high school. "I was to take over the project as my initiation. It was obvious that Evangeline had no skills and would never acquire any.

She was worthless, at best, and, with her lack of business acumen and penchant for making enemies, a liability at worst."

"So, you lured her to the cabana and killed her."

Pepper nodded. "But when the deed was done, and her screams finally silenced, I heard a strange noise. A sort of *clacking*."

I knew that distinctive sound, too.

"I looked outside, and someone was running away, into the darkness. It wasn't until you told me about meeting Benedict Blodgett in the alley, and I saw him filming at the funeral, that I knew who'd been there." She shrugged. "At which point, I silenced him and his clickety-clackety camera, conjuring a little indoor whirlwind to tear up his endless canisters of film and strew the footage all over the floor."

So that's why I'd slipped and slid my way through Take 666, and the furniture had been upended. Pepper had summoned a small tempest to get rid of possible evidence.

"I really had no choice," she added, with a mock pout.

"You've had choices all along," I reminded her, through gritted teeth. "You could've chosen to be loyal, not to mention *less than morally bankrupt*. And talk about greedy! Astrid might take home some appetizers, but you wanted . . . everything!" My voice was rising, and I stood up, too, on legs that weren't as steady as I would've liked. But there was no turning back, and I forged ahead, ticking off Pepper's desires on my fingers. "An endless supply of money. An alliance with a bunch of heartless, lawless witches. And—"

"Power!" Pepper cried, her voice booming nearly as loudly as the thunder she'd summoned above us. Luna flattened herself against the table, as if she wasn't sure whether to duck or pounce, and I could practically feel Mortimer shaking. Or maybe that was the wind that howled around us, rattling the barn. "I don't want to spend my whole life in this crazy town making pudding pops with you and Astrid Applebee!"

We'd never made the pudding pops, but it wasn't the right time to quibble. Pepper swept the knife around, gesturing to the Owl & Crescent. "Do you think I want to grow old in this *dump*, surrounded by pigs and cats and owls and now a stray *dog*—"

So, she had run across Marinette. I wondered again where Lucien's partner was, but briefly, because Pepper was still ranting.

". . . not to mention no-talent party guests who couldn't draw a stick figure to *save their lives*! Do you think *anyone* would really want that?"

Of all the terrible things Pepper had said and done to me, her complete dismissal of the home and the business—the life—I'd created, and which *I* loved, even if it was simple and a little cluttered with people, animals, and things . . .

Somehow, that cut me the deepest.

Then again, I was probably about to be cut even more deeply, in a different way.

"So, what now, Pepper?" I asked, with a glance at the knife. "Have the witches in your coven decided I'm disposable, too? Because I really can't unlock the alchemy spell. I don't know how to do it."

"Maybe not," Pepper agreed, snapping the knife toward the table, where Luna crouched, her eyes huge. "But you haven't even tried. Like you'll do right now."

"I won't."

Pepper's voice was even. "Yes. You will."

"Detective Turner will solve Evangeline's murder," I

reminded her. "And Benedict's. And mine, if it comes to that. You can't get away with this forever."

"Ah, yes, your mysterious detective." Her lips twitched with a tiny smile. "Do you really still think he's not hiding his own secrets?"

"I don't know," I said. "And I don't think you really know anything about him, either."

I'd hoped to get Pepper to share anything she might know about Lucien and the alliance he'd told me he'd helped form. I was testing whether his cover had been blown—and working through lingering doubts. It would have been almost reassuring if she'd at least mentioned a group of vigilantes who dogged her new coven. But all she said was, "You're so naive, Willow."

"Better trusting than untrustworthy," I told her.

Her mouth set in a grim line, and she pointed the knife again. "Help me get the alchemy spell. Now."

I didn't intend to help her do anything, but I moved to the table, edging around the blade, which she had pointed in the general direction of my throat. She followed closely on my heels.

"Open the book to the right page. Then we'll spill a little blood."

I'd been flipping pages in the *Book of Miscellany*, which was still open from earlier that night, but I wheeled around, just as I found the pink stain and the recipe for fritters I never did get a chance to make. Under the table, Mortimer squealed again, and Luna yowled.

"What are you talking about?" I demanded.

"My new coven thinks there's a good chance the pages are sealed with Bellamy blood, and can only be unlocked the same way." Pepper edged closer, the knife clutched in her hand and a weird look in her eyes. "It's a very powerful way to seal a spell. The *most* powerful way."

"Um, I'm pretty sure that's calamine lotion," I informed her, daring to glance at the page. In fact, my eyes lingered an extra few seconds, before I turned back around. "That stain is way too pink to be blood."

Pepper's eyes narrowed to slits. "Do you *dare* to joke, at this moment? Are you honestly testing *me*—a member of a coven so secret its name cannot be spoken?"

"You aren't a member yet," I reminded her, my anger overcoming my fear.

Pepper's hand shook, the knife twitching, and her voice sounded demonic. "DO. NOT. TEST. ME!"

I raised my hands, trying to calm her down. "Okay, okay." I needed to get my own emotions under control and do something quickly, because Luna was about to pounce, and Mortimer, hidden beneath me, was quaking against my legs. I didn't want either of them to get hurt.

Closing my eyes for just a moment, I took a deep breath. Then I forced myself to meet Pepper's diabolical gaze, telling her, in a calm voice, "I *might* be able to help. I might've overheard my grandmother talking about some locked pages once, with my mother. I listened closely, because they were being so secretive. I could *try* to repeat what they said before we resort to blood."

"I think you're lying," Pepper said. But she nodded at the book. "Go ahead, though. I have nothing to lose if you mutter a bunch of nonsense, and everything to gain if you're somehow telling the truth."

I didn't reply. As the storm above us suddenly quieted, like the clouds were holding their breath, I hovered my hands above the calamine lotion stain, then rested them on the pages, whispering, *"In a garden of delights, protect me from the plant that bites."*

As I finished invoking the spell that inexplicably *caused* poison ivy, I reached one hand out to clasp Pepper's wrist, so we *both* burst into red blotches that itched so badly they stung—which didn't cause Pepper to drop her knife.

I was pretty sure that happened because, while I quickly released her, and she lunged for me, screaming curses, a plucky little cat leaped at her head, and a rescue pig stepped in front of her, causing her to stumble just as the door to the studio flung open.

We were all in a heap on the floor, and I was itching terribly, not to mention still exhausted. But I managed to pull my bedraggled self up to see Lucien and Astrid step into the Owl & Crescent, accompanied by a very wet dog and an owl who flew up to the rafters, where he peered down at us all with an *I knew this would happen* look in his dark eyes.

Then, much to my surprise, Astrid, not Lucien, stepped forward and raised one hand, not unlike Lucien had done to summon fire. She spoke directly and authoritatively to Pepper, who was struggling to rise and perhaps take us all on.

"Ligatis manibus eius!"

Pepper looked completely baffled, not to mention blotchy and miserable, as her hands locked together, as if bound with invisible handcuffs. "What the . . . ?"

Astrid cut off the confused complaint, addressing me, Mortimer, and Luna. She sounded more like her usual self. "Are you all okay?"

I nodded, Mortimer snuffled, and Luna licked a paw, as if nothing dramatic had just happened.

Clearly reassured, Astrid turned back to Pepper, who

kept eyeing the knife on the floor with wild eyes, like she hadn't given up hope of escape. Then her shoulders finally slumped when Astrid commanded, "Come with me, traitor. A swift trial awaits you!"

As they left the studio, Astrid looked over her shoulder and winked at me, while I finally struggled to rise with the help of Lucien, whose dark eyes were unreadable by the light of the guttering candles circled around Evangeline's painting.

I knew I was in for a lecture about the dangers of leaving a sealed-up house, but first I had a few questions for him, starting with, "What in the world happened to Astrid Applebee?"

Chapter 40

"Like Rembrandt, Astrid was determined to protect you," Lucien said, pouring tea while I dabbed calamine lotion onto my red, freckled arms.

We'd retreated to my kitchen, along with Mortimer and Luna. Rembrandt, who'd flown through a gale to find Astrid and bring her back to the Owl & Crescent, had remained in the barn, resting.

Marinette, who had run for Lucien, was, of course, close by, but for once giving her person a little space. She'd joined the cat and pig in the living room, where they were all recovering from the night's adventures.

I sat at the table, and Lucien joined me, sliding a mug of steaming, soothing chamomile in front of me before taking the seat next to mine.

"Astrid kept dogging me, demanding to know who I really was, until I finally revealed my identity to her, too," he continued. "I was more worried that she'd poke around too much, and get herself in danger, than I was about losing my cover." He grinned. "I needn't have been concerned on either count. When Astrid learned about the alliance, she first wanted to know if there were uniforms."

I globbed some pink liquid onto a particularly rashy spot near my elbow. "Yeah, that makes sense."

"Then she asked if she could *join*."

My hand jerked, and I looked over at Lucien, alarmed. I loved Astrid, but I didn't think she had the skills or temperament to be a vigilante. "You're kidding, right? Please tell me that whole 'arresting Pepper' thing was a one-time deal."

"Don't worry," he assured me, with an appealing lopsided grin. "I merely deputized her, temporarily. And I might've quietly backed her up, with the spell to bind hands. I knew she'd be fine delivering Pepper to a pair of warlocks who were waiting in the darkness, just outside, to take her away."

I'd been wondering about Pepper's fate, since no traditional, uniformed, human-type police officers had shown up yet. I watched Lucien, almost warily. "So, I take it Pepper's not going to have a traditional trial?"

He grew serious again and shook his head. "No. She'll face justice within the magical community. Not only did she kill a fellow, if novice, practitioner, but she betrayed your coven. And there's reason to believe she used dark arts to murder Blodgett. There was no blood at the scene, no traces of poison, or visible wounds. The coroner is stumped and can't even declare it a homicide. But anyone who's seen paranormal crime scenes would strongly suspect foul play. Which is another reason to try Pepper in a court that understands witchcraft."

I was about to ask what type of sentence Pepper might face, then I changed my mind. She had betrayed me and committed some terrible acts, but we'd been friends for a long time, and I had no desire to imagine her suffering, no matter what she'd done to others.

"You suspected Pepper all along," I noted, rising to toss out my calamine-soaked cotton balls and wash my hands. The lotion wasn't helping at all. "I was stupidly blind, even when you told me about the coven, which seemed tailor-made for a witch like her."

"To be honest, I didn't think Pepper was powerful enough to interest the other members," Lucien said, standing up, too. "She was all show and bluster, with her ostentatious manipulation of the weather. That kind of display actually sits poorly with the group I investigate. They like to fly under the radar. So even though I suspected Pepper, I had serious doubts—especially given the strong bond of friendship I also believed you two shared." Lucien drew closer to me, looking down at me with his dark eyes, while I kept scratching. "I suppose, in the end, the coven just manipulated Pepper and Evangeline to gain access to you."

We were standing almost close enough to dance, and before I knew what was happening, he clasped my wrists. I pulled back, on reflex, then relaxed under his cool, firm touch. I had no idea what he was doing, but I didn't want it to stop. Not yet.

"I shouldn't do this," he said quietly, wrapping his fingers more tightly around me. "But I can't bear to see you suffering the results of a spell that seems to defy all logic. Why even create it?"

"It totally backfired on the creator," I explained. "It was supposed to cure poison ivy."

"Well, I suppose it helped to distract Pepper, if in a dangerous way." Lucien sounded disapproving, but there was a glint of amusement in his eyes. "Regardless, it's done its work, and I can't stand to see you pink and itching anymore."

I wasn't sure what he planned to do, and my heart fluttered with anticipation, and his touch, as he closed his eyes, muttering words in a language I didn't recognize. The Cajun part of his accent seemed more pronounced, though.

And as he spoke, I could feel his restless energy being transferred to me, and the chill in his touch seemed to travel through my veins—while the spots on my body faded to nothing.

"That's quite a spell," I said quietly, when he opened his eyes again. "You *do* have some tricks up your sleeve."

"I have more skills than I first admitted, but perhaps fewer than you've come to believe," he said, releasing me. But we still stood very close to one another, until Marinette entered the kitchen and *growled at me*.

Lucien stepped back and scolded the dog, if gently. "Marinette. Enough. I am fine."

His canine partner lowered her head, clearly not happy. Her tail hung, too, as she retreated.

"Sorry about that." Lucien rubbed his jaw. "She's just trying to look out for me."

My gaze flicked to the living room, where Marinette was lying down again—but watching me. "What have I done to her?" I lowered my voice. "And tell me the truth. Is she a *loa*?"

"No, she's purely canine," Lucien assured me. "A very intelligent—and tired—dog who ran all the way to the police station to find me. The real Marinette would be far too unpredictable a partner."

I was sort of relieved not to be hosting a volatile spirit.

"As for what you've done to her," Lucien added, "it's really what you've done to *me* that has her worried."

"I don't understand," I said. "I haven't done anything."

Lucien opened his mouth, then seemed to change his mind about speaking.

I tried another tack, searching his eyes and finally asking the question I'd wanted to pose before he'd disappeared earlier that evening.

"Lucien, what were you about to tell me, back at the gala, when you said, 'Willow, you must know that you and I are . . .'?"

Chapter 41

"You must know that you and I are connected in a powerful way," Lucien said, moving to take my hands again—then pulling back.

I would've been fine if he'd touched me, because, of course, I felt the bond we shared, too. I'd painted him before I'd known him, and I'd trusted him, on some deep level, when Pepper had given me cause to doubt him. And when I felt vulnerable around him, it was because I knew that, if we got too close, he would have the power to break my heart.

I reached for him, but he again withdrew his hands and took a step back.

I tried not to feel hurt or rejected, although I heard a tinge of both those emotions when I spoke his name. "Lucien?"

"We can't act on whatever we feel," he told me, crossing his arms over his chest. "I shouldn't have danced with you at the gala and shouldn't have touched you to perform the healing spell a moment ago. And that's why I left so abruptly after sealing up your house. I was too close to kissing you, and if I'd really stayed the night . . ."

We both knew what would've happened. That was one reason I'd also wanted him to leave. I didn't think I was ready for that. But I didn't understand why we couldn't take things slower, and I dared to step closer, again closing the gap between us. Now that we'd admitted what we felt, *I* wanted to kiss the tall, handsome, still mysterious man who seemed to really want that, too, in spite of his defensive posture.

"If you think I'm with Derek, I'm not," I assured him, guessing at what might keep us apart. "There's no one in my life right now."

He was shaking his head. "No, Willow. It's not that. It's the alliance. Our rules are very clear about relationships with those we protect. They are strictly forbidden, for obvious reasons."

I didn't think anything was obvious. "What reasons?"

"What if you'd already been working with the coven, as I'd feared?" he asked. "If I'd allowed my feelings to get in the way—emotions I felt from the moment I feared you'd *killed yourself* with that spell—you could've easily manipulated me." Even as he explained why we had to be apart, we were both drawing closer together. "You could have pried secrets from me . . . perhaps even drawn me to the other side. That's why the laws that govern me are so strict on this matter." He glanced toward the living room. "And that's why Marinette's been cold to you and growled at me. She's sensed, from the start, that I'm drawn to you, and she was warning me not to get too close."

Lucien looked down at me again, and I searched his eyes, although I feared what I might see there when I asked, "What would happen to you, if we . . . ?"

I wasn't sure how to end that question, but Lucien answered it, anyway. "If you don't want to know the fate

Pepper faces . . ." He must've guessed that, earlier. "You don't want to know what would happen to me, if I acted on the feelings I have for you."

I was pretty sure that Pepper was in deep, deep trouble, and I finally grasped just how deadly serious Lucien was. He might be talking about losing his *life*. Yet, neither one of us seemed capable of stepping back. We kept staring at each other, across an invisible wall that crackled with the electricity I'd felt before. And I saw something in his eyes I'd never seen before, not even with Derek.

"I dreamed about you, before we met," I confided, my voice dropping to a whisper. I didn't want Marinette—or some paranormal police force—to overhear and come bursting in before Lucien and I said all we needed to say. "You were holding out your hand, and I wasn't sure if I should take it."

"I dreamed of you, too," he said softly, studying my eyes. "Before I was assigned to come here. Yet I was surprised to see the painting, which told me you'd anticipated me, as well. But there's nothing we can do."

All at once, I wasn't sure that was true. "But I'm not in danger, anymore. Pepper has been taken away. So, you're not really—"

"No, Willow." Lucien interrupted firmly, before I could get my hopes up. "As long as the alchemy spell exists, I'll be watching over you. Maybe not as closely, for a while, because you're right, the imminent danger has passed. But, as far as my associates are concerned, this case is far from closed. And the moment it was, I would be reassigned. Perhaps without even a chance to say goodbye, given how close I've come to kissing you. I am already under scrutiny, and have been warned about possible censure, because it's been difficult for me to conceal my true feelings for you."

I took a moment to grasp that my being in danger was the thing that would keep Lucien anywhere close to me, while paradoxically keeping us apart.

"But I think we're meant to be together, or at least try—"

"I'm sorry, Willow." I saw profound regret in Lucien's eyes, and he dared to break the barrier between us, risking his own safety by reaching up to lightly brush my cheek with the back of his fingers.

But just before he could touch me, the back door flew open, and we both stepped apart, the moment between us ended by the arrival of two unexpected, and very upset, visitors.

Chapter 42

"Has anyone heard anything about Pepper?" Grandma Anna asked me, Astrid, and my mother. We were all moving around my kitchen, assembling yet another tray of hors d'oeuvres for the Templeton painting party, which was taking place in the studio on a balmy July evening. My grandmother sprinkled Parmesan cheese onto a baking tray, to make tuiles, while I sliced lemons. "Deputy Astrid, any news?"

Needless to say, I'd told my mother and grandmother the whole story about Pepper's schemes, and Astrid's semi-impressive arrest, the night they'd interrupted Lucien's and my conversation. Which was probably a good thing. I wasn't sure what would've happened if he'd dared to actually touch me.

"I'm afraid I've already been drummed out of the force," Astrid said, with a sigh. She was cutting up a cold watermelon, eating most of the pieces. "When the rest of the alliance found out about my illegal use of a crystal ball, they revoked my badge."

I was juicing the lemons into a pitcher, but I stopped to give Astrid a funny look. "You actually had a badge?"

"Of course," she said. "I made it, using a lid from a tin

can and some crystals from the Emporium. It looked very official, and I was sorry to lose it!"

My mother was right next to me at the counter, measuring sugar for the lemonade, and she rolled her eyes. Like me, Mom probably suspected that Astrid's dismissal was related to more than just her shady surveillance tactics.

"Funny how I can't stop worrying about Pepper, even though she did such terrible things," Grandma Anna added, popping the tuiles into the oven. Someone at the party had a big appetite for cheese, and the lacy crackers were going fast. "It's force of habit, I suppose. She was practically a member of the family!"

"I feel the same way," I agreed, looking out the window. Daphne Templeton's basset hound, Socrates, and his poodle pal, Snowdrop, had come along, after all, and they were romping in the yard with Mortimer, while Luna looked on from atop the potting shed. I was very surprised to see the basset, who had such a serious air, running around. The sight made me smile, until I noticed Rembrandt flying in the direction of the woods, again following the path he'd led me and Derek down, the night we'd found Evangeline's body. "But I'm glad Pepper won't be able to cause any more harm," I added. "At least for a while."

"I never thought I'd say this, but I feel terrible for Evangeline," Astrid said. "And Benedict Blodgett!"

"Yes, I really don't think he meant any harm," I noted. "I think he was just in the wrong place at the wrong time."

"And thank goodness Rembrandt went to the right place," Astrid added, with a shudder. "If he hadn't tapped on my window, waking me up, you could've been Pepper's next victim!"

Grandma Anna closed the oven door and wiped her hands on her apron. "It's almost like the dog and owl knew they should split up to get as much help as possible."

I smiled. "I wouldn't put it past Marinette or Remi."

I thought my mother was about to disagree when the door opened and Mr. Van Buskirk entered the kitchen, lugging a crate. "Hey, everyone," he said, winking at my grandmother. "I got the cantaloupes you asked me to pick up."

Grandma Anna greeted her beau with a kiss on the cheek. "Thank you, George. This is a small, but hungry crew. The fruit salad disappears as quickly as we can make it."

He set the melons on the table, then frowned at me. "Are you okay, Willow? You've been through quite a bit."

"I'm fine, thanks," I assured him. "And you went through a lot, too!"

"I'm sorry I didn't share my suspicions about Pepper and Evangeline earlier," he said. "I knew something funny was going on in the cabana when I saw them using that book you keep in the barn. Evangeline acted so guilty when I caught them studying it. I had keys, and I kept debating whether to go back to snoop around."

Astrid shot me a look that said she was thinking the same thing as me. He'd been pondering his options when we'd spied on him.

"But I'm pretty new to witchcraft," Mr. Van Buskirk continued, with a quick glance at my grandmother. "I certainly didn't know Pepper and Evangeline were doing anything dangerous."

I wasn't sure how much Mr. Van Buskirk knew, even then. Grandma Anna had obviously told him about the spell book and her interest in the craft, but she wouldn't have shared information about the alliance. We'd stretched the rules by telling *her* about its existence.

"Well, at least you're no longer under suspicion of murder," I reminded Mr. Van Buskirk, adding water to the pitcher. Mom dumped in the sugar. "That must be a relief."

"Yes, it must be," Astrid agreed. She was retrieving

cantaloupes from the crate. "But what will happen now? Will you keep living in the caretaker's cottage?"

"For a few more weeks." He smiled down at my grandmother, who'd taken his hand. "Then it's probably time for me to move on."

Grandma Anna beamed up at her boyfriend. "We've been discussing a different living arrangement. For both of us. At the farm."

"Grandma!" I cried. "Isn't this a little sudden?"

My mother also seemed surprised, and perhaps disapproving. "Yes, you two! You're acting a bit rashly!"

Grandma Anna hugged Mr. Van Buskirk's arm, both of them laughing. "We're nearly in our eighties—and madly in love. We don't want to waste time."

"Speaking of which . . ." Mr. Van Buskirk checked his wristwatch. "Can you get away now, Anna? We have reservations at Typhoon in fifteen minutes."

I was stirring the lemonade, but my hand slowed. "You know, about Typhoon. I actually suspected Linh Tran of being involved in the murder. Evangeline had scheduled a meeting with her, and Linh and Penny Dandridge talked about 'destroying' Evangeline at the painting party."

"Linh might've done that, in a way," Mom noted. "From what I understand, Linh—who is a phenomenally tough businesswoman—figured out the Silver Spoon was in trouble when Evangeline started leaving bad reviews online."

That issue had been the subject of a recent story in the *Weekly Whisper*, much to Derek's dismay.

"Linh was fighting hard to buy the Fletchers' restaurant," Mom added. "And, from what I understand, Derek is considering selling it to her."

"In the meantime, I could go for some dragon noodles," Mr. Van Buskirk noted, dropping a not-too-subtle hint.

"What do you say, Willow?" Grandma Anna looked to me for permission. "Can you all handle the party from here?"

"Yes, of course." I shooed them along. "Go have fun."

"They're adorable," Astrid said, when the happy couple was gone. "I'm so pleased for them."

I resumed stirring my latest, harmless concoction. "Yes, me, too."

Astrid was cleaving open a melon, but she gave me a sidelong glance. "How about you, Willow? Any romance in your life, right now?" For a second, I thought she was talking about Lucien, until she added, "Maybe with some-one else who lives just across the creek?"

"No, I'm afraid not," I told her and my mother, who was pulling the tuiles from the oven. "Derek has a lot to work through. I spoke to him yesterday, and he's going to coun-seling with a PTSD specialist in Philadelphia twice a week. And the rest of his time is spent figuring out what to do with the estate. When that's settled, his plan is to move somewhere new for a fresh start."

Mom was arranging the tuiles on a platter. "It will be strange, not having any Fletchers in Zephyr Hollow. But I understand his decision."

"I always thought you two would get back together," Astrid said sadly, setting down her knife and wiping her hands with a towel. "Such a shame." She checked my finger. "Oh, and you must feel badly, too. Your ring is azure, for heartbreak!"

Mom checked the ring, too. Then she handed Astrid the plate. "Would you mind taking this out to Willow's guests, dear?"

"Sure," my sole remaining coven member agreed. Ac-cepting the platter and grabbing the pitcher, too, she left me and Mom alone in the kitchen.

The door had barely swung shut when Mom said, "You're not really sad about Derek, or heartbroken over Pepper's betrayal, are you? It's Lucien Turner, right?" Before I could protest, she reminded me, "I saw you two at the gala. Saw the way you looked at each other. And when Detective Turner and I would meet, I heard the way he spoke your name, and his genuine concern for you."

"It can't happen," I told her, leaning against the counter and crossing my arms. I was very near the spot where Lucien and I had stood the night before. "At least, not for now. Alliance rules."

She shook her head. "I feel badly for you both. But I have to say, I am not sure I could've approved of you seeing him. While I admire Detective Turner—or whatever title he really goes by—I think his lifestyle is more itinerant and dangerous than Derek's was."

"Well, the point is moot." I fidgeted with the mood ring. "He's not allowed to be involved with someone he's protecting."

"I'm sorry, Willow." Mom took my hands and gave them a squeeze. I thought she was just expressing sympathy, until she closed her eyes and whispered, *"Endless circles binding me. From this jewelry, set me free."*

The mood ring that had been stuck on my finger clattered to the floor, and she released me. "At least you're free of that."

I bent to pick up the ring, which I set on the counter—and which I'd probably wear again, someday. I really had grown to like it. "Thank you," I nevertheless said. "And that's a very particular spell!"

"Your Great Aunt Josie was always in denial about her chubby fingers. She actually used that quite a bit."

Gazing out the window again, I saw Daphne Templeton

standing just outside the barn with a woman who was about my mom's age. I needed to go check on her and the party, but I had to ask my mother, "Why don't you start practicing witchcraft again? You seem very good at it."

"I don't want to end up like Pepper," she said. "I am ambitious, in some ways." That was true. "I think it's best if I pursue my goals through normal channels."

"I respect that," I said. "Even if I don't think you'd ever be like Pepper."

"I'd rather not risk it," she said. "I cast my last *real* spell before dawn this morning."

"What do you mean?"

"Your grandmother and I unsealed, and destroyed, the alchemy spell. I think we did it correctly, too. I did a lot of research on spell destruction, and, while we're not skilled enough witches to guarantee anything, it seemed to work."

Mom must've seen the shock, and no doubt confusing to her, dismay in my eyes. "We had to try, to protect you," she hurried to explain. "And we were going to show you the spell book later tonight, after your guests are gone. We knew you were preoccupied with the party today."

"It's not that . . ." My throat felt tight, and I was backing away from her. "Mom, could you please take care of my guests? I have somewhere I need to go."

"What's wrong, dear?"

I reached behind myself for the doorknob. "Please, if you and Astrid could just take care of things for a few minutes. I'll be right back."

Mom nodded. "Of course."

I dashed out into the night, running for my Subaru, where I found a cat, a rescue pig, and an owl waiting for me, as if they knew I might need their support one more time.

Chapter 43

"Lucien said he could only stick around while the alchemy spell existed," I told Luna and Mortimer, as I wheeled my old Subaru into a parking spot right in front of the police station. Rembrandt had flown ahead, and he was circling the cupola, where a dim light glowed. Hopping out of the car and releasing the animals, too, I noted that a faint light also gleamed in the windows of Lucien's office. I slammed the door, still concerned. "He warned me that, if the spell was destroyed, he might be called away, without the chance to even say goodbye."

I doubted Luna and Mortimer were listening to my explanation. They ran ahead to the station door. Catching up, I hauled on the iron handle, half expecting the building to be locked up.

However, the door flew open, and I took a moment to look skyward for Remi, to see if he'd swoop down. Noting that he'd vanished, I slipped inside with Mortimer and Luna close on my heels. I was going to lead the little pig to the elevator, but he and Luna darted past me and began running up the spiral staircase, Mortimer's hooves clattering loudly.

I bounded upward, too, and we quickly reached the top floor. Opening another door, we raced down the hallway to Lucien's office, my heart pounding in my ears.

Grabbing the doorknob, I twisted and discovered that the room was also unlocked. I thought that had to bode well until I threw open the door and cried softly, "No!"

Everything was gone. The books and bookshelves. The antique rug. And the giant desk where Lucien had stared me down, challenging me to tell him the truth about Derek's handwriting on the envelope.

That wasn't to say the space was empty. It was cluttered with dusty old junk, like abandoned filing cabinets, broken office chairs, and one discarded lamp that was neverthe-less switched on. The fireplace, which I'd admired, was boarded up, the marble surround obscured.

"No," I whispered again, doubting for a moment that Lucien had ever existed.

But, of course, he had.

Right?

Luna and Mortimer knew things were amiss. Luna was mewing softly and twining around my legs, and for the first time ever, Mortimer's eternal piggy grin looked almost like a frown. He snorted softly and bumped against my legs, too.

As I stood there, fighting to breathe, I pulled out my cell phone and dialed Lucien—which I should've done in the first place.

But I'd been too afraid of what actually did happen. Which was nothing.

Lucien's phone seemed to have been erased, too.

There was nothing more to do, no way to contact him,

which was probably for the best. I knew that, by summoning him away, his associates were probably trying to protect him from making a costly mistake, just like Marinette had tried to do, back in my kitchen.

I turned slowly, still reluctant to leave. That's when I felt a cool breeze tickle the back of my neck, and I turned back, spying an open window and the white face of an owl who sat on the wide sill.

I picked my way across the room, thinking I would shoo Rembrandt outside and shut the window. But when I reached him, I saw that he was perched on a *book*.

Having done his job, Remi flew off, while I picked up the volume.

The Conjured Canvas: Intersections of Art & Magic, by D. W. Turner.

Lucien had left it for me. And there was a slip of paper inside.

Opening to the page, I was again disappointed, because there wasn't a note. Then I read the chapter title by moonlight.

> *Spells to Summon a True Love,*
> *Using Painting and Sculpture*

Lucien had left me a way to reach him, if I ever really needed to do that.

I knew that I never would. If it was ever safe or the right time for him to return to me, he would come back.

Still, I clutched the book to my chest, absently petting Luna, who'd jumped up onto the windowsill. Mortimer stretched up to look outside, too, his little hooves scratching the old wood.

Together, we all watched a majestic owl—my other protector—soar above the lights of Zephyr Hollow. And when he was out of sight, we all followed him home.

Don't miss the first in Bethany Blake's
Lucky Paws Petsitting Mystery series

Death by Chocolate Lab

Pet sitter Daphne Templeton has a soft spot for every
stray and misfit who wanders into the quaint, lakeside
village of Sylvan Creek. But even Daphne doesn't like
arrogant, womanizing Steve Beamus, the controversial
owner of Blue Ribbon K-9 Academy. When Steve turns
up dead during a dog agility trial, Daphne can think of
a long list of people with motives for homicide, and so
can the police. Unfortunately, at the top of the list is
Daphne's sister, Piper—Steve's latest wronged girlfriend.

Certain that Piper is innocent, in spite of mounting
evidence to the contrary, Daphne sets out to clear
her sister's name—and find Axis, Steve's prize-winning
chocolate Labrador, who went missing the night of
Steve's death. Aided by Socrates, her taciturn basset
hound, and a hyperactive one-eared Chihuahua
named Artie, Daphne quickly runs afoul of Detective
Jonathan Black, a handsome and enigmatic
newcomer to town, who has no appreciation for
Daphne's unorthodox sleuthing.

Can a free-spirited pet sitter, armed only with a Ph.D.
in Philosophy and her two incompatible dogs, find the
real killer before she becomes the next victim?

Connect with Us

Visit us online at
KensingtonBooks.com
to read more from your favorite authors, see books
by series, view reading group guides, and more.

for sneak peeks, chances to win books and prize packs,
and to share your thoughts with other readers.

facebook.com/kensingtonpublishing
twitter.com/kensingtonbooks

Tell us what you think!

To share your thoughts, submit a review,
or sign up for our eNewsletters, please visit:
KensingtonBooks.com/TellUs.